The Seymour Tapes

The Seymour Tapes

TIM LOTT

VIKING
an imprint of
PENGUIN BOOKS

VIKING

Published by the Penguin Group
Penguin Books Ltd, 80 Strand, London WC2R ORL, England
Penguin Group (USA), Inc., 375 Hudson Street, New York, New York 10014, USA
Penguin Group (Canada), 10 Alcorn Avenue, Toronto, Ontario, Canada M4V 3B2
(a division of Pearson Penguin Canada Inc.)
Penguin Ireland, 25 St Stephen's Green, Dublin 2, Ireland
(a division of Penguin Books Ltd)
Penguin Group (Australia), 250 Camberwell Road,
Camberwell, Victoria 3124, Australia (a division of Pearson Australia Group Pty Ltd)
Penguin Books India Pvt Ltd, 11 Community Centre,
Panchsheel Park, New Delhi – 110 017, India
Penguin Group (NZ), cnr Airborne and Rosedale Roads, Albany,
Auckland 1310, New Zealand (a division of Pearson New Zealand Ltd)
Penguin Books (South Africa) (Pty) Ltd, 24 Sturdee Avenue,
Rosebank 2196, South Africa

Penguin Books Ltd, Registered Offices: 80 Strand, London WC2R ORL, England
www.penguin.com

First published 2005
2

Set in Monotype Dante 12/14.75pt
Typeset by Palimpsest Book Production Limited,
Polmont, Stirlingshire
Printed in Great Britain by Clays Ltd, St Ives plc

A CIP catalogue record for this book is available from the British Library

ISBN 0-670-91270-0

Dedicated to the memory of Thomas Haynes

Acknowledgements

Lorraine Electronics Surveillance, Mayfair; Communications Control Systems Ltd, Mayfair; Patrick Binet-Decamps and Andrew Milton at Le Prince Maurice, Mauritius, for providing a refuge; likewise Christina Østrem at Hotel Portixol, Mallorca, and Miguel Angel Prohens, at the Hotel Cuitat Jardi; Dr James LeFanu; Juliet Annan, Amelia Fairney and all at Viking Penguin; David Godwin; Laurence Bowen and Josh Golding for taking the trouble; Rachael Newberry, as ever.

Preface

The story of the death of Dr Alex Seymour is – inevitably – more profoundly lodged in the public consciousness than the story of his otherwise unremarkable life. Attention thus far has focused on the circumstances that led to his demise, at the age of fifty-one, in the basement of a run-down house in west London. The issues that seem to shuffle around that basement like questioning mourners – of privacy, voyeurism and sexual compulsion – have been constantly scrutinized since the story emerged, nearly two years ago, of his complex and eventually fatal relationship with Sherry Thomas.

I would be the first to confess that I find it both peculiar and surprising that out of the many first-rate and experienced writers who have commented on this strange, and strangely modern, saga, it is I, never having written a word previously on the case, who was granted access to the much discussed, but hitherto unseen Seymour Tapes.

When I was approached by Samantha Seymour in the autumn of last year and requested to collaborate in writing a book about her family, her husband and Ms Sherry Thomas, I was nonplussed. My only contribution to the world of non-fiction to date was my first book, *The Scent of Dried Roses*, concerning the suicide of my mother, and a short, briefly controversial article in a literary magazine about the break-up of my marriage at the end of the 1990s. I also write a London newspaper column and occasional travel pieces. All in all, it is little enough qualification to tell the story of a celebrated and, above all, visible act of violence and defilement. Whether that visibility – culminating in the Internet broadcast of the infamous Skin Tape – came about because of theft or bribery, or through Sherry Thomas is not a matter for me to address here.

I am not a sleuth, or even an investigative journalist. But after the Skin Tape leaked out, to the distress of the Seymour family, it seemed to Mrs Seymour that the record needed somehow to be 'set straight'. She chose to approach me to undertake that task – even though my faith in the ability of anyone to set anything straight through any medium is strictly limited. Reality is too crooked.

I assumed, therefore, that Samantha Seymour had made some error. However, when we met at my publisher's offices in the West End of London, she assured me that this was not so. She told me that after the death of her husband, and the subsequent discovery of the Seymour Tapes, she suffered a complete nervous breakdown. It was shortly after this that an acquaintance gave her a copy of my memoir about my mother, which details not only my mother's suicide but my own struggle with mental illness. She claimed that it helped her recovery, and that she had admired it sufficiently to seek me out to discuss producing a book about her family and Sherry Thomas.

I tried to explain to her that I had never attempted to tell anyone else's story, at least not at book length. I had only told my own. But she was insistent: so many lies had been told about Alex, she said – that he was a pervert, a snooper, a weirdo, a control freak – that only a complete explication of the facts would provide an effective correcting focus for these misperceptions. Such a picture would prove that Alex Seymour, although misguided and foolish, had acted only out of a desire to protect the family he loved.

Mrs Seymour has been offered considerable sums of money by representatives of the broadcast media for access to the tapes. She has consistently refused. However, in order to tell her husband's story to the fullest extent, she offered to grant me access to Alex Seymour's videotapes of the Seymour household. She said that she could never allow them to be broadcast but that, given the level of public interest and the distortions that followed upon this intense curiosity, it was sensible that they should be viewed, and reported on, by a neutral observer.

She said she wanted to ask me one simple question before she offered me otherwise unqualified access. It was anything but. It was 'Can you be honest?'

I replied immediately that I could do no more than try and, furthermore, that I was bound to fail. I added that pure honesty might exist wherever Alex had gone, but that it was unlikely to be found on this earth. And, anyway, honesty was not the same as truth, which, unfashionably perhaps, I did believe in – at least as something for a writer to aspire to.

Apparently this was sufficient answer. There and then she offered me access to the tapes and the rights to the book. She told me that after I had made use of the tapes, they would be locked into a vault until her death.

I cannot deny that I was excited by the prospect. From a purely professional point of view it would be a scoop, and if the sales of the book reflected anything like the amount of interest that existed in the case, I could expect to do reasonably well financially. All the same, I continued to express my scepticism. The Seymour Tapes were only part of the story: there were the tapes recorded by Sherry Thomas – of which the Skin Tape was the best known. And there were, of course, Alex Seymour's video diaries in which he recounts his experiences directly. Without these crucial pieces of the jigsaw, I felt I would be in danger of indulging in simply another exercise in prurience – or, at least, wilful misrepresentation for profit.

Mrs Seymour agreed. In fact, she revealed to me later, had I not put forward this caveat she would have questioned whether I was the right person for the project. It was her little test, she said – and I had passed. As for the Thomas tapes, which were not in her possession, she felt confident (correctly, as it turned out) that the police would agree to release them to help the family achieve 'closure' on the whole traumatic business.

So, we were both reassured. I began to feel increasingly confident that I might have some chance of building up a true picture of Dr Seymour's story and his peculiar relationship with Sherry

Thomas. However, so complex was the nature of the case that I found myself asking for still more material, whose compilation, I knew, might be painful for Mrs Seymour and her family. In short, I asked her if she and her teenage children, Guy and Victoria, would be prepared to allow me to interview them in depth. (Polly, the Seymours' youngest child, was only six months old at the death of her father so exempt, of course, from this request.)

Several weeks later, she agreed to my request on behalf of herself, but not her children, who, she said, were too young to be exposed to this. I accepted the point, and decided that access to Samantha Seymour alone was sufficient for me to take on the project. But she had another condition, to which, after some negotiation, I acceded: that although I should receive a generous fee for compiling the book and be entitled to all copyright fees from newspaper serializations, all royalties, serial and film rights should go to the newly founded Seymour Privacy Institute (SPI). As she pointed out, the Institute is the first charity of its kind to address one of the most corrosive obsessions of the modern world – suffered not only by individuals but by states, television companies and big business: the addiction to, as the institute's manifesto puts it, 'watching, to snooping, to gawking, to prying', sometimes openly, sometimes secretly. And not only for security, but for pleasure and entertainment, even mockery and humiliation. Mrs Seymour – understandably, perhaps – now believes that tendency to be an insidious, intolerable blight on our national way of life.

The Seymour Institute has one aim: to restore privacy in private and public life. That Mrs Seymour has essentially opened a window into the world of her family and her husband by consenting to, indeed soliciting, this book in no way represents a paradox, as far as she is concerned: she is simply using every tool at her disposal to mitigate some of the damage that invasion of her privacy has occasioned. Since this exercise is carried out with her consent, and indeed the consent of all parties, no privacy issues are involved. On the contrary, it represents reparation of the damage done by other media.

In the end, I signed the contract, with a single caveat on my side: that I should be free to report what I found with neither let nor hindrance from the Seymour family. If they were to trust me, that trust must be absolute. I would allow them to see the finished work and check the facts, but the decision to censor or retain anything that I considered relevant to understanding the story would remain in my hands. To take any other course would be to compromise my integrity as a writer, and since that integrity had led her to approach me in the first place, it would be absurd to undermine it by removing my right to control the final product. I would, of course, listen to the family's representations, but if most of the profit of the book was to go to the Seymour Institute, I would at least determine its content.

Mrs Seymour agreed – not without reluctance, but she finally accepted my point that any attempt to represent the truth is hardly likely to be taken seriously as long as those with most to lose are given control of the final product. She also accepted that I was writing in good faith, and that public sympathy was likely to be on her side; in practical terms, I could do little damage beyond that which had already been done.

It is a given that every representation of reality, even our own first-hand perception, indicates a point of view. I have tried my best, in this case, to make my reporting of the facts neutral – perhaps, it lately occurs to me, in a subconscious attempt to vie with the camera for the right to represent correctly what we label 'reality'. Nevertheless, the facts I have selected, the quotes I have used, the sections of the videotapes I have judged irrelevant, dull or too intrusive, all of these factors mean that the version of reality I have constructed is distorted. At times I have allowed myself to be opinionated and critical about the meaning of certain events, and my impressions of the Seymours and Sherry Thomas.

But this does not imply that truth and lies are indistinguishable. Throughout, I have kept in mind as best I can Mrs Seymour's original remit, those simple words 'Can you be honest?' And I can answer sincerely that I have tried, just as I can acknowledge the chastening corollary that I will have failed.

In the final analysis, I can do no more than hope that the failure is honourable, and that the result sheds more light than it casts shadow.

Tim Lott

Interview with Samantha Seymour

Mrs Seymour's appearance is now extremely well known, as a result of the television and press coverage of this case. However, in person she gives a rather different impression from the one-dimensional, tight-lipped, grief-stricken widow she has been most consistently depicted as. On the numerous occasions I spent interviewing her – at my office near London's Portobello Road, and at the family home in Acton – she was, at different times, warm, polite and generous, as well as occasionally shrewd, defensive and difficult. Now thirty-nine years old, she remains an attractive woman, although her normally round, doll-like face has become thin and drawn with the pressure of her ordeal. She is of medium height and in good shape for a woman who has borne three children. She has straight, chocolate-brown, shoulder-length hair, and favours casual, well-cut high-street clothes, usually in quiet unpatterned materials – black, dark blue, white, taupe.

Although she is highly intelligent – Mrs Seymour holds a Ph.D. in psychology from Birkbeck College, London – she is endearingly vague. She will often put down a mug of coffee then forget where it is. She admits to being clumsy and 'a bit of a slob'. Although her clothes are always smart and well pressed, whenever we met there seemed to be smear of food or ink on a lapel, her blouse or skirt. However, none of this prevented her pursuing a successful career in public relations with a small London-based consultancy, Jackdaw, although her tendency towards disorganization infuriated her husband, despite what she describes as their otherwise healthy relationship.

Before she answered any question, Mrs Seymour almost always paused to weigh and consider her reply. Undoubtedly she has a tidy mind, which belies her slightly slapdash appearance.

Since the birth of Polly, and then the death of her husband, Mrs Seymour has all but given up her career to concentrate on the founding, promotion and maintenance of the Seymour Institute. She confesses that, prior to her bereavement, late motherhood had diluted her ambition, and that her husband had become more or less the sole breadwinner.

This first interview took place at my office in Notting Hill. She was wearing dark slacks and a white, peasant-style blouse. She was lightly, rather amateurishly made-up, her lipstick smudged round her mouth. She was nervous, sometimes skittish and occasionally awkward, and chain-smoked Silk Cut Ultra. Overall, though, she came across as a woman of formidable confidence and insight.

Can I start by thanking you, on the record as it were, for agreeing to participate in this? I know the prospect must be painful.

I must admit I'm not looking forward to it.

We can take it as slowly as you like.

I appreciate that. But, of course, it was I who approached you. In reality, you're the one who agreed to participate.

It doesn't feel that way. After all, I have nothing in particular to lose.

That's true. Although . . .

Author's Note: Samantha Seymour pauses here and takes out a cigarette, which she lights with an unsteady hand.

Sorry.

You were about to say something.

Yes. Simply that the more I've thought about this whole sad spectacle, the more it seems that no one ever gets out of anything scot-free. Everyone is implicated in everything.

Can you explain?

When I started on this journey – the journey of my bereavement – everything appeared black and white. He was good, she was bad. I was good, he was bad. I was a victim, he was a betrayer. He was a victim, she was the betrayer. It reassures you to make everything stark and clear.

And then?

As time goes on, grey seeps into the picture. At that moment most people stop thinking about it. But I haven't been able to give myself that luxury. I'm still wrestling with it. And the more I wrestle, the greyer it gets. Yet I can't stop myself.

Hence this book?

Perhaps . . . Perhaps I hope it will be the final chapter. There is a sense in which these things can bring about a sort of resolution, isn't there? Didn't you find that when you wrote The Scent of Dried Roses?

I don't know. People were always asking, 'Wasn't it therapeutic?' and it's impossible to say. I wrote it, and then it was published. Some people appreciated it, others didn't. The question isn't answerable. If you're doing this to feel better, I can't guarantee that you will.

I think it's worth trying. And I'm committed – I hope you're convinced of that.

Yes, I am – but why put yourself through all this?

I'm not sure. I only know that it feels right.

Perhaps we should get started.

I'm ready. Oh – I only have a short time today. I do apologize, but the Institute is moving into new premises and I have to supervise. Where shall we begin?

Perhaps before we attempt to impose a chronology on the events, you might tell me what kind of a man your husband was.

That's a big question.

Just a thumbnail sketch, so I can get a picture in my mind.

He was a fairly ordinary man – not to me, of course, but he was decent, conventional, dutiful, middle-class. He was hard-working, he worried quite a lot, particularly about money, he was irascible when he was tired. What can I say? He read the Daily Mail *and the* Daily Telegraph, *but didn't buy into their world-view entirely. Still, he shared the prejudice that things were going to the dogs. He played squash, he watched his weight – not particularly successfully. Loved his kids, loved me – but we all drove him up the wall occasionally. Regularly. Not much time for friends after work and family duties were completed. Slumped*

9

in front of the telly at about ten o'clock most nights, often fell asleep in front of Newsnight *or some undemanding movie, preferably without subtitles. Read about four novels a year, not terribly good ones. Felt a bit hard-done-by. Probably* **was** *a bit hard-done-by. Drove a Volvo, bought lots of insurance. Didn't bother much about clothes – I chose most of his stuff for him. Liked a glass of wine. Loved a cigarette. Hated giving them up. Wasn't a bad cook. Honest, tidy, worried about order. Big on cleanliness, too. Um. That's all I can think of at the moment. Above all, he was an unsurprising man – which makes what happened even more incredible, I suppose. But, then, he had started to change, I think, some time before all this happened.*

So you'd noticed he was behaving oddly before he installed the cameras?

Not oddly, exactly, but he wasn't quite himself.

Was there a crucial moment at which you noticed a difference?

It's hard to put an exact time on it. Like everything that happens, you can trace the roots back a long way, or you can take a shorter view.

He'd been unhappy, though.

For some time – probably several years. I can't say when, exactly, only that I had noticed a change. He was more tense, more moody. But my getting pregnant might have been the catalyst for all that followed. It was a bit of a shock for all of us. We thought we'd put all that behind us. I was delighted. But Alex . . . well, it was always hard to tell with him. He was pleased, but I think he also anticipated an enormous amount of pressure. You know what it's like with very young children.

I do. I'm not very good at it. Do you like *The Simpsons*?

Everyone does.

One of my favourite moments is when Bart rushes up to Homer and says, 'Dad, something terrible's happened.' Homer's face falls and he says, 'Your mother's pregnant?'

[Laughs.] I think Alex felt the same. I knew he'd love the baby in time. But we were struggling financially, and I had made the decision to give up my work with Jackdaw. I wasn't going to miss out on my new baby's early years, as I'd had to – or, at least, chosen to – with Victoria and Guy. Alex agreed, but he was beginning to worry about the weight that

would fall on his shoulders. I don't suppose I was very helpful. Just told him to sort himself out and get on with it. All my thoughts were for the baby. Not fair on Alex, but there you are. Anyway, it's an oversimplification to say that Alex began to change exactly. He was the same — just more distant. As if he was gradually drifting outside everything. It's hard to put into words. I think he felt he didn't know us any more. Children turning into adults. Wife reverting to a nursing mother. And he was becoming something he could barely understand or countenance.

What?

I can only guess that he had started to feel he was a failure. Which terrified him.

How old was he when you first noticed this?

He would have been approaching fifty. One of those 'landmark' ages.

You're telling me.

You're surely nowhere near fifty, are you?

This is why I love PRs.

No, really. You don't look it. Alex didn't either, but he felt it. He was a very good-looking man, and I suppose the ravages of time were showing — crows' feet, sagging belly, loosening chin. The standard middle-age spread. Not that he was a vain man, but he took pride in his appearance. I think he felt that the fading of his looks symbolized something.

The end of youth?

Actually, I think he had accepted the end of youth quite a long time before. The end of . . . romance, perhaps. Not in the sexual sense. It wasn't anything to do with us as a couple. It was . . . the romance of life that I think he was grieving for. Of ideals. And of a certain kind of potency — yes, potency. As life progressed . . . or passed, Alex felt more and more helpless in the face of . . . what? Circumstance. Circumstance becomes so big when you get older. So confining. So belittling. Maybe that was why he got involved with Sherry Thomas. Maybe that was why he started watching us. To take a swipe at that . . . blind unstoppability. In some ways it's understandable. I've felt something similar myself. It's universal, I expect.

Was he generally a faithful man?

You don't feel the need for kid gloves, do you? Even after all I've been through.

I apologize if I'm being tactless. You asked me to try to get at the truth. That's what I'm attempting to do.

I know. It's just that it's painful. The whole thing is painful.

Would you like me to change the subject?

No. No, it's OK. Was he faithful? Well, there was the matter of that woman at the surgery, of course, but otherwise, yes. Always. I'm sure of it.

The woman at the surgery being Pamela Geale?

Pamela. His receptionist. Yes.

Did you believe him when he said he'd not had an affair with her?

I did. As I've already suggested, he was a highly moral man. Sounds strange, given what he did, but it's true. Then there was his Christianity. He was a Catholic, in fact – in a woolly, liberal, non-public way. His faith – or its residue – was important to him, although he never tried to impress it on other people and rarely talked about it to me. He was humble like that. Very private. So when he told me that he'd merely kissed her at that party . . .

Party?

To celebrate twenty years of Greenside. The practice he set up with his brother, Toby. It was in March last year.

Did you go?

I couldn't make it. Polly was waking up all the time and demanding milk. Wouldn't take it out of a bottle. Anyway, I believed him when he said it never went beyond a kiss. I also believed him when he told me she had become possessive and sloppy at work after the . . . what shall we call it? Dalliance? That was why he had to sack her.

So it was after Pamela Geale was sacked that she . . .

She started to threaten him. Which led to an intensification of the whole situation.

When did Alex actually turn fifty?

The year before that. Just after I found out I was pregnant.

So that was when it dawned on you that things weren't quite right with him.

As I've said, I suspect things had begun to unravel before then – if we're still looking for 'the beginning'. Not that there were any obvious symptoms. Nothing big or dramatic, anyway. We'd had our problems. All families do. Guy and Victoria were at difficult ages – thirteen and fourteen respectively – when the situation boiled over. And the birth of Polly . . .

She's – what? Eighteen months now?

Nineteen and a half. Her birth added to the other stresses. Polly was not an easy baby, and in those first six months she was getting us up three or four times every night. We were both tired. Alex was under increasing pressure generally in his job.

What kind of pressure?

Perhaps 'pressure' is the wrong word. But he was certainly experiencing a kind of disillusionment. He didn't talk about it much, but I felt it. I think there's a stage that GPs can reach in their career when they feel they're not challenged any more. The same complaints, the same diagnoses, day in, day out. Alex was a clever man. A curious, inquisitive person. Also, there was a certain . . . well . . . Perhaps 'disgust' is too strong. A lot of the patients he found quite trying. The Greenside is an inner-city practice, after all, and he saw a lot of poor and desperate people. That was why he set it up in the first place – to help people. But as the years went by he felt less able to help them, beyond formulaic prescriptions and referrals. He was resentful that people saw him more like a car mechanic than a healer. Then there was the constant stream of skivers, wanting a note so they could pull a sickie. And they wouldn't listen to his advice, or take any responsibility for their lives. It was like, 'I'm ill, so fix me.' They saw themselves as customers rather than patients. Many weren't civil to him, let alone grateful.

Did he expect gratitude?

He would have denied it, of course, but I think he did.

And he was hurt that it wasn't forthcoming?

A lot of things hurt Alex. There was always something of the martyr about him. There's a certain emotional income in suffering, isn't there?

It puts you incontrovertibly in the right, I suppose.

Perhaps I'm not being fair. He was a sweet man. I think he wanted to be good enough to work as a GP for its own sake, but I also think he had imagined that 'doing good' would have more of a payoff than it provided – especially given the income he had to forgo to remain in the National Health Service. He hoped for a payoff in gratitude or goodwill. Yes. But little of either was forthcoming. In fact, he irritated his patients, I think, by virtue of his special knowledge. They disliked him because they needed him. Whatever the case, some of the ideals he'd started out with had eroded. And there was the matter of his status. I think that concerned him.

In what respect?

It's connected with what I was saying before. People with whom he went to university were earning three or four times his salary. We couldn't afford to put our kids through private school. The house was shabby. Everything was a struggle.

Was his status lowered in your eyes?

[Samantha Seymour ignores this question.]

Somehow, in the last twenty years, respect for the medical profession in general has eroded. When Alex was a child, the local doctor was like a god: everyone looked up to him. Perhaps that was what Alex wanted.

Was that why he became a doctor, do you think?

Who knows? He always told me this story. A story his mother told him. Anyway, it seems that he had a pet – I can't remember now whether it was a cat or a dog. This pet got sick, very sick. His mother took it to the vet, who told her that it was going to die. Something wrong with its head, a tumour or something. But Alex – so his mother said – wouldn't stand for it. He was determined to make the pet better. He would sit there for hours, stroking its head, talking to it, rubbing it, caressing it. And you know what?

The pet got better?

It got better. Well, it didn't die immediately. Toddled on for another year or so. Probably some natural remission, but his mother told him he had healing hands.

And that was why he became a doctor?

I don't know. If this was a film, doubtless that would be a scene they would use to explain his 'motivation'. But he had some kind of faith in himself as a healer.

And he lost it?

I think so. Many of his patients didn't see him as a healer, anyway. He thought people took him for a mug. That was the word he used. 'Mug'. 'Muggins'. I remember something he said to me once, quite out of the blue – he just sat up in bed and said it: 'Samantha. I'm bored. I'm so fucking bored.' And he never swore. Never. I was shocked. I asked him if he was bored with me. He said no. It was bigger than that. It was like a great black whale about to swallow him up.

Like Jonah.

He did think in biblical analogies sometimes. Yes, like Jonah. A blackness was growing inside him. I didn't know what to say to console him.

What did you say?

To be honest, I didn't take him that seriously.

Do think boredom was behind this whole thing?

Yes. Yes, I do. Boredom . . . and age. And helplessness.

You've mentioned helplessness before.

That's what we fear most, isn't it? Or, at least, what I think Alex feared most. Perhaps that was why he became a doctor in the first place. To give him a sense of control. And I think, obviously, it had a connection with why he got involved in the taping. It gave him a sense of power while the world was drifting away from him.

How else was the world 'drifting away from him'?

In all sorts of ways. The kids, of course.

Can you be more specific?

Victoria had always been his little girl. Our firstborn. He'd doted on her. I sometimes think his connection with her was what kept our marriage going through the most difficult times. They were very close. Or had been. She was growing up. She was fourteen, becoming a woman, wearing makeup, cropped tops, short skirts, that sort of thing. He found that difficult. It's very primal, isn't it, the father-daughter thing? Do you have kids?

Three daughters.

The oldest being?

Old enough for me to understand what you're talking about.

There you are. So, Victoria was starting to have boyfriends. He found that problematic. He was nervous that she was going to get into things she wasn't ready for.

You mean sex?

Yes. Not so much for what it was, but for what it represented. That she was no longer his. So when she and Macy . . .

Macy Calder, the boy in the first tape?

Yes. He's a nice boy. Alex hated him, though, because he was trespassing on what Alex thought of as his territory. He wanted to keep Victoria pure. Any father would. He just went a bit too far in trying to protect her, I suppose.

Do you think that was how he saw it?

Without a doubt. I know some of the papers have tried to put a sexual slant on it, like he snooped on her for some kind of thrill, but that's nonsense. Or if there was a thrill, it wasn't sexual. It was the thrill of being able to keep tabs on her. That's intrusive, I agree, and it's wrong, but it wasn't entirely for the wrong motive, I think.

Was the same true in Guy's case?

I'm sure it was, although with Guy the fears were different. It's paradoxical, I know, but as I've said, honesty was important to Alex.

Why is honesty the issue here?

Because he thought Guy was stealing. Which, as it turns out, he was. I'd always told him he was being paranoid. To some extent, my relationship with Guy acted as a counterpoint to his with Victoria. Not that I preferred Guy: I love all my children equally. It was just Alex's thing with Victoria, their closeness. I felt I had to compensate for it so I tended to take Guy's side. And it's difficult to believe that your own son is a thief. Although, looking back on it now, it was obvious.

What kind of thieving?

Petty stuff. Coins down the back of the sofa. Bits and pieces that belonged to Victoria – magazines, pens, CDs. A packet of my cigarettes, although I don't think he smoked them. I never know where anything is, so I just thought they'd been mislaid. But Alex was always meticulous, and he suspected from the beginning that Guy was pilfering. I suppose he was just doing it for attention, but Alex was outraged that Guy should be dishonest. I defended him, of course. I'd probably have defended him even if I'd known what he was doing. But at the time I just wouldn't look at the facts straight. Always blamed it on someone else.

Who?

Miranda, the nanny. Or myself, or Vicky.

I suppose there's a sense in which the hope of 'looking at the facts straight' motivated Alex when he first went to see Sherry Thomas.

In a way. Yes, I suppose that's right. The thing is, I believe a point came at which Alex felt he couldn't see anything clearly any more. He wanted to get it all back into focus – to find a window on me, his children, himself. Himself most of all. He knew that in embarking on the course of action he adopted he might hurt himself – emotionally, I mean – but I don't think he thought he would hurt us.

Not even when he became involved with Ms Thomas?

'Involved'? I'm familiar enough with tabloid jargon to know what the word implies.

How would you put it?

I think she cast a spell on him.

Literally?

Obviously not. But he was at a weak moment in his life, and she took advantage of it. She had a talent for spotting weakness. In a sick way, a kind of genius for understanding the way people were. She misled him. She got him caught up in a situation he couldn't find his way out of. She sensed his frustrations and exploited them.

A *femme fatale*?

Exactly that. In the most literal sense, as it turned out.

Author's Note: Samantha Seymour begins to sob violently. Her hands fly up to cover her face, her whole body rocks back and forth, then from side to side, as if thrown by the four winds. She clutches herself, as if the circumference of her arms will stop her flying apart. I rise from my chair, thinking I should attempt to console her, but falter. She is, after all, a stranger. Registering my discomfort, she waves me away, and I sit down to wait for the storm to blow itself out.

Mrs Seymour . . .

Oh, this is absurd. Sorry.

I understand. I know this must be difficult for you. Shall we stop for a while?

17

No, no, it's fine. This happens occasionally. On street corners, in super-markets. At least this time it's in relative privacy. Let's get on.

Are you sure?

Please. I'm fine. Really.

[Samantha takes out a handkerchief from her bag, blows her nose, returns the handkerchief, then smooths down her slacks.]

Shall we talk a little more about Guy, then?

Guy . . . Well, Guy has always been a sensitive kid. I know that Alex thought he was bolshie and rude and selfish. Your basic teenager. But that was because Guy was angry. He knew who his father favoured.

You think he stole because he wanted to be caught?

I don't know. Possibly.

You said in one newspaper interview that you thought your husband became 'addicted' to surveillance. How soon did that happen?

Almost immediately. He was a compulsive man. He got into deep grooves, found it hard to climb out. Giving up smoking, for instance, was hell for him. We'd both given up at the beginning of that year, as a New Years' resolution because we didn't want to smoke around the baby. He was suffering terribly. And in the house everything had to be just so. He always said I was a slob. I suppose he was right. With him everything had to be tidy and clean and in its right place. He couldn't bear dirt and mess. And families are messy. Perhaps he wasn't constitutionally inclined towards family life. Sometimes he almost admitted as much. Too chaotic. Nothing was ever tidy enough, nothing was ever organized enough. He saw himself as the single coagulating force that kept the family together. Without him, he reckoned, everything would fall apart. Perhaps that came out of a feeling of being unloved. I don't know. Perhaps it accounted for his final addiction – to virtue, to seeing himself as good.

Unloved by whom? By you?

By all of us. Certainly we took him for granted. And I suppose we ended up conspiring to cast him in the role of house prefect. We laughed at him behind his back. Not in a nasty way – but it might have looked nasty . . . viewed as he viewed it. Through the cold eye of a camera lens. Whatever. Although we loved him, we saw him as a bit of a busted flush,

18

a bit Lear-like. The irony was that while his compulsive streak arose out of his insecurity it fostered it too.

Why?

Because it's hard to be close to someone who's telling you off all the time. Particularly someone who is finally ineffectual. And because it's hard to love someone who's better than you.

Please forgive me for this question but . . . did you?

Did I what?

Did you love him?

How can you ask me that?

All right. Let me put this to you instead. Did you think he was better than you?

Shame on you. Haven't you got something to say to me?

I apologize for asking if you loved him. It was tasteless.

All right, then . . . Did he think he was better than us? He certainly had high standards, which made us all feel guilty most of the time.

Those standards didn't stay that high, did they?

I know. But I don't think his was an affair in the normal sense. I believe him when he said he and the Thomas woman hardly even touched each other. Even so, I also know that he must have suffered the most terrible guilt over it. That was why I can't hold it against him. Alex was always so hard on himself. He must have suffered so much. But even when he was betraying me –

If you think that no sex took place, was it really a betrayal?

In a way it was worse than sex because, in a sense, he allowed Sherry Thomas to . . . rape all of us.

That's an emotive word.

But don't you think it's the correct one, in the circumstances? Whatever it was, the odd thing is that I can find it in myself to forgive him for allowing her into our lives to do her raping. Because I suspect he did it from complex motives. And, of course, he thought I was betraying him.

Can you set the record straight here? There has been a good deal of speculation in the tabloid newspapers and others. Might you have 'driven' him to it?

I respect what you're trying to do, but I don't feel comfortable discussing this.

It's going to be hard not to confront it sooner or later.

I'll say this much. And I don't want to have to repeat it. I wasn't having an affair. My lawyers are in touch with the newspapers that made those allegations.

Is that it? Is that all you have to say?

Isn't it enough?

It may be. But it's not only me you have to satisfy. The public are –

The public are insatiable. Whatever you tell them, they want more. Until they've destroyed you.

They get bored when they think there's nothing else to know. Then they'll leave you alone.

[Sighs.] *As for what anyone else thinks, I don't give a damn. But as for him believing in the possibility of my infidelity – well, as much as anything else, that's what put him in the power of that woman.*

So this . . . what? Limits Alex's culpability?

All I'm saying is, it's difficult to judge people's behaviour without knowing their motives. And I believe, even now, that Alex's motives were – at least, in his own mind – good ones.

For allowing this woman to 'rape' you all?

I think he was just lonely. Don't you?

It doesn't matter what I think.

The Ali Tape, Saturday, 28 April, Time Code 10.03

In the course of my research, I discovered some hitherto unreported audio-visual material. This came to light as a result of my interview with Mr Hamid Ali, who runs a small supermarket at the end of Dr Seymour's street. As is now a matter of record, it was Mr Ali who originally put Dr Seymour in touch with Sherry Thomas. However, the police and, indeed, Mr Ali were unaware that he was in possession of a tape of that crucial encounter, recorded on the shop's security system. After I requested that he make an extensive check of his security tapes, he came up with this one, from the morning of the same day that Dr Seymour first met Ms Thomas. It survived unwiped because shortly after the visit the CCTV broke down and has never been repaired. The equipment and the tapes had been languishing in a small storeroom at the back of the shop.

In keeping with Samantha Seymour's wishes, this tape, like the remainder, will not be released to the broadcast media, but I have permission, as with the others, to describe its contents. On the day in question there were two cameras in operation – one trained on the checkout and one on the aisles. I have combined the contents of both tapes to make it appear as a single narrative.

The poor-quality black-and-white tape begins with Dr Seymour entering the shop. It was his habit to buy a selection of newspapers on Saturday morning. He picks up a copy of the *Guardian*, *The Times* and some chewing-gum, then pays for them at the checkout.

Mr Ali is a middle-aged man, thin, tall and completely bald. On this occasion, Dr Seymour is looking tired but otherwise normal. He is wearing a pair of clean denim jeans and a plain, well-pressed white T-shirt. The dialogue from the tapes is clear, and is reproduced below, along with my attempt to describe the action.

– You look like shit, Doc.

– Thanks, Hamid.

– How's the little one?

– You know how it is.

– There it is. I don't know. I am a single man, Doc. Footloose and fancy-free. I can't be doing with all this family hoo-ha. Too much vexation.

– There are compensations. But today I can see your point.

– Under the cosh, Doc?

– Something like that.

– That's two pounds eighty. Anything else? Packet of fags?

– I'm still on the wagon.

– How's that going?

– It's hell.

– You want to try some of that nicotine gum. My cousin was a smoker for twenty-five years. Now, he thought he'd never – HOY!

At this point, Mr Ali drops the newspapers he is holding to scan the barcodes and runs out from behind the counter. We see him seize a young white boy, about twelve years old and wearing a Puffa jacket, by the collar.

Boy: *Fuck off, you Paki* [inaudible]. *Get your hands off me. I'll call the police.*

– I'll call the bloody police, you little [inaudible]. *I'll get you locked up. Take it out your jacket. Drop it.*

– There ain't nothing in there. Fuck off, Gandhi.

– Don't you bloody well Gandhi me, fucker. Gandhi was a man of peace. I'm no fucking Gandhi. I'll break your fucking face if you shit me. Drop it.

Mr Ali thrusts into the Puffa jacket, with the hand that isn't latched on to the boy's neck, and pulls out a four-pack of Carlsberg Extra Strength lager.

– What you going to say now, fucker? Still want me to call the police?

– I was going to pay for it.

– Show me the money, fucker.

Mr Ali starts shaking the boy by the scruff of the neck.

– You got no money, fucker. This shop is for people who got money. Now, get your shitty arse out that door and don't come back.

Mr Ali lets go of the boy, who straightens up, smooths down his jacket and walks nonchalantly towards the door. He spits on the floor.

– No good calling the police anyway. I ain't old enough to get arrested.

– I won't call the police, fucker. I'll take you out the back room. We got things for kids in there, things that make kids not want to come here no more. Understand, fucker?

The boy gives one last defiant preen, sticks his finger in the air and swaggers out of the door. Mr Ali, who appears to be breathing heavily, makes his way back to the side of the counter facing Dr Seymour.

– You've got sharp eyes, Hamid.

– Yeah. I got second sight. Seventh son of seventh son.

Mr Ali points to somewhere below the level of the counter.

– Cuts my shoplifting bill by eighty per cent.

Dr Seymour walks to the other side of the counter. We cannot see what he is looking at, but Mr Ali has confirmed to me that it is a monitor, which receives images from the two CCTV cameras in the shop. The contemporaneous tape from camera two shows another shoplifting attempt at this exact moment, this time an old woman dropping a can of something into a wicker shopping trolley. Immediately Mr Ali rushes out from behind the counter again.

– Fucker.

Shortly after this, Dr Seymour leaves the shop. The moment when Mr Ali hands him the business card for Sherry Thomas and Cyclops Surveillance Systems is not captured by the camera. However, Mr Ali has confirmed that he provided Dr Seymour with the business card that morning. On the afternoon of the same day, Dr Seymour paid his first visit to Ms Thomas.

Interview with Samantha Seymour

Could you put in context Alex's visit to Mr Ali?

He went to get the papers.

But why was he interested in spy cameras?

That was down to me, I suppose, although I didn't say anything about nanny-cams.

Nanny-cams?

It was all about Miranda, the nanny. Miranda Kelly. I thought Alex had a thing about her. She was very attractive. I was probably being unfair – it came out of my own insecurity. Despite what I said about trusting Alex, you can become irrational when you've just had a baby. I was a little jealous.

I thought you said you wanted to be with your baby after she was born. Why did you have a nanny?

I discovered quite quickly that there was a limit to my maternal instinct. That, in fact, my decision not to spend their early years with Victoria and Guy was not quite as self-sacrificing as I had previously imagined. The first year with a baby is very demanding – I'd forgotten how demanding. I decided I wanted a part-time nanny.

What did you do with your spare time?

Oh, this and that. I think I was just trying to re-evaluate things. I definitely felt this time that I didn't want to go back to work. I needed to get some perspective – I needed a bit of breathing space. I still spent three days a week with Polly and on the other two I kept house, did a bit of cooking, reading, shopping. The time passed easily enough.

Did Alex resent you having time to yourself while you were hard pushed financially?

Funnily enough, no. I think it gave him an extra opportunity to be in the right. Working all hours, nailing himself to a cross.

You wanted to get rid of the nanny because you thought Alex had designs on her?

Not simply that. I got rid of the two we had before her as well. They were never good enough – not for me. It frustrated Alex. He felt all the changes were damaging Polly. Three nannies in as many months. I'm not what you would call a perfectionist – that was what used to drive Alex up the wall about me – but when it comes to looking after a baby, there's nothing more important so I'm very critical.

How were you critical on this occasion?

There were little things. I'd come home and find Polly in a nappy that clearly hadn't been changed since the morning. Or she would just be propped in front of the telly. Alex thought Miranda was the best we'd had so far and, I suppose, looking back, he was right. She was always on time, friendly and polite. And Polly seemed happy with her – in fact, everyone liked her. Guy thought she was the bee's knees.

So why did you want to sack her? Because you thought Alex had a crush on her?

Perhaps subconsciously. But that wasn't the reason I gave Alex. I told him that stuff kept disappearing.

Stuff?

Small amounts of money, mainly. A pound here, a pound there. Nothing significant.

Did Alex suspect Guy?

I wouldn't believe him when he said it, so I convinced myself that if it was anyone it was Miranda.

And you decided to sack her?

That was the ostensible reason. Looking back on it now, I can see that, along with the jealousy, it was probably my guilt at not being able, or wanting, to cope with my baby. I couldn't bear that some . . . stranger could do it relatively easily. And Miranda had a way with Polly. She found it all simple. Never came close to losing her temper, whereas I get stressed very quickly. At work, I'm the picture of patience and fortitude, but at home . . . Anyway, I insisted, the night before Alex went to Ali's, that she had to go. Alex became visibly angry, which was unusual for him. He normally kept it tightly reined in. It was another symptom of the changes that had been taking place in him. He really put his foot down. As a rule, he let me have my way in the end. That was another thing about Alex. I think he feared that he was being weak because he always tried to do the right thing, to be the diplomat.

Was he weak?

Probably. We all took advantage of him, to some extent. Perhaps it got on top of him, when you add it on to everything else. But I don't think he thought initially that going to Cyclops Surveillance was a solution to anything other than the problem of Miranda. It was Sherry Thomas who pushed him over the edge. In trying to make himself strong, he just found another facet of his weakness.

Is that what it was about? Him trying to be strong?

To take some power back, I suppose, in a household and a life where he felt he had lost it.

We'll talk about that a bit more in a moment. You wanted to sack Miranda Kelly. What did Alex say?

He said it was stupid and unnecessary. He said he'd come up with a different solution.

Do you think he had any ideas about surveillance at that time?

Not as far as the household went. It might or might not have crossed his mind as regards the surgery. There had been this woman who had come to see him – there had been a big mix-up. He became worried about how he might appear.

And, of course, later he did install cameras at the surgery, without the knowledge of his brother.

By then, I think, he was losing control.

At the point when he thought he was taking it back. The dilemma of every addict, I suppose.

Ironic, isn't it?

So, let me get this straight. He had some worries about a situation that had been developing at the surgery but, as far as you know, he had no thoughts of employing electronic surveillance in any context until that morning at Ali's shop?

That would be my reading of it. Obviously, as it turned out, I was not always party to his innermost thoughts.

What was the atmosphere like when he left the house that morning after the row?

Tense. He was angry. I was angry. But, then, anger was becoming normal in the household.

How so?

Everything was a negotiation. Everything was always unclear. That upset Alex, with his precise mind.

What do you mean, 'Everything was always unclear'?

Just normal family life. In the few days before he visited Mr Ali and CSS, for instance.

Cyclops Surveillance Systems.

Sherry Thomas's shop. Yes. There was a fight over something – it was really stupid. A PlayStation. Someone had been using it on the television in our bedroom – we didn't allow the children to have one in their own room.

They shared a room? Weren't they a little old for that?

They were. It was very inconvenient – even inappropriate. But we needed a separate room to put Polly in. Alex wouldn't give up his loft study, because he needed to work there on a daily basis. If she was crying in our room all the time, neither of us could get any sleep, and Alex needed every bit of shuteye he could get. Guy's was small anyway, and next to our bedroom. Understandably he didn't want to share with baby, so he had to go in with Vicky, at least for a short while until we sorted something out. It's not as bad as it sounds. Vicky's room is a good size and we put some screens up for privacy. But it was another factor that contributed to the tension in the house, I suppose.

What happened with the PlayStation?

Alex tripped over it and banged his head on the edge of the wardrobe. Given that he hated untidiness – on a purely symbolic level – to suffer an injury as a result of someone else's mess hit one of his most sensitive nerves. He was livid. He controlled it, of course. But I could see how angry he was.

Who had left it there?

That was the point. At breakfast that morning, before school, Alex confronted Guy about it. He denied it. He said that Victoria had set it up, not him. Victoria said that although she **had** been playing on it, Guy had used it last so it was his responsibility. That kind of thing really got to Alex. It was important to him to be fair. So when he could find no way of being so, he got very vexed.

What did he do?

At first he threatened them both with docking their pocket money if someone didn't own up. Guy went bananas – screaming, shouting, the lot. Victoria, of course, just looked as if she was about to blub, gazing up at Alex with those big spaniel eyes of hers. Worked every time. I knew exactly what she was doing, but Alex didn't see it.

And the upshot was?

It was getting late for school. Alex hated being late. And if they were late for school, Alex would be late for surgery. So, there was a bit of a showdown. Guy refused to budge until Alex backed down, and Victoria just sat there being all moony. In the end Alex blustered but gave in. They got their pocket money. Alex often took what seemed the easiest path at the time. In the long run, of course, it's not a good idea. But it's human. And this kind of thing happened all the time. In fact, now that I think of it, there were several other instances of . . . what? Confusions, the sort of confusions that tormented him, that particular morning. Trivial stuff. It's odd that I remember this but . . . Victoria started putting sugar on her Frosties and Alex told her not to, and she said I'd said it was OK.

And had you?

That was the trouble. I couldn't remember. And she was so passionate about it. So Alex gave up on that one too. 'Just this once,' he said. Then there was the matter of his mobile phone. Victoria wanted to send a text message to a friend. Alex said no.

This was all on the same morning?

Yes. A typical morning in the Seymour household.

Why did Alex say no?

Because he didn't like them tinkering with his stuff. He always thought they were going to break it. And as a kind of feeble punishment for leaving out the PlayStation. But it was more, I suppose, because having given way once already, he felt he had to say no to something and stick to it. Then this whole dialogue started. Not a row – Victoria rarely shouts and

*screams in the way that Guy does. But she whines. And she's relentless
and insistent. She doesn't let it go. And this time Alex really had decided
to make a stand. Victoria said she'd promised to send this girl the message
and that Alex had always told her she should never break her promises.
He said that she shouldn't have promised in the first place. Then Victoria
began to cry, and went on about how she had lost her own phone through
no fault of her own, and he wouldn't replace it even though he'd promised to on the household insurance. So he'd broken a promise too, and if
he hadn't there would have been no need for her to borrow his mobile
phone. Alex reminded her that he'd offered to claim on the insurance until
he discovered that there was a hundred-pound excess so she'd have to
wait till her birthday. But Victoria said he'd never told her anything of
the sort, only that he'd promised her a replacement.*

And had he?

*I'm not sure. I've no memory of him telling her she had to wait till
her birthday.*

It's as if Alex had difficulty with conflicting versions of things.

*That's a good point. Although he tried hard to be efficient – it was
one of the things he prided himself on – his memory was fallible, as it
is for all of us. Only that morning he lost his keys. He thought I'd been
using them, but I hadn't. Eventually he found them in a place where he
swore he hadn't left them. But I hadn't put them there. He sometimes
acted as if he thought I'd hidden them just to annoy him.*

Was there anything else in those few days before he met Sherry
Thomas that, in hindsight, might provide clues to his later behaviour?

There were a few incidents with the kids.

Can you be specific?

Victoria had a friend round, Macy. She's known him for years.

You've mentioned Macy before. He's the boy in Alex's first tape.

*That's right. Anyway, a few days before Alex went to Cyclops
Surveillance, there was some kind of altercation. I didn't see it myself,
but Alex gave me his version of events.*

Which was?

*He said that Victoria had gone into her room with Macy and barri-
caded the door. When he knocked, Victoria told him to go away, and*

when he continued knocking there was a long pause before she opened it. Then Alex said that both kids' clothes were dishevelled, and that one of Macy's fly buttons was undone. Of course, Alex was upset. As I've said, he couldn't bear the idea that Victoria was growing up – becoming interested in boys and so forth. I told him that they were probably dishevelled before they went into the room. That he had no proof, that he was being paranoid. Once again, he was on uncertain ground. But that didn't stop him throwing Macy out. Victoria was mortified.

Anything else?

Yes. Something with Guy and money. Guy had asked Alex to lend him some cash to buy a CD that was on discount in one of the local shops. Alex said no. Later that afternoon Guy came in with the CD. Alex wanted to know where he'd got the money. Guy said he'd had some saved up that he'd forgotten about. Alex didn't believe him but didn't want to accuse him of lying. Anyway, he gave Guy the benefit of the doubt. Then, later on, he wanted to go down to the off-licence and pick up a bottle of wine. I told him there was five quid in my purse, but when he looked it wasn't there. I assumed I'd made a mistake, but Alex said he thought Guy had stolen it. I told him not to be ridiculous – I'd probably spent it earlier and forgotten about it. I'm always doing things like that. Anyway, he became quite agitated, and, again, he had no proof.

None of this immediately led to him putting in the cameras. In the beginning, I think, it was just about Miranda. It snowballed from there. If only that boy hadn't been shoplifting at Ali's, though, maybe none of this would have happened.

You can't say that.

Why not? Ali would never have given him the card. And he would never have had the crazy idea of going to Cyclops Surveillance in the first place.

Cyclops Surveillance Systems, Tape One, Saturday, 28 April

Author's Note: I was granted access to this and other tapes from Cyclops Surveillance Systems after extensive discussions with the Metropolitan Police. As far as I am aware, every tape relevant to the case of Alex Seymour has been made available to me.

Two principal cameras were located within CSS, as well as an external camera to monitor the entrance and a police CCTV camera a short distance away on the street outside. Again, I have merged the tapes from each camera to bring together a unified picture of what happened on that first afternoon when Alex Seymour met Sherry Thomas.

The first camera shot comes from the police CCTV, which covers the area roughly adjacent to the CSS shop on the Park Royal trading estate near the Central Middlesex Hospital in Acton. The quality of the footage is far inferior to that from cameras installed by Ms Thomas, who used high-grade colour equipment. However, it reveals some important details of the state of Dr Seymour's mind when he made his first approach to CSS: he was clearly having second thoughts about employing covert surveillance in his home.

The police tape for that afternoon shows Dr Seymour approaching the shop slowly. His appearance is timed at 13.07, just a few hours after he had taken the business card from Mr Ali. He is wearing the same smart but casual clothes, and seems somewhat nervous and distracted.

The street in which CSS is situated is bland and unexceptional. There are no residential buildings, only business parks, warehouses, pubs and cafés. There are few people about – indeed, Dr Seymour seems virtually the only person to have walked down the street during his appearance on the tape. Clearly he was uneasy: the tape shows him checking the business card several times, as if he wants to be sure that he is in the right place. In another section he turns round and walks a good twenty yards away from CSS, then halts and turns back.

The day is unseasonably warm – records show that the temperature reached one of its highest peaks ever for that time of year. The tape shows Dr Seymour repeatedly wiping his brow with a handkerchief. In as much as one can read his expression, it is one of hesitation and anxiety.

It is at 13.09 that an image of Dr Seymour is picked up by the external camera at CSS. The colour image shows that he was an unusually good-looking man, tall, with a full head of floppy brown hair, side parted, and large, rather soulful eyes. His movements are oddly graceful – this is apparent even on the jerkier images of the street CCTV. He is clean-shaven, and has a strong jaw-line and high cheekbones. His mouth is wide and full, and he seems quite slim and athletic – there is no sign of the 'middle-age spread' to which his wife referred. However – no doubt partly because of his apparent anxiety and the heat of the day – his face is red, and he is sweating profusely: there are dark patches of sweat at both armpits. He is carrying a large leather bag over his shoulder.

The picture shows him pause in front of the shop and gaze at the interior for several seconds. The security shutters are down even during trading hours, and it may be either that Dr Seymour thought the shop was closed, or that he was still hesitating over the path he was about to embark upon.

From his demeanour, then, it appears possible that he was about to abandon the project. But one of Cyclops's internal cameras shows the proprietor, Sherry Thomas, looking up from her desk while Dr Seymour stands outside. Apparently she notices the figure outside her shop and her face becomes animated. She checks her hair and makeup in a mirror mounted on a wall adjacent to her desk. Then she looks back at him, and beckons. We see her hit a button, which automatically unlocks the front door.

Before I continue the description of this first meeting, it is worth recording what the camera reveals of both Sherry Thomas and the CSS shop, immediately prior to Dr Seymour's arrival. Like Dr Seymour, she is attractive, if not spectacularly glamorous or showy. She appears younger than her actual age of forty. She is full-bodied, though not fat, and is formally dressed in a light grey matching jacket and skirt. The skirt is tight, and cut several inches above the knee. She is wearing black shoes with heels high enough to look a little inappropriate in a business context. They emphasize the length of her slender, toned legs. She appears quite heavily made-up, but this may be partly the effect of the colour resolution on the tape. Her hair is strawberry blonde, long – almost covering her shoulder-blades – swept back, teased and bouffed in the American-cheerleader style. Her narrow, hooded eyes give her a feline, almost squinting appearance.

Sherry Thomas spends most of her time walking around the shop restlessly. She checks her watch continuously. She is never still or relaxed. Sometimes she seems to see a smudge on a glass case, breathes on it, then wipes at it urgently with a small square of cloth.

She seems bored and ill at ease. She picks up a magazine from the waiting area, only to put it down again. Occasionally she sighs or yawns. She lights a cigarette, then stabs it out almost immediately. She stares out of the window, then inspects the floor. She is never at rest.

She spends a few minutes making a cup of coffee. Then she rubs her temples and takes out a small bottle from her bag. She tips out some pills and washes them down with the coffee, then washes, rinses, dries and hangs up the mug. Then she returns to her desk, where she fidgets, squirms and doodles absently on a blotter pad, until Dr Seymour arrives.

The interior of the CSS shop is familiar from TV broadcasts, and particularly the Channel 4 documentary *The Cyclops Factor – Inside The Spider's Web*. I confess to having used this programme to supplement my description, since the relatively immobile eyes of the CCTVs, although there are three, tend to limit perspective.

The fittings and fixtures of CSS have been removed or ripped out now, but the documentary was made when they were still intact.

The interior, unlike the untidy, bleak and – on the day of Dr Seymour's visit – sweltering streetscape, is cool, ordered and professional-looking. It is clean and tidy, with not a single object out of place. Sherry Thomas's desk is almost architectural in the precise arrangement of the objects on it, as if they were permanent fixtures on an invisible grid. There are several litter-bins, but they all appear empty.

The room – about twenty feet by fifteen, with the desk on the west side furthest from the door – gives the impression of being chilly. This may be because it is washed in blue light, although again this may be the effect of colour distortion produced by the camera. A number of glass cases are placed about the walls, displaying neatly arranged technical equipment, which rests inside boxes lined with a purplish velvet fabric. The effect is after the style of a jeweller's shop.

The equipment is much as you would imagine. There are miniature tape-recorders, telephone bugs, headsets, cameras concealed within a multiplicity of ordinary household objects – beer cans, teddy bears, books. There are transmitters and receivers, battery packs, lenses, desktop cameras.

However, there are more sinister elements to the display: in one glass case, in the centre of the north wall, a model of a child wears a frightening-looking bright yellow plastic mask with a long, flexible hose. A sign above it can be made out: 'Emergency Defense Preparedness: Nuclear, Biological, Chemical Protection'. The mask is identified as the 'Potomac Emergency Escape Mask'.

Elsewhere, there are rape alarms, elaborate body armour, covert electronic lie-detectors. A magazine article, from American *Time* magazine, has been enlarged, framed and placed on the wall. The headline reads, 'Someone Is Watching You.'

There is no decoration in the room, apart from a framed picture of an American eagle that gazes down at the scene below from the wall behind Ms Thomas's desk.

To return to the CCTV images featuring Dr Seymour: we see him respond to Sherry Thomas's beckoning gesture with a slight smile of acknowledgement and a raised hand. The audio picks up the sound of the door catch unlocking electronically. Dr Seymour hesitates. Then he is lost to the outside camera as he pushes hesitantly through the door to the shop and is picked up by the internal cameras. He flaps his arms around, as if to indicate to Sherry Thomas, who remains sitting behind her desk, how oppressive the heat is outside. She again beckons him in. The door closes behind him. We hear it lock with an almost symbolic resonance.

Dr Seymour seems embarrassed, and moves awkwardly to the near side of the desk. Sherry Thomas rises, holds out a delicate hand. He takes it.

– *Hi. Welcome to Cyclops.*

– *Thank you.*

They maintain contact, it seems, for longer than would be normal in such a formal business situation – several seconds. And it is Dr Seymour who withdraws first. He takes a seat, after Sherry Thomas gestures for him to do so.

He coughs, then shifts in his chair. He seems uncertain of what to say.

It's worth noting here that from the beginning there appears – and I grant that it is possible that I am imagining this – to be a certain tension between Dr Seymour and Sherry Thomas. It is hard to say whether or not it is sexual – just as it is hard to say if their final relationship was fully sexual – but a ballet of gesture and facial expression suggests some mysterious connection between them.

Certainly, she is not obviously seductive, or even outstandingly attractive for someone later characterized as a *femme fatale*. But – and this is only my impression – an implication in her words and gestures suggests a powerful, unspoken subcurrent of emotion, passion or *need*. It is significant that Dr Seymour's greatest weakness, by all accounts, is for the needy – both physically and psychologically. If Samantha Seymour is to be believed, the desire to make himself indispensable runs deep in him. It is another reason why Sherry Thomas might have exerted on him a magnetic influence.

Eventually Sherry Thomas speaks again.

– *It's very warm outside today.*

– *It's chilly in here, though. I'm shivering.*

– *I like the a/c on high. It keeps me calm. I don't know why.*

– *Right.*

– *My name's Sherry Thomas.*

She hands over a small business card. Dr Seymour takes it, then introduces himself.

– *Dr Alex Seymour.*

– *A medical doctor?*

– *I'm a GP.*

At this point he shuffles in his chair and looks around the room uneasily. The impression is that he is having second thoughts once again about his intention. He picks up the bag that previously he had put down on the floor and fiddles with it. Sherry Thomas remains still, with a confident smile.

– *I didn't expect a woman.*

– *Most people don't.*

– *So what . . . I mean . . .*

– *We're not supposed to understand all those complicated male things.*

– *I didn't mean that.*

– *Don't worry. I don't take myself that seriously.*

For the first time, Dr Seymour loses his nervousness and smiles.

– *For an American.*

Sherry Thomas laughs.

– *Good Lord, two prejudices for the price of one!*

– *I was joking.*

– *I know. We're not **completely** without irony, you know.*

– *Of course not.*

– *So. What can I – DAMN!*

She rises suddenly from her desk, a look of alarm and anger on her face.

– *Those goddam traffic wardens. I'm, like, paid up to one fifteen and the restrictions end at one thirty yet those vultures – Look, she's writing up a ticket!*

– *Oh dear.*

She moves as if she is intending to go out and confront the parking attendant, but as she does, Dr Seymour rises.

– *Look, maybe –*

– *I'm going to give that vulture a piece of my mind.*

– *Just a moment. Perhaps – perhaps I can sort this out. Do they know you?*

– *What?*

– *Do they know that that is your car?*

– *I don't think so.*

– *OK. Just bear with me a second, will you?*

Dr Seymour leaves Sherry Thomas in the shop and heads outside to where the parking attendant is writing out the ticket for her red 5-series BMW. He approaches, gives the attendant a wide smile, speaks a few words to her and takes out his wallet. He shows her something – presumably his identification as a doctor. The parking attendant looks suspicious, but stops writing. Dr Seymour says a few more words, smiles again and returns to the shop. The parking attendant watches him return and, as he approaches Sherry Thomas's desk, does not take her eyes off him. Dr Seymour glances briefly behind him, then turns back.

– *I'm sorry. This is a bit embarrassing. Do you mind if I pretend to examine you?*

– *What?*

– *I told her it was my car and that I'd been called out on an emergency. I said you were sick. She's not quite convinced. Do you mind terribly?*

Dr Seymour reaches out his hand, and Sherry Thomas stares at him blankly.

– *Could you give me your hand, please? So it looks like I'm taking your pulse?*

– *Oh, I get it.*

She stretches it towards him and closes her eyes, as if she feels faint. Dr Seymour puts two fingers on her wrist and checks his watch. He has his back to the shop window.

– *Has she gone yet?*

– *Hold on . . . just a second . . . she's still staring. How's my pulse?*

– *More or less operational. How about now?*

– *Hold it. Yes. She's gone.*

Dr Seymour lets go of her wrist and sits down hastily. She is flushed, and is having a little trouble reverting to her previously businesslike mode.

– *Thanks for that. I'm impressed.*

– *That warden was tough as old boots. Or maybe I'm losing my charm.*

– *I wouldn't say that. I thought you were very smooth. And kind.*

– *At least we can relax now.*

– *Certainly. So what exactly is it I can do for you, Dr Seymour?*

– *I'm not sure.*

– *Are you new to this kind of thing?*

– *Absolutely. To be honest, I'm not very comfortable about it.*

– *I can understand that. But, look, you're under no obligation. Why don't I just show you around a bit? Once you've understood the options you can come to a decision. No pressure.*

– *OK.*

– *How did you hear about CSS, by the way?*

– *From the man who owns my local corner shop. He got his CCTV system through your company. Mr Ali. He gave me your card.*

Sherry Thomas wrinkles her nose.

– *Bread-and-butter work. We do that kind of thing mainly on the Internet. I don't know Mr Ali. Only the real enthusiasts make the pilgrimage here. Can I offer you something? Tea? Coffee?*

– *I'm not an enthusiast. On the contrary. I just thought that . . .*

She holds up her hand and gives a nod of reassurance.

– *Please. I didn't mean to offend you. I'm not implying that you're some kind of crank.*

– *I feel like one, to be honest.*

She smiles.

— Surveillance isn't a fringe activity any more. It's a multi-million-pound business. It's entirely mainstream. Everybody's doing it. They just tend to keep quiet about it. That's the nature of the beast. Secrecy. But people are spying on their neighbours, their employees, even their families. It's a growth business. The money spent is phenomenal. And you British are even ahead of the Americans on this. Most surveilled country in the world.

— Is that so?

— Absolutely. The thing is, it's normal. Some people come in here thinking there's something shady or strange about it. Nothing could be further from the truth. Because what we sell isn't equipment. It isn't wires, transmitters and cameras.

— It isn't?

— No. What we sell is peace of mind. There's nothing wrong with wanting peace of mind, is there?

— I suppose so. I suppose that's what I'm looking for. What we're looking for.

— We?

— My wife and I.

Ms Thomas picks up a pen and poises it over a notepad in front of her.

— I see. And what is your wife's name?

— Samantha. Why? Is that important?

— Not particularly. Not in itself. It's just that I like to take what you might call a holistic approach. It helps me to help you. Kids?

— Why do you want to know about my kids?

Sherry Thomas puts down her pen and regards Dr Seymour directly.

— I know this sounds strange, but you get a sense about the characters you meet in this business. It's a people business, after all, surveillance, when it comes down to it. The machines are just that. Machines. They're at the service of human emotions. Which are complex. Getting a wider picture helps me establish how I can be most useful.

— I don't know. It seems creepy to me.

— I understand that. Look, take things in your own time. Shall I just

show you around first? Then we can come back to the matter of your situation. No pressure.

Sherry Thomas rises from her chair, and motions to Dr Seymour to join her. He gets up, and she leads him over to a set of glass cases on the left-hand side of the shop.

– Now, over here is our audio equipment, essentially for bugging. Hidden microphones, transmitters and receivers. They're voice activated . . .

– Wouldn't they go off every time a car drove past?

– Voice, not noise, activated. You can hide them just about anywhere. In a plug, a toy, a pen, a telephone, you name it. The quality is remarkably high nowadays. You don't have to be around, it will record automatically to tape or even hard disk. And it's not expensive. But, then, I'm not sure what you're looking for.

– Neither am I. But I don't think it's this stuff. It's to do with the nanny, you see . . .

– Ah. You want a nanny-cam? Of course. They account for a lot of our domestic business. People are worried nowadays about who they let into their home. Nanny-cams are the ideal solution. If you come with me, I'll show you the sort of thing we have.

Now Sherry Thomas leads Dr Seymour to a glass case on the other side of the room.

– This is our audio-visual equipment. Obviously it's more expensive, but not prohibitively so. It's not complicated. A camera and mike, and a receiver. You can hide the camera in pretty much anything. As you can see, we've got them in calculators, children's lunch-boxes, baseball caps – you name it. You can organize it so that you can either watch live on a monitor or have PIR so that you –

– PIR?

– Movement activated. Infrared.

– We have cats. Surely the moment they –

– You can adjust it to respond to certain degrees of movement. You'll get the hang of it.

– Right. And where do you put the receiver?

– Anywhere you like. You can hook it up to your computer – use it as a web-cam. This would mean you could log on to the pictures from your

place of work – or anywhere else, for that matter. Alternatively you can link it to a conventional tape- or DVD-recorder. You could put this anywhere in the house, and when you got home it would have recorded automatically any activity.

– *Extraordinary. And this costs how much?*

– *Typically, anything between a thousand and three and a half thousand pounds, depending on how much equipment you need and the level of sophistication.*

– *Phew.*

– *Unconditional two-year guarantee. Also we can make stuff customized to order.*

– *All the same, quite pricey. Have you got anything a little more economical?*

– *We've got plenty. Have you got a mobile phone?*

– *Yes.*

– *Could I borrow it for a moment, please?*

Dr Seymour hands it over, and Sherry Thomas removes a device from a glass case. Then she takes off the back of the mobile phone and inserts the device. She goes to her land line, asks Dr Seymour for his phone number and dials it. The mobile phone rings. Dr Seymour goes to answer it, but she holds up her hand to stop him. The phone stops.

You'd have the ringer turned off, of course, so as not to alert the target.

Then she holds out the receiver of the land line to Dr Seymour. He puts it to his ear. She stands by the mobile phone and whistles 'The Star Spangled Banner'. Dr Seymour looks startled.

– *You see, you can leave your mobile phone anywhere, and when you want to check what's going on, just give it a call and it will listen in to whatever is going on around it. What we call a GSM engine. There's an extra device that will send you a text the moment any movement is detected. That's six hundred bucks.*

– *Amazing.*

Now Sherry Thomas picks up the phone and appears to remove the bug.

– *What else have we got? Cameras in flower vases, CD boxes. That clock, it's seven hundred and ninety-five pounds. Lie detectors? Very effective nowadays. You'd be amazed. Completely covert. You don't have to strap people into sensors. The machine can recognize a stressed voice even over the phone. Needs a bit of practice, but it's ninety per cent accurate.*

   — How about the Potomac Emergency Escape Mask?

   — Why? You gotta gas leak?

Dr Seymour laughs. It is clear that the sales pitch is working. Sherry Thomas does it well – informal, concise, friendly. By the time Dr Seymour sits down again, he is substantially more relaxed than he was when he arrived.

   — So what do you think, Dr Seymour? Anything float your boat?

   — Look, Ms Thomas . . .

   — Do you mind if I smoke?

   — What?

   — Two or three Americans still do.

   — Well, it's your shop.

   — Bad for you, of course. But, then, you'd know that, wouldn't you, being a doctor?

She slides open a drawer in her desk and brings out a packet of Marlboro Red. The fact that Dr Seymour had himself given up smoking only a few months before and that Marlboro Red was his own chosen brand can only be a matter of coincidence.

Now she winces, then touches her forehead. Dr Seymour registers this – his body language suggests that he is on the point of making a remark – but the moment passes and she recomposes herself. Then slowly, almost sensuously, she removes a cigarette from the packet, places it in her mouth and lights it. She draws deeply and exhales a cloud of blue smoke in Dr Seymour's direction. He waves it away with a fan-like action of his right hand.

   — Never smoked yourself, Dr Seymour?

   — Gave up a while ago.

Dr Seymour stops flapping his hand, and instead seems to take a deep breath of smoke.

   — Got a spare?

Sherry Thomas immediately and unaccountably stubs out the cigarette although she has only just begun it.

– *Sorry. Last one.*

He glances at the almost unsmoked butt in the ashtray as she resumes.

– *Now, listen. Can you tell me a little bit more about your situation? It's completely confidential, of course. Would you indulge me? Please.*

– *I have three children. Guy is thirteen. Victoria is fourteen. Polly is six months old. But I don't see –*

Without looking up from the note she has started to take, Sherry Thomas interrupts.

– *Keeping you up much, is she?*

– *God, yes.*

– *That must be difficult. You're under quite a lot of stress, then.*

– *What?*

– *Two teenage kids. A newborn. Plus a GP's life can't be a bed of roses. You look tired.*

– *I am tired. But I simply don't see what this has to do with anything.*

– *Like I say. It's a holistic approach. As in medicine. There are alternative therapies, right? I've visited one or two healers myself.*

– *Most of them aren't much use.*

– *I guess. But surely there is a case to be made that to treat only the symptom does not necessarily get to the root of the malady.*

– *The only difference being that I'm not ill, you're not a doctor, and I don't want you to 'cure' me.*

Sherry Thomas laughs.

– *Yes. That's the only difference.*

Dr Seymour smiles, apparently feeling that he has scored a point. Then she looks up at him, with a serious, intense expression.

– *But what **do** you want, Dr Seymour?*

He turns and looks at the door almost longingly.

– *It's very simple.*

– *Yes. You want to get your life back under control.*

Now Dr Seymour seems to regard her with surprise.

43

– It's not out of control.

She nods, smiles, and takes another cigarette out of the packet of Marlboro Red.

– I thought you said you didn't have any more.

– I'm only thinking of you. You don't really want a cigarette.

She lights the Marlboro, and exhales the smoke into the air.

*– Let me put it to you again. What **do** you want?*

At this point, Dr Seymour explains briefly, and as simply as possible, about the situation with Miranda Kelly and his need to allay his wife's fears about theft. Sherry Thomas listens gravely; this time she finishes the cigarette right down to the stub.

– And is that your only surveillance concern?

– What?

– Is that the only thing that is currently concerning you in terms of covert information?

– I don't know what you mean.

– No. Well. All in good time, I suppose. I think I can help you, Dr Seymour.

– Is it legal to snoop on people like this?

*– It's absolutely legal. And forgive me – it's not **snooping**. It is legitimate surveillance. After all, what if you found out that your nanny was – God forbid – not merely stealing but doing something untoward with your child? Wouldn't you consider the investment justified? That the 'snooping', as you call it, had headed off a potentially disastrous and tragic development?*

Sherry Thomas now stares out of the front of the shop for several seconds, as if growing bored with her audience. There is a desk diary in front of her, which she shuts suddenly. It makes a loud report. Dr Seymour starts at the abruptness of the sound.

– So. Which of Cyclops's products do you think you could make use of?

– Depends on what they cost.

– That depends on whether you want to rent or buy. And on the level of sophistication you require.

– How much for the camera in the smoke-alarm?

– Sound or PIR activated?

– PIR?

– You weren't paying attention. Movement activated. An infrared beam detects anything moving in the room, then switches on automatically. Is that what you want?

– I don't know. I suppose.

– To buy, six hundred for the transmitter and four for the receiver. PIR is nine hundred and eighty. All prices plus VAT, so something on the high side of a thousand altogether.

– It's quite a lot of money.

– Not for something that could transform your life.

– It's not going to transform my life. If I go ahead, it will be a temporary measure to help me sort out a specific problem.

– Whatever you say. Rental for a week – let me see – that would be one hundred and fifty pounds for the lot. Plus a deposit, of course.

– I don't know. It still seems a bit strange.

Sherry Thomas doesn't reply. Instead, she looks at her watch, as if impatient.

– I'm not sure that I can afford it, to tell you the truth.

– Is that the issue?

– It's much more than I had anticipated. My wife simply wouldn't stand for it.

– Tell you what I'll do. You can take it on approval.

Sherry Thomas gets up from her chair and starts packing the smoke-alarm camera, along with two small black boxes, a transmitter and receiver, into a carrying case.

– What do you mean?

– You did me a favour with the traffic warden. Maybe I can do you one. Just see how you get along with it. If it doesn't produce the results you hope for, you owe me nothing. Or if your wife gives you the no-no, just return it in the box. No pressure. But if it works out the way I think it will, you pay me in full. What do you say?

– I'm not sure.

– All I need is your credit-card imprint as a guarantee. Then you can take it away. No strings attached.

– *That seems . . . remarkably generous.*

– *You have to understand. My job – well, it's a bit like yours. You don't do your job just to bring home a pay cheque, do you? You want to help people.*

– *Of course, but –*

– *Well, then. You understand when someone has a sense of vocation about something. A sense of mission, if you will. And something else . . .*

Sherry Thomas seals the box, and puts it into a large plastic carrier-bag with the CSS logo – a simple drawing of a large eye superimposed on an image of the globe. Dr Seymour hands over his credit card, and she takes an imprint. Then, returning the card, she looks at Dr Seymour and flashes him a wide, generous smile.

– *You need this. It's right for you, I can tell. Like I say, you get a feeling for people.*

She holds out the carrier-bag to him. Then, suddenly, she drops it and grabs at her forehead. Her face contorts.

– *Aah. Jesus. God Almighty.*

– *Are you all right?*

– *No. Yes, of course. I'm used to it.*

– *Headache?*

– *I need to sit down. It's all right. You can go. It'll pass.*

She sits down unsteadily. Dr Seymour steps forward and inspects her carefully, as if some diagnosis might be possible from looking as her.

– *Can I get you a glass of water?*

Instead of responding, Sherry Thomas, still with one hand on her head, picks up the bag she has dropped and hands it to Dr Seymour.

– *Instructions are all in there. It's easy as pie. If you don't want it, just bring it back to me this time next week. Before one thirty. Closed on Saturday afternoons. Please don't be late. I'll be here. We can settle up then. Now, go, please. This will pass. I'm fine.*

– *Can't I just –*

– *Go. Please. And thanks for the ticket thing. 'Bye.*

Dr Seymour remains still for several more seconds, then reaches out and slowly, as if it was of enormous weight, takes the carrier-bag. He looks behind him one last time as he opens the door and makes as if to speak, but Sherry Thomas waves him away. After he has left, she sits there for several minutes, holding her head in her hands, rocking back and forward. Then the tape ends.

Interview with Samantha Seymour

What can you tell me about the situation at the surgery that was concerning Alex?

In fact, there were a number of 'situations' at the surgery.

Specifically the situation with Pamela Geale, the receptionist, and with the patient, Mrs Thibo Madoowbe.

I don't think either of those 'situations' really amounted to anything.

Do you find this difficult to talk about?

A little. I resent some of the allegations that Pamela made. After all, she had her part in driving Alex to this. No remorse, though. Instead she picked up I don't know how many thousands for her 'story'.

How do you know she's lying?

Because I knew Alex. Her version of events – it just doesn't make sense. Alex wouldn't have done anything like that – with either her or the Somali woman. I know because he told me everything about both situations. He told me when he didn't need to. Simply because the truth was weighing too heavily on him. I don't see why he should have gone to the trouble of lying to me when he could have kept quiet about the whole thing.

Can you tell me, then, as best you can remember, Alex's version of events? I understand, for instance, that worries about Mrs Madoowbe might have contributed to his decision to go to Cyclops Surveillance.

It's true he was worried about work, but I don't think he thought of putting cameras into the surgery until a good while after he'd started taping us. At least, that was what he told me and, as I say, I can't think why he would lie about it at that stage when he was making a clean breast.

Why was he worried about work?

His vulnerability to allegations of one sort or another.

And this all came to a head with Mrs Madoowbe.

It's a permanent risk for doctors – we live in sensitive times. They can be accused of sexual abuse, paedophilia, homophobia, racism, you name it. Doctors are in a powerful position, and some patients resent that – or that GPs are not always able to make them better or are unwilling to prescribe the drugs they want so they can dope themselves.

Are you saying Mrs Madoowbe –

No, no. Not at all. As far as I can make out she was – is – a perfectly nice, somewhat frightened woman, who has made no allegations against my husband.

No one has succeeded in locating her yet.

I believe the reason he put cameras into the surgery was largely as a result of what Pamela Geale was threatening him with.

Pamela Geale, of course, alleged that she herself had a full-blown, if brief, affair with your husband.

Have you met her?

I approached her about co-operating with the book. She declined. She's writing her own, of course, so it wasn't entirely unexpected.

What did you make of her?

I didn't find her especially likeable.

Did you think she was attractive?

Not particularly.

Quite. If he was going to stray, I can't imagine him risking everything for Pamela Geale.

What people find attractive in other people is mysterious. And what they will risk is incomprehensible. Anyway, even in your own version of events . . .

Yes – he kissed her. No big deal, really. He told me about it the same night. As I say, Alex always tried to be honest.

This was the night in March last year. The surgery's twentieth-anniversary celebration.

It wasn't much of a celebration. Just a drink at the pub round the corner for everyone who worked at the practice. Anyway, Pamela. She'd been flirting with Alex ever since she started work at the surgery. His brother Toby had often joked about it with me. And Alex told me several times, long before all this blew up. Anyway, he came home that night and told me he'd done something stupid – that he'd got drunk and kissed her, and he didn't know why he'd done it and he was very, very sorry.

How did you react?

I was furious. I hit the roof. I slapped his face.

So it was a big deal.

It wasn't, really. I was just too . . . too ungenerous. For the first time in our marriage he'd committed some trivial infraction and he'd told me about it immediately. I reacted like a virago. Maybe that was why he got so secretive afterwards. Decided he couldn't afford to be honest with me. Maybe if I had . . .

[Samantha Seymour begins crying. The tape is switched off. Recording resumes several minutes later.]

Don't be too hard on yourself.

Oh, Alex. What did I do to you?

Do you want to stop?

No. I need to talk this through. Ask me another question.

All right. What was the aftermath of the whole thing?

The kiss? Well, I didn't speak to him for a few days. And I asked him to sack Pamela Geale. But he refused. He said it wasn't her fault – or, at least, it was as much his as hers. Typically fair-minded. I said he was putting his principles before me. But he wouldn't budge.

He did sack her in the end, though, didn't he? A week or so later.

He didn't have any choice.

Because of pressure from you?

No. It was her. She started to get sloppy. Over-familiar. Like there was something between them when there wasn't, and he'd made that clear to her on several occasions.

How did this sloppiness manifest itself?

According to Alex, she continued to flirt with him. She turned up late in the mornings, or left early in the evenings. She pestered him to go out for a drink, and when he refused, she turned nasty. Nothing specific – just in her tone and general demeanour. Alex didn't want to sack her, even then. But the thing happened with the Somali woman.

Incidentally, Miss Geale said that your husband was racially prejudiced.

Yes, he was. That's true.

Are you saying –

He was mainly prejudiced against white people. The 'trailer trash', as he had started to call them. Said they were stupid, incapable of taking responsibility for themselves. Overfed, overweight, docile, dim. He had a lot more respect for East Africans, particularly the Somalis. Some held down two, three jobs to keep going. They were refugees, displaced people with nothing, but they were proud. Also, they held themselves together through the Church, which I think he identified with, being . . . what shall we say? . . . borderline religious himself. He was not a racist. I defy anyone to produce a shred of evidence to back up Pamela Geale's allegations. Any of them.

Can you reiterate them?

I don't want to. The point is that they were one of the things that sent him down this road.

They weren't made public until after his death.

But he feared them. Pamela Geale had threatened to 'expose' him over Mrs Madoowbe – though she never dared say anything in public while Alex was alive. Apart from his professional standing, he must have thought I'd go ballistic – because of the way I'd reacted to that kiss.

Author's Note: As is a matter of record Pamela Geale alleged, in several newspapers in the aftermath of Dr Seymour's death, that apart from conducting an affair with herself, Dr Seymour behaved with sexual impropriety towards Mrs Madoowbe at his surgery on 2 April of that year. She claimed that she accidentally witnessed this incident, which resulted in her sacking by Dr Seymour on the same day and the immediate termination of their affair.

Mrs Madoowbe made no such allegations at the time, and at the time of this book going to press, she could not be found. However, the surveillance tape of Dr Seymour and Mrs Madoowbe that he made later in an attempt to protect himself from such allegations seems to back his claim that no impropriety took place. It is described on pages 129–33, below.

So what, to the best of your knowledge, happened on the second of April of last year?

I know exactly what happened because he told me.

What was his version of the events of that day?

It's hard for me to imagine it as merely a version of events. It's what happened. I'm sure he wouldn't have lied to me.

With respect . . . he kept the truth from you on a number of occasions subsequently.

That was different. It was because he didn't think I'd understand. And he was right. Also, I'd given him such a hard time over that stupid kiss. It shook his trust in me. Anyway, I think if he'd been guilty of having sex with Pamela Geale – or, for that matter, 'interfering' with the Somali woman – I'd have known it without him saying a word. Also, it would have been utterly out of character.

But people do act out of character – he spied on you all.

There's an odd way in which that was consistent with who he was. Although to some people it might seem much more outrageous than an affair, it was less of a surprise to me than a mistress would have been.

What was your reaction to him sacking Pamela Geale?

Relief and gratitude. I'd wanted him to sack her from the moment I found out about the kiss, but his notions of fairness didn't allow it. As for the allegations about the Madoowbe woman, I simply didn't believe them.

So what did he tell you about that day?

He told me he'd had a row with Pamela shortly before he attended to Mrs Madoowbe in the surgery.

What about?

Her attitude. Her timekeeping. Her demeanour since the kiss. On that day he'd buzzed repeatedly for a new patient to be sent through and no one had come. When he had looked out into the surgery, Pamela was gossiping on the phone with a friend. He remonstrated with her. She told him it wasn't a friend but a patient, and that Alex was spying on her. He took her to one side and told her that this behaviour had to stop, that there was nothing between them. She was offended. Angry. Anyway, there was certainly tension between them.

52

So do you think Pamela Geale made up the whole story about Mrs Madoowbe?

Not entirely. In fact, Alex told me that Mrs Madoo – God, I can never pronounce it – the Somali woman had ended up naked on the examination table. It was just his bad luck that Pamela Geale walked in at that moment.

Why was she naked?

I can only tell you what Alex told me. That she spoke hardly any English. That she asked to see a woman doctor, but there was no woman doctor on duty that day, and Alex judged that she needed examining because she had fainted earlier on, and there was risk of an ectopic pregnancy.

If she couldn't speak English, how did she tell Alex this?

She brought a note from her sister with her symptoms written on it in English.

What did Alex do?

He told me that he was reluctant to examine her. Apart from anything else, she was his last appointment and he was late for dinner. I had just started on one of my hobby-horses – as Alex called them. I wanted the family to share a meal together every night, instead of peeling off and eating in front of the television. Alex was doubtful that it could be made to work, but he was prepared to give it a go. That day – the second of April – he was running late and it would have been easy for him to tell her to come back the next day. But he was a good doctor. And ectopic pregnancy can be life-threatening, so he decided to examine her.

This would have been an internal examination?

That's right.

Which involved the patient being naked?

Of course not. She misunderstood him. He asked her to remove her pants and lie down on the table. Then he went to get a speculum and some swabs, and made some notes. When he returned to her, she was naked.

And at that point Pamela Geale walked in without announcing herself?

That was one of the ways in which she had become sloppy. Anyway,

Alex was furious – partly out of embarrassment, but partly because he'd talked to her about her attitude just a few minutes earlier. And here she was barging in without so much as a by-your-leave. It's an infringement of patient privacy.

So Alex sacked her.

There and then.

She was an attractive woman, wasn't she?

Pamela Geale?

Mrs Madoowbe.

What are you implying?

The surveillance tape that was produced after Alex installed a camera in the surgery shows that she was rather beautiful.

It's hard to tell from the tape. The light isn't good. Anyway, that's irrelevant. As I've said, he didn't do anything improper.

Was he a sexual sort of man?

With me he was – at least, before Polly was born. Things went a little quiet after that. Which is normal, I think. A wife smelling of posset and nappies isn't the most attractive prospect in the world. I didn't feel attractive anyway. But I'm sure he didn't have any sexual feelings for anyone else. Although he was far more worried about the lack of sex than I was.

At this point – in early April – did he suspect you were having an affair with Mark Pengelly?

Do we have to talk about this?

I think you must to address some of the concerns that –

[Sighs.] All right, all right. I just hate the idea of the tabloids setting the agenda. No. I'm sure he didn't. That didn't come until after the first camera was installed in the front room, when he got the wrong impression.

Then there was no sense in which his . . . concerns about you and Mark Pengelly gave him a sort of . . . I mean, in his own mind . . . a justification for . . .

If you're suggesting that because he thought I was having an affair with Mark Pengelly he also thought it was OK for him to have sex with his receptionist and molest a patient, you're barking up the wrong tree.

I didn't mean to imply –

Yes, you did. If you keep pursuing this line of inquiry, we can forget the whole thing.

I'm sorry. I'm just trying to do the job you asked me to do. Tell me more about what he said happened the day Pamela Geale was sacked.

Whose side are you on?

I'm not on anyone's side. I'm just trying to look at it from all angles.

And that's your idea of truth, is it? Looking at it from all angles?

I suppose it is, yes.

So you give as much weight to a lie as to the truth?

That's not what I meant.

It is. That's what 'neutrality' adds up to. Well, you know what? You can stick it.

Author's Note: Here, Samantha Seymour switched off my tape-recorder so the interview was suspended. It resumed several hours later, after a break for lunch.

Are you OK now?

To be frank, I'm beginning to regret this whole thing. You're not who I thought you were.

No one is. Surely that's the lesson of this whole thing. The question is, are you prepared to continue?

Possibly. But you should be aware that there are lines you shouldn't cross without being prepared for the consequences.

I understand. Can we move on, then?

Slowly. Gradually. And tactfully.

OK. After Pamela Geale was sacked, what happened?

She started threatening him.

In person?

She tried to meet Alex, but he wouldn't. That enraged her. She began pestering him with telephone calls.

This is according to Alex?

Obviously.

And what did he tell you?

That at first she pleaded with him to meet her, hoping that even though they no longer worked together they could be friends. Alex told her that it was out of the question, but he would give her good references so that she could get another good job. He bore no malice in that respect.

But she was not placated?

Not at all. She felt humiliated and wanted revenge.

So how did she go about getting it?

She threatened to go to the practice manager at the Greenside and tell him what she'd 'seen' in the surgery with Mrs Madoowbe. And that Alex had tried to sexually harass her.

Do you think she'd have gone through with it?

I don't know. But Alex was extremely worried. Even without proof a doctor can be suspended for months after any allegation. There are armies of politically correct bureaucrats out there trying to get a GP's scalp for their belts. It would have appealed to a certain element at the General Medical Council – it had racism, sexism, molestation, the lot. It would have tarnished Alex's name horribly, even if he was found innocent of all charges, which he knew he would be.

How could he be so sure?

Apart from anything else there wasn't any evidence. But he was a little worried about Mrs Madoowbe. She had been frightened, clearly, at the time of the examination, and Alex said there was some evidence that she had been a victim of violence by her husband – bruises on the thighs and so forth. Pamela might have seen the notes. He got this idea that she might be able to talk Mrs Madoowbe into making an allegation against him.

Why would Mrs Madoowbe do that?

Alex had heard of something similar happening to one of his colleagues, a few years back. A young Muslim woman – little more than a girl – came to him complaining of a gynaecological problem. He examined her and found evidence of abuse. He took advice, then informed the appropriate authorities, who visited her home. However, the woman was so terrified of her husband that she ended up alleging the doctor had abused her to protect herself from her husband's wrath. In the end he was found not guilty of all charges, but it haunted the rest of his career. Alex was worried that something similar might happen to him.

And that was when he decided to install cameras at the surgery?
He didn't make that decision on his own.
Sherry Thomas talked him into it?
That's a matter of record. It's on one of the tapes. She was very clever in building up a bond of trust between them, always appearing to be looking out for him, to have some special intuitive knowledge.
While in fact she'd put a bug in his phone on that first day when she was doing the demonstration in the shop.
That was how she kept abreast of the situation. It gave her a weird kick. It gave her power.
Can you help me with the time frame here?
Alex put in the cameras at the surgery about two weeks after he first put one into our front room. Some time in early May, I think.
I understand you believe that initially he didn't *mean* to spy on you and the family at home.
*I know he didn't. Just before I saw him for the last time – after he had decided to end it with Ms Thomas, whatever 'it' was – he told me everything. He said he had simply wanted to surprise me with the nanny-cam, that he had been going to make a short secret tape to give us all a laugh. After that, if I approved, we would use the equipment together to find out if Miranda was up to no good. If I didn't approve he would return it. But the images he captured on that first tape captured **him**. He became hooked.*
What did he see that 'captured' him?
You know that already.
We've both seen the tape. But I want to know what you think was relevant.
He saw Victoria with Macy. And he saw me with Mark Pengelly.
And he interpreted both in the worst possible light.
He made sense of them in accordance with the information he had at the time. In Victoria's case he was probably right. She's very precocious. In my case he was wrong. There has never been anything sexual between me and Mark Pengelly. He's a single parent with a young baby, a neighbour and a friend. Nothing more.
Do you think he was attracted to you?
Mark pretends he's attracted to all women. He's a compulsive flirt. It

doesn't mean much. I can see how Alex got the wrong idea – especially with him being in a paranoid state of mind after the business at the surgery. I had often told him I felt that Mark was flirting with me, and he hadn't made any fuss about it. Maybe seeing it on camera gave the whole thing a new perspective. Direct evidence can be more misleading than hearsay. It's a precept of the public-relations industry, after all – that there's no absolute standpoint.

That's a nice distinction. A useful one, in your industry.

What are you saying?

I'm not saying anything. Did you flirt back?

No.

Not even unconsciously?

If it was unconscious, I wouldn't know about it. But again, once you've finished watching the tapes, you'll have a clear answer.

You seem uncomfortable talking about this.

You'd be uncomfortable if you'd read what I've had to read in the papers about Mark and me.

Do you think that some people might think it odd that both Pamela Geale and Mark Pengelly should go to the papers with bogus stories?

Not with the amount of money they were being offered. And Mark's story wasn't bogus in the way that Pamela's was. They simply twisted it out of all recognition. I think he was just trying to be honest – clearly he had some feelings for me. But he never alleged an affair – they just hyped it up, made it look that way. I understand how it works. I've been in the media for twenty years.

So you're still on good terms with Mr Pengelly?

Not particularly. I don't bear him any ill will, but too much damage has been done. Our friendship was just another casualty of all this . . . information pouring out of everywhere, like sewage.

Do you want to talk about the first tape that Alex made at your house?

There's no point, is there? You might as well let the tape speak for itself.

Everything needs to be put in context.

I don't care. I know what the truth is. The purpose of this book is to lay out the facts. No one will ever agree on the conclusions. But that's the best we can do. So just describe the tape. I have no further comment to make about it, other than that I believed Alex – and still believe Alex – on two important counts. First, I believe he meant to tell me about the camera until he caught Victoria and Macy and Mark and me on it. Second, I believe he only kept it secret out of the best intentions – to see if Victoria was getting out of her depth, and if I was betraying him. I'd have done the same.

You're being very generous to your husband. He deceived you all. He watched you secretly.

Not because he wished us any harm. And after he'd started, he couldn't stop. Like I say, he had an addictive personality. And that woman poisoned his mind.

Are you not angry with him at all?

Of course I am. I'm angry that he left us. I'm angry that he got himself killed. But I understand everything he did. I love him, for God's sake. Loved him. We all did.

Seymour Surveillance Tape, Week One

Author's Note: This is the first tape that Alex Seymour made in his home on the day after he visited Sherry Thomas's shop. According to his wife, the remainder of the family was out in the early afternoon – Victoria and Guy visiting friends, and Samantha Seymour and Polly at the local park with Mark Pengelly and his seven-month-old boy, Theo. This gave Dr Seymour more than enough time to set up a transmitting camera in the front room, disguised as a ceiling smoke alarm, which was so similar to the original already in place that no one in the family noticed or commented on it.

Dr Seymour had a loft-room den, which was kept for his use and from which the children were 'banned': he kept in it a lot of important confidential and technical papers that he did not want interfered with, and worked on his articles for several magazines and medical journals. Even Samantha avoided it, mainly because it gave him a space of his own that he could keep tidy and in order, and she, with her more casual, forgetful nature, was liable to disturb it. The loft room, then, was more or less the private domain of Dr Seymour, and it was here that he set up the receiver, linked to a TV and a VCR.

The material that survives of this first week is of relatively short duration, occupying no more than about twenty minutes. We do not know how much videotape Dr Seymour began with before he edited it down to this core of material. As he later confessed to Sherry Thomas, and as any documentary-maker knows, a great deal of early raw material – the 'rushes' – is dull and unusable. It is not extant and was doubtless overtaped.

Sequence One: Sunday, 29 April, Time Code 15.03

The camera is activated after Victoria Seymour enters the house with Macy Calder and makes her way into the front room where the transmitter is located. The room is decorated in a fairly ordinary London middle-class style. There is a modern, IKEA three-piece suite, somewhat the worse for wear having been ravaged by the cats, and the red-patterned Moroccan rug is frayed and balding in several places. The floorboards are stripped and varnished, the walls are off white, and wooden venetian blinds hang over the Edwardian sash windows. An original tiled fireplace dominates the room. There are modern abstract prints on the wall, and a large antique mirror. As Samantha Seymour has indicated, the room is somewhat shabby, and seems to be well overdue for renovation. There is a large crack in one corner; one of the less pressing difficulties facing Dr Seymour was that the house is in the early stages of subsidence.

Victoria is wearing a pair of white jeans and a T-shirt with a FCUK logo on it.

– *Anyone home?*

There is no answer to her call, although we can assume that Dr Seymour is watching her and Macy from his eyrie in the loft room. Victoria sits down on the sofa. She is ordinary-looking, not un-attractive, a little on the heavy side. She has a tattoo of a phoenix on the upper part of her right arm – illicitly procured after a protracted bout with alcopops, according to her mother. Despite the demure face she displays to her father in later scenes, she is – and her mother confirms this – rebellious. She has a certain anim-ation and life about her that marks her out from her more sullen, disaffected brother. She appears to be wearing mascara and lipstick, somewhat amateurishly applied after the style of her mother. Macy, a tall, dark, thin boy with curly brown hair, is dressed in black trousers and a plain red sweatshirt. He goes to sit on the armchair that is positioned perpendicular to the sofa.

Victoria: Why don't you come over here?

Macy: Are you sure there's no one in?

– The front door was double-locked so there can't be.

– Will your dad mind me being here?

– Why should he?

– He seemed annoyed the other night.

– He thought we were up to no good.

*– We **were** up to no good.*

At this point, Victoria reaches up to Macy and pulls him down on to the sofa beside her. He seems nervous, but complies. They sit next to each other, touching but not moving, for several seconds. Both are clearly unsure of themselves. However, Victoria leans over and attempts a clumsy kiss. Macy responds. They embrace, and kiss for several minutes. Although it is clearly a 'French' kiss, it does not appear overly passionate. On several occasions Macy, who has a cold, withdraws to catch his breath. They make relatively limited contact with the rest of their bodies, but at one point Macy strokes Victoria's leg. Then he pulls away.

– We'd better cut it out, Vicky. Your parents will be home in a minute.

At this point, Victoria pulls Macy back on to the sofa and kisses him again. Her hand moves gingerly up his thigh, towards his groin. Again, Macy pulls away.

– Your dad would kill me if he caught us.

– My dad's a pussycat. [Laughs.] He'll do anything for a smile and a hug. He's so desperate for approval, the poor sod.

– [Nervously] He looks quite strong.

– My dad isn't strong. He's weak.

Macy smiles, and they begin to embrace again. This time, Victoria has her hand on Macy's zip. Almost immediately we hear the front door opening, and they pull apart. Seconds later, Samantha Seymour appears in the doorway, holding Polly in her arms.

Samantha: Hello, you two. Up to no good?

Victoria: Yeah, we were going at it like rabbits.

Macy: Hello, Mrs Seymour.

Samantha: Hello, Macy. Is your dad home, Vick?

At this point, Mark Pengelly appears in the doorway. In his

mid-twenties, he is handsome in a bland fashion. He has carefully messy mid-length black hair and is clean-shaven. His skin is olive, he has a bold, almost Roman nose, and full, Cupid's-bow lips. No one could be amazed to be told that he is, and remains, an unemployed actor. He is dressed in tan chinos and a short-sleeved blue shirt. He is holding his baby, Theo, in his arms.

Victoria: Nah. All right, Mark? Aah, look at Theo. Isn't he cute?

Mark: He reeks.

Victoria: Can I change his nappy?

Mark: I really wouldn't go there, Vick. You have no idea of the potential ugliness. I've been putting it off. And I intend to continue putting it off.

Victoria: Poor little tinker.

Victoria gets up and begins making a fuss over both babies. She takes Polly from her mother, and sits with her on the floor. Macy shifts uncomfortably on the sofa. There is small-talk for a few minutes, then Victoria and Macy announce that they are going up to Victoria's room. Victoria hands back the baby.

Samantha: Don't let your dad catch you.

Victoria: I can deal with Dad.

Samantha: I know you can. You make it sound like a special achievement.

Everyone in the room, including Mark Pengelly, laughs. Then Victoria and Macy leave. Mark Pengelly and Samantha are alone with the babies. There is more small-talk – about nappies, the dog mess in the local park, the weather. Then Guy appears at the door. He is a tall, lanky boy, with floppy brown hair similar to his father's. He displays an almost perpetual expression of surliness and disappointment. He is wearing baggy jeans and an outsize T-shirt with the words 'White Stripes' (a pop group) on the front.

– Can I borrow your mobile, Mum?

– Hello to you too, Guy. And this is our neighbour, Mark. I believe you've met before.

– All right, Mark? Listen, I just want to text someone.

– God, what is it with you kids and this texting business? It's boring. You're as bad as Victoria.

– Can I, though?

– There wouldn't be much point in us confiscating your phone if I let you use mine.

– Just one text, Mum. It's important.

– I'm afraid not. It'll have to wait until you get your own phone back. It's only another fortnight.

– Mum, please. It's really urgent. It's this competition, see . . . everyone's entering it.

– You should have thought about that before you ran up the bill without asking us. The answer is no.

– Fine. [Then, under his breath, but audible] *Bitch.*

– Guy!

Guy leaves the room, slamming the door behind him. Mark Pengelly and Samantha shake their heads at each other.

– What am I going to do with that kid?

– Why did you take his phone away?

– He was ringing premium lines – sex chat, I suspect – yakking all hours and running up huge bills when he should have been asleep. It had to stop. We've confiscated it for a month. He hates it. But with Victoria having lost hers as well, it certainly reduces the background noise in the house.

– Are you going to let him get away with calling you a bitch?

– God, Mark, sometimes I just can't be bothered. Anyway, I am a bitch.

– What do you mean by that?

– You know what I mean.

– Yes, I suppose so.

There is a long period of silence. Finally Samantha breaks it.

– Something on your mind, Mark?

– The usual thing.

At this point, Samantha puts her hand on Mark Pengelly's shoulder. It is a tender gesture, not obviously sexual.

– She'll come back.

Author's Note: According to Samantha, Mark Pengelly's wife,

Catrina, left the family home shortly after the birth of their son. She left a note saying that she had made a mistake, and that she was sorry. Since then, Mark Pengelly has not heard from her.

   – [Laughs.] *I don't **want** her to come back.*

   – *But surely – for Theo's sake, if nothing else.*

   – *It's not in anybody's interest to be in a family that isn't working.*

   – *Everybody's family goes wrong sometimes. Even this one.*

   – *Come on, Samantha. You seem to have it pretty much made.*

   – *You'd be surprised.*

   – *What does **that** mean?*

   – *Nothing, really. You know what it's like with a new baby.*

   – *Yes. But you've got lots of support, haven't you?*

   – *That's one word for it. Is that what you feel you need?*

   – *Yes. It is.*

   – *Any love interest on the horizon?*

   – *Sure. I'm a real hot catch. Single parent, unemployed, with a seven-month-old baby. They're flocking to me.*

   – *Mark, I'm sure you get loads of women after you. Anyway, I've heard a baby is a real magnet for them.*

   – *I haven't noticed. Anyway, I'm not that interested at the moment.*

   – *Still not over Catrina?*

   – *I haven't forgiven her, if that's what you mean.*

   – *I mean, do you still love her?*

   – *No. I hope I never see her again.*

   – *That's harsh, Mark.*

   – *I mean it! How can I have been so stupid as to get mixed up with her?*

   – *We all make mistakes.*

   – *You haven't.*

   – *Haven't I?*

   – *Have you?*

There is a silence for several seconds, then one of the babies starts to scream, and Samantha takes her hand off Mark Pengelly's shoulder and picks up Polly.

   – *Do you fancy a cup of tea?*

– Sure, why not?

– MACY! VICTORIA! Want some tea and biscuits?

The response is inaudible, but Samantha replies.

– OK. Ready in five minutes.

Then she and Mark Pengelly leave the room, and the camera cuts out.

Sequence Two: Monday, 30 April, Time Code 08.45

We know that this takes place only a few minutes after Dr Seymour has left with the children for school and work. The tape shows Samantha Seymour searching around the front room, apparently having lost something. After several minutes she reaches up behind a row of books on a high shelf and comes up with a packet of Silk Cut Ultra. She takes one out, lights it, and smokes it down to the filter. Then she opens all the windows and puts the cigarettes back behind the books. She leaves the room, taking the ashtray with her.

Sequence Three: Tuesday, 1 May, Time Code 16.16

Victoria bursts into the front room, clearly distressed. The audio picks up Guy's voice through the door, but the words are not clear. However, the tone is angry – apparently the siblings have had an argument.

There is a stuffed animal on the floor, a pink gorilla, one of Polly's toys. Clearly infuriated, Victoria kicks it across the room. She looks adult for her age, even in school uniform. Her face is hard and set in a scowl. So it is a surprise when, glancing at the door as if terrified of being caught, she picks up the gorilla, hugs it to her shoulder and weeps, silently but violently. It is as if the developing skin of adulthood has fallen away to reveal a vulnerable, frightened child. This continues for several minutes, until

Victoria hears footsteps approaching the door. She drops the toy, wipes her face on her sleeve, and composes her face into blankness. Her mother enters the room with Polly.

– Are you all right, Victoria?

– I'm fine.

– Have you been crying?

– Don't be ridiculous. When are you going to realize that I'm not your little girl any more?

– Never, I expect. Can I get you anything?

– No.

– Well, OK. Look, I have to give Polly her dinner.

– Oh, Polly. It's always Polly.

– No, it's not always Polly.

– She's all you care about now.

– That's not true, Victoria.

Now, once again, the mask slips, and Victoria begins to cry bitterly. Samantha takes a step towards her, but she shrinks away.

– I want my dad.

– You know that he's working. You know how hard he works.

– Fine.

– Victoria . . .

– Just go and feed Polly, why don't you?

– All right. All right.

Now Samantha, apparently reluctantly, leaves with Polly. Victoria waits a minute or so, fighting back the tears. Then she reaches for the phone and dials.

– Hello? Is Dr Seymour there? . . . I see . . . No, no message . . . Yes, I'm fine . . . OK, thank you.

She hangs up. Guy walks into the room.

– Has Diddums being crying?

She looks imploringly at him.

– Just leave me alone, will you?

– Just because Macy's dumped you, don't take it out on me.

– I haven't been dumped.

– Then why are you crying?

– I'm not crying.

– Then why did you ring Dad?

*– I didn't ring Dad . . . Oh, God, I can't **stand** this any more.*

Victoria leaves the room. Almost immediately the phone rings, and Guy picks it up.

– Hi, Dad. . . . You want to speak to Victoria? . . . Dad, will you tell me something? Why is it always Victoria you want to speak to? . . . No, she didn't ring you. . . . She just told me she didn't ring you . . . No, I'm not going to give her a message . . . No, I'm not going tell her that Daddy sends his love.

Guy hangs up angrily. Now Victoria reappears.

– Was that Dad?

– No. Wrong number.

Victoria looks disappointed and leaves. Guy sits down and stares out of the window for some minutes, not moving. Then he gets up and leaves the room.

Sequence Four: Friday, 4 May, Time Code 19.30

Victoria and Guy are playing with Polly, who is giggling. Victoria is holding her and Guy is tickling her. The older pair are laughing uproariously as the baby giggles more and more heartily in response to the tickling. Then Guy takes the baby, and Victoria makes funny faces at her. More giggling. Eventually the three are on the floor together, the two older children passing the baby from one to the other. Then Polly is put down and Victoria and Guy begin to tickle each other. The laughter becomes cacophonous, Polly joining in.

Then there is a call from their mother. Victoria picks up the baby, still laughing, and carries her out of the room. Guy follows, singing 'The Teddy Bears' Picnic' at the top of his voice.

This is the last of the four sequences recorded in Week One.

Interview with Samantha Seymour

So you believe that until he recorded those first sequences on the Sunday he intended to tell you about the equipment and his visit to Cyclops Surveillance?

I do believe that, yes.

Because he told you so.

Yes. I always trusted my husband. I would trust him today if he was alive.

So why didn't he say anything?

It's fairly obvious, isn't it?

Because *he* didn't trust *you*.

I wouldn't put it quite so harshly. He was worried about Victoria. That's just a father being protective. And obviously he took away the wrong impression about Mark and me. Watching the tape out of context, I can see why. I might be sounding him out, reaching out to him.

And you weren't.

Not consciously. Perhaps – I don't know. Things obviously weren't going that well between me and Alex, but I wasn't worried because it was all understandable – the new baby, the teenage children, the sex drying up, the pressure at work. It would have cleared up eventually.

Were you attracted to Mark Pengelly?

I suppose he's quite good-looking. And I felt a certain sympathy for him. It's hard being a single parent, particularly for a man. He was hurting.

If you'll forgive me pressing you – you didn't quite answer my question.

No. I suppose I didn't.

And . . .

And nothing. As I've already told you, we didn't have an affair. That's all you need to know.

Why did you say on the tape that you were a bitch?

Because I am sometimes. Oh, I see what you mean. You think I was being a bitch because . . .

Did anything happen between you and Mark? Even a kiss?

My children are going to read this one day, you know. I don't think it's fair of you to be so . . . prurient. I had taken you for a different kind of writer. Perhaps I was mistaken. Perhaps this whole book was a mistake.

This isn't the first time you've gone down this road.

What road?

The what-have-I-done-I've-made-a-mistake-you're-not-who-I-thought-you-were road. But I can't hold off when I'm trying to find out what happened. You asked me a question when you first approached me about this project, Samantha.

Did I?

You asked, 'Can you be honest?'

Being honest doesn't mean prying. There are limits.

I asked for your trust.

I'm a PR, you know. Or, at least, I was a PR. I understand about information. I understand that there is an infinite number of ways of presenting it. I understand the great Blairite truth that everything's spin. And I genuinely didn't expect you to be putting negative spin on this whole thing.

I'm not a PR. I'm a writer. For me this isn't about spin.

That's naïve.

I don't think so.

You're just telling a story. From a certain perspective.

I'm trying to do what you told me. I'm trying to be honest. And I can't be unless I'm in as full possession of the facts as possible. The tabloids are still digging about. Whatever you don't tell me, they're going to find out sooner or later. It's too late to protect Victoria and Guy. Everything's stirred up. The muck will settle sooner or later – and solidify. What that final shape will be is partly down to you. If you view this as an exercise in spin, then your view is that everything that doesn't fit in with your interpretation is a distortion. And what I would say to that is, what's the point? Why not hire another PR rather than a writer? Why not get Max Clifford to do it, like Pamela Geale has?

Well, I –

The point is, I have different intentions. I have different purposes. I have different beliefs.

Such as?

I know this sounds a bit pretentious, but I believe in the truth. I believe you can achieve a reasonably authentic snapshot of the truth. That's what I'm doing this for.

That and the money.

Yes. That and the money. They're not mutually exclusive.

But you're safe, aren't you? You aren't exposed, like we are. You're the author. So you'll come across pristine, god-like. You say you're honest but you'll spin yourself. You'll be the good guy. The truth-giver.

Well, I don't see –

How about this? What do you say to some kind of quid pro quo?

What are you talking about?

I'm sitting here talking of secrets. Of things that are shameful to me. And you sit with your pen and tape-recorder, safe. Protected. You get paid, you get status.

Wasn't that the deal?

The deal was about honesty. So why don't you try it? Why don't you expose **yourself** *– if you really want me to trust you.*

That's crazy.

It's not. I'm standing in front of you metaphorically naked. And you are fully clothed. I want you to show me something, tell me something, that you're ashamed of. That you've told no one else. I want you to violate your own privacy.

You want me to give you some secrets.

Not just me, the world. Tell me, then put them into the book.

I don't know what to say.

You'd better think of something or I'm calling this off. You have to put yourself on the same footing as me. Then you'll really have my trust.

Are you serious?

Absolutely.

I'm switching this off now.

Author's Note: The idea of exposing myself for the sake of balance in the book – not balance between elements of the story but between myself and the subject of the book – I initially found preposterous. Yet the more I thought about it, the more I saw a rough justice in it.

I have always been uncertain about the ethical aspect of journalism, and non-fiction writing in general. There is no doubt that Samantha Seymour had a point when she claimed that a power imbalance existed – must always exist – between writer and subject. After all, the writer has the last word – what can be more potent?

But the idea that I should give up secrets of my own to continue with the book seemed a painful option. I cannot profess to be a particularly private person, given the nature of the 'confessional' journalism I often practise in which I 'sell off' parts of my life to the media. As newspapers become increasingly hungry to feed the maw of their readers, the more frequently I have been tempted down this route, telling myself that to stand above and beyond it, to turn down such offers on the grounds of dignity, was self-important and pointless.

But, of course, I controlled – more or less – the output. Now Samantha had presented me with an authentic challenge. I have always sold off the parts of my life that I considered bankable and that would not portray me, or anyone I loved, in a too wretched light. But much of my life remained in shadow, either because it was forgotten or because I protected it. I wanted to define my own image, as we all do: we edit out uncomfortable stories from the grand weave of narratives that is our life. Most people do this personally; I happen do it professionally too.

Why did I agree to her demand for a *quid pro quo*? Because it was clear that the book would not continue if I refused. She had the whip hand: if she withdrew from the interview process – although I had legal redress since contracts had been signed guaranteeing her co-operation – the project would be disastrously affected. Without the sympathy and collaboration of Dr Seymour's wife, it would be at best a half-baked dish.

Also, I could not deny the strength of her ethical position. I *was* being prurient: I was poking about in corners of her life into which she was unwilling for a light to shine, and she had already suffered disproportionately from the glare of exposure. Also, she had felt 'raped' by Sherry Thomas. Was she to be violated again by her amanuensis? If the truth involves a kind of metaphorical stripping off of all clothing, why should I not be naked too? There was a certain irresistibility about the proposition, I couldn't deny it. So, after several hours of soul-searching, I agreed to Samantha Seymour's request.

Interview with Samantha Seymour (resumed)

So, have you come to a decision?

I suppose so.

Are you prepared to do as I asked?

I've thought it through. I'm not prepared to tell you anything that's going to hurt anyone else.

You can't guarantee that.

No. But I'm not prepared to do it knowingly.

All the same . . .

All the same, I'm prepared to do as you ask to put us on a more equal footing. I'm not quite sure what kind of information you want . . .

Yes, you are. I want something that you don't want people to know because it will damage your self-image, because people will look at you differently. That's what's happening to me, Victoria and Guy, through no fault of our own.

Isn't this malicious? Don't you think it's unfair?

It's not malicious. It's about trust and power. So, go ahead.

Then we can continue with the book?

Yes.
With absolute honesty on your part?
Yes.
OK. Once, when I was a kid . . .
Something the matter?
I really don't want to do this.
Then you're beginning to know how I feel.
Right. OK. I suppose that's a fair point . . . I had an uncle. He was a kind man but he was eccentric. Not just eccentric. Nowadays you'd call him 'special needs'. My friends used to call him a 'mong'.
Did you ever call him that?
Did I ever call him a mong?
Yes.
Yes, I did.
Not just 'your friends'.
No.
Go on. I'm listening.
He looked crazy, I suppose. Hair sticking up on top of his head. Long, ungainly limbs. Smiled all the time. He worked as a park-keeper and everyone said he was a loony. Yes, all right, me too. Lived near us – a couple of streets away. I loved him, but I was ashamed of him too. He was just so weird. Mind of a twelve-year-old. Still bought toys and read comics.
What was his name?
Thomas Haynes.
What did you do to him?
I told a lie about him.
That doesn't sound so bad.
I told a lot of lies in those days. The whole thing started with a lie. See, he used to go away at weekends. Camping, by himself. And you know what I wanted most when I was that age?
How old were you?
About thirteen, I suppose. What I wanted was privacy. My mum and dad were always watching me. My two brothers were always around. We had a small house. I never seemed to be on my own

and I liked being on my own. Anyway, I found out that my uncle Thomas was going away one weekend. And the idea that there was this empty house just round the corner from me was incredibly seductive. A whole space like that, all to myself. I knew Mum had a copy of his front-door key. I got hold of it. Told my parents I was going to the park for the afternoon with some friends. But instead I went round to his house and let myself in.

How did that feel?

Powerful. Invigorating. Exciting. Scary. I had this whole space all to myself. And I knew it would be full of secrets. Places I'd never been. Things I'd never seen, or been allowed to see.

What was the inside of the house like?

Ramshackle. It was a mess. Dirty clothes lying all over the place. Unwashed crockery, stains on the carpet. It was an ordinary terraced house, nothing special. But the sense of the forbidden was thrilling.

What did you do?

Not much. I just snooped about. I remember he had a Scalextric set. With the little racing cars. I always wanted a Scalextric. I played with that for a while. Then I got bored, and started snooping in his cupboards. I found the magazines under a load of old shirts.

What kind of magazines?

Porn. Or what passed for it in those days. *Mayfair. Parade.* Soft core, compared with what we have nowadays. But I was fascinated. I'd never really seen a naked woman before. I just . . . I was amazed. Thrilled.

Did you masturbate?

What?

Did you use the magazines to masturbate?

I don't think that's any of your –

You sit in that chair like a judge. You ask me outright if I've had sex with Mark Pengelly. Now we're levelling the playing-field so that I can trust you.

[Pause.]

I did. Yes.

For how long?

75

I don't remember. Until Thomas came back.

He came home?

I didn't even hear him come up the stairs. There I was with my trousers down. I've never . . . It was the most embarrassing –

Is this the thing you wanted to tell me?

No. It's worse. I'm finding this very difficult.

How did he react?

How would you react?

I'd probably laugh.

He didn't laugh. He was absolutely furious. He yelled at me. He smacked my leg. He went berserk. I'd never seen him like that. He was always kind to me. He was a good man. I was terrified. But I was angry too. Angry that I'd been caught. Angry that he'd hit me. Hugely embarrassed. Then he said he was going to tell my mum and dad. I couldn't let that happen.

How could you stop it?

I said I'd tell them he'd been . . . interfering with me.

Sexually.

Yes. I knew they'd believe me. I could be very plausible. And, like I say, Thomas was weird. He was an easy victim.

How did he react to the threat?

He went very quiet. He was simple, but he wasn't an idiot. He had enough self-knowledge to know that it would be devastating for him.

So he let you go?

Not exactly. But he didn't stop me.

And then?

I went home. I never said anything to my parents. And neither did he. But . . .

But?

Nothing was the same after that. He stopped coming round. My mum – his sister – couldn't understand it. He was lonely – we were all he had. But he must have been terrified that I might carry out my threat. Some months afterwards he moved away. Died a few years later. Alone. No one found him for two weeks.

You feel responsible?
I *was* responsible.
You were only thirteen.
I was responsible.
Yes. You were . . . We can go on with the interview now.
Thank you. In a while.

Author's Note: If Samantha Seymour's intention in forcing me to give up some of my own stories for the sake of the project was to take revenge on me for my own intrusions, it was effective. Others who read the story about my uncle and me may find it relatively innocuous, given the purple climate of today's confessional culture. I was, after all, only a child. Perhaps I did no more than throw a token bone towards Samantha's hunger for 'balance'.

But that doesn't *feel* to be the case. Telling the story, which I have long suppressed – I've not told my life partner, my father or either of my brothers – was agonizing. Is agonizing. I fell into a depression that lasted several days, and was unable to continue with my work. The injustice to my poor, simple uncle, so traduced, came to me with terrible freshness, and the idea of seeing that story in print seemed like crucifixion.

Perhaps my imagination was overactive – probably no one would care. But *I* cared, and that was the point – what others made of it was neither here nor there. I had given up part of my life that I would have preferred to stay hidden. Was the result a kind of catharsis, a cleansing of my guilt? Not at all. It was a refreshing and sharpening of it. If I may pile confession upon confession, I dread publication of this book; I dread the eventual revelation of my toxic shame.

But storytelling, as writers are wont to tell anyone inclined to listen to them, is addictive. I could no more let go of Samantha's story than I could stop telling my own in my head. This wasn't simply for financial or professional reasons. The Seymour Tapes had seized my imagination – as they have that of the wider public – and I was set on finding out the truth behind them. It wasn't a bone that I threw Samantha Seymour, it was red meat, and it still bleeds. But it was a price I felt I had no choice but to pay.

Interview with Samantha Seymour (resumed)

Are you satisfied now?

Are you?

No. I feel – raw. Violated.

Then, yes. I am satisfied.

I'm glad you've achieved what you wanted. Now, were you attracted to Mark Pengelly?

Yes. I was. Very attracted.

Did you sleep with him?

No.

Did you have any sort of sexual contact with him?

I kissed him. That was as far as it went.

How often?

Once. I felt alone. So did he. We were supporting each other.

But you betrayed Alex.

If that's how you want to put it. But I never loved Mark, and I never had sex with him. Never got close. Alex got hold of the wrong end of the stick.

But not *completely* the wrong end.

No.

Thank you for being frank.

You earned it.

We'll come back to this later. Let's return to the first day that Alex started taping. What effect do you think seeing the tape of Macy and Victoria had on him?

He must have been disturbed. As I've said before, he was very protective of Victoria. Also, his mother got pregnant at sixteen, and she always said it ruined her life. He was terrified of something similar happening to Victoria.

Why didn't he just confront her?

78

He did, in his way. But I suppose he couldn't be too upfront about it without giving himself away. Also, he had enough sense to realize that the more you forbid a teenage girl, the more she'll want to do what is forbidden. I think he just wanted to keep a watch on her.

Do you think there was anything sexual in it?

I don't get you.

In watching them.

No! God, no! What kind of man do you think Alex was? He would have found it painful and embarrassing to watch. Anyway, in a sense the sex wasn't the biggest thing.

What was, then?

He hated ambiguity, uncertainty. He couldn't make proper decisions, fair decisions, because there was always so much doubt about the facts and so much dissembling among those on whose behalf he had to make those decisions. With solid information in front of him, I think he thought he could be a better father. A stronger father.

By being a snoop?

He wouldn't have seen it in that way. You watch your children when they cross the road – you watch them everywhere to see they don't get harmed. He just saw it as an extension of his protection.

Like God?

He wouldn't have viewed it as such. But I suppose so, yes, God and the government.

Did you notice anything significant in the first days of surveillance? Anything, for instance, that might have given the game away?

Nothing that actually did give the game away. But it might have done, had I been a bit sharper. For instance, the business with the cigarettes.

What was the situation there?

You already know that we were both meant to have given up. As a New Year resolution.

But you hadn't.

I did. It lasted about a week. Then I went out one night with a friend, had a few drinks and . . . well, you know how it is.

You didn't tell Alex?

79

It would have discouraged him and he was doing so well. I knew how hard it was for him to give up.

But you were lying to him.

If you want to put it that way.

What did he do after he found out you were cheating – when he'd seen you on the tape?

Nothing. Perhaps he enjoyed knowing something that I didn't know he knew. Or perhaps he was just trying to be nice. However, he couldn't resist making a few comments.

What kind of comments?

Just goading me, really. He'd look at me in this very pointed way, and say how he thought we ought to start smoking again, then watch me as I delivered a stern lecture about how there was no going back. Or he would ask me if I missed it very much, and I would make up all this guff.

It can't have done much to convince him of your honesty about Mark Pengelly.

It was such a stupid thing. I suppose we all like secrets. I had one and it must have given Alex a kick to know that he knew it and that he had a bigger one. It would have soothed his guilt too. I can understand that. In a way, I can understand the appeal of the whole thing.

What did he say about the nanny? After all, the camera was meant to be there to catch her stealing, wasn't it?

He told me to let her go, even though he thought my suspicions were ill-founded. But I suppose he couldn't see any way round that one. I was very stubborn about it. I believed she was stealing, and if Alex couldn't show me any evidence to the contrary, I had sworn that she was going. He had that evidence, I know now. Or, at least, he got evidence later that it was Guy. But he couldn't show it to me, of course, without disclosing his secret. So I sacked Miranda. Now I feel terrible about it, of course. She was very upset and puzzled. I didn't even give her the chance to defend herself because I didn't accuse her. Typically feeble, I just pretended we couldn't afford a nanny any more. I said I'd give her references and everything. But she was very fond of Polly. I was stupid. Overprotective of Guy. Unfair.

What other effects did putting that front room under surveillance have on Alex?

I would say he became more confident. There was definitely something different about him – a new gleam in his eye. For instance, when he sorted out the children's fights, he was much more resolute.

Presumably, though, relatively few of those fights would have taken place in the front room.

That's true. Of course, it wasn't until a week or so later that he put the other camera in. But his new confidence came before that. I think . . . I think it was because of that first sequence he recorded. With Macy and Victoria. It was what she said about him being weak. I think she meant it kindly. Alex wasn't weak, but he was soft. We all knew that. Anyway, I believe it was important to him to be strong, to be a real father, and her remark about him being weak really hit home. He told me so before that last visit to Sherry Thomas – he told me it shocked him that Victoria had called him a pussycat.

And you sort of underlined that, didn't you?

Did I?

When Victoria said, 'I can deal with Dad.' You said, 'You make it sound like a special achievement.' Like anyone could deal with him.

God, yes. I suppose you're right. That's terrible, isn't it? Poor Alex. It was only a joke, really. We all loved him. But he was dissatisfied with himself – as a doctor, as a family man, as a husband. Watching those things on tape – well, it was all so misleading for him. Some things are better not known. That way, they can't be misunderstood.

Did he react to having seen Victoria with Macy on camera?

Not obviously. But he became watchful. Made sure that her door was kept open – at least until he put the camera in there too. But there was something else. He said it the morning after he must have watched the tape. We were all having breakfast. Alex was making pancakes. There were the usual arguments. Guy came down wearing Victoria's dressing-gown. Claimed that Victoria had borrowed his then mislaid it. Victoria came down, saying she wanted her dressing-gown back, claiming she hadn't touched Guy's. The usual unprovable mess. Anyway, out of nowhere, after the argument had died down, he looked at Victoria and said . . . What were his exact words? I remember he said it very quietly. I had to strain to hear.

What did he say?

He looked right at her, and he said, 'How could you?'

What did Victoria say?

I don't think she heard. And I didn't know what he was talking about, of course.

Was there anything else about that morning?

Yes. He seemed tired – as if he had hardly slept. I now know through his video diaries that he was self-prescribing amphetamines, or some kind of stimulant – I didn't know about that at the time – just to get him through the day. But he was even worse than usual. Polly had slept well. I didn't understand it. I assume now that he'd spent half the night looking at the tapes. Anyway, Alex was always circumspect. He often found it hard to come directly to the point. And I remember that morning particularly, because shortly after we'd had breakfast, and Victoria and Guy had gone back upstairs, he asked, out of the blue, if I thought he was weak. Those were his words. 'Do you think I'm weak?' I was taken aback. Not so much because of the question but because of his directness. Again, now I can understand why he asked it when he did.

And how did you respond?

I shrugged it off. Told him he was being silly. Then he said he'd overheard Victoria saying she thought he was weak, that he was a pussycat. If I'd taken it up with her at that point, I might have found out what he was doing. After all, there was no way he could have known that without bugging. It would have raised my suspicions, and all of this might have been avoided.

What did you say when he said Victoria had called him a pussycat?

*I said he **was** a pussycat, but that it didn't make him weak. Then immediately – I've just remembered this – he asked me another direct question. God, yes, that's right. It was so uncharacteristic.*

What did he want to know?

He asked me why we didn't have sex any more. And I said, rather brutally, that it was because he didn't seem capable. He should prescribe himself some Viagra, I told him. He said he didn't need Viagra. The only reason for **that** was my clear lack of interest. Then I said I didn't want to talk about it. I quoted his own maxim back at him, that sometimes it was better not to talk about things. 'Silence can heal' was what he would say. Alex was always the buttoned-up one, so this was a turning of the tables. He pushed me. Pushed and pushed. 'What's wrong with me?' 'Don't you fancy me any more?' That kind of thing. Then he started going on about weakness again, saying how no one ever wanted to abide by the rules. That he was the only one who was tidy, fair, reasonable. He said the family would fall apart if it wasn't for him, and that it was outrageous to call him weak. He got quite worked up. Then he started calling me a slattern.

Slattern?

Yes, I know. I laughed. I said, 'Who do you think you are? Samuel Pepys?' Then he said that it was the right word, that he'd looked it up in the dictionary and that it was from the dialect word 'slatter', to slop. He said that was what I did, I slopped everywhere. I thought it was funny. I said, 'Not everyone wants to live their lives like you, Alex, looking things up in a dictionary.' Then he said, 'No one wants to live like me, you just want to walk all over me,' because, he said, he was nice, he was decent, he wanted to create 'order out of the chaos' – that was the phrase he used, 'order out of the chaos'. I told him to stop being such a victim, then he said he **was** the victim. I told him to grow up and then . . . then he did something he never did.

What?

He told me to fuck off. I was completely shocked. I snapped back at him. I wanted to hurt him.

Did you hurt him?

Yes. Of course I hurt him. I was his wife. I knew how.

What did you say?

I said, very calmly and evenly, 'Do you really want to know why I don't have sex with you any more?' And he went all quiet and said, 'I don't think I do.' But I carried on. And I said, 'It's because when I look into your eyes I don't see anyone there.'

83

Is that really how you felt?

I don't know. At the time I probably did.

And what did he say?

He said, 'There's someone here. I'm here.' And told me that I didn't know how to look. Then he walked out. End of conversation. He went up to the loft room briefly. He always went up there when he was upset. Perhaps he started watching the nanny-cam again. Although there was no one in the front room to look at.

Looking back, even at this point, are there any other things you can think of that might have ensured that he continued with the whole thing? After all, as you said yourself, he must have been suffering considerable guilt, and the fear of being found out.

Not really. Other than the fact that he was a doctor.

Meaning?

They're used to it. Prying into people's lives. Hearing their secrets. Looking where no one else can. Of course, that didn't give him licence to do what he did, but it would have been a smaller leap for him than for other people. Being a doctor is like being a snoop.

And also a bit like being God.

Yes.

Can we switch topics? When did the phone calls from Pamela Geale begin?

According to Alex, the week after he sacked her.

He told you about them?

Not until he decided to confess about the tapes. After which he made a clean breast of it all. The weight of the secrets was crushing him. It went so completely against the grain of who he was.

Did you have any clues before that?

Only with hindsight. A few weeks after Pamela Geale was sacked, he had a call on his mobile. He checked the number, then went to take it in a different room. Afterwards he claimed it had been Toby, his brother. I couldn't understand why he needed to go next door to talk to him, but there are issues of confidentiality when it comes to medicine so I didn't think much of it. But it seemed a little strange.

You didn't suspect at the time that it was Ms Geale?

No. I didn't imagine she'd start threatening him.

Was she threatening him with claiming that they had had an affair?

It wavered between allegations of sexual harassment and a full-blown affair. And the additional suggestion that he had molested Mrs Madoowbe. It was all a way of trying to get him to see her again. He stalled her. That was when he must have thought of wiring up the surgery. To get himself off the hook. His idea was that if he got Mrs Madoowbe to come into the surgery again and recorded their meeting he would be in the clear.

But surely taping patients secretly is against every rule in the BMA handbook?

I'm not sure that he was thinking clearly at this point. He might have believed that he would rather be hauled up for a breach of client confidentiality than rape. And I think he felt that if the tape exonerated him he would be treated leniently, if it came to that. The end justifying the means, that sort of thing.

Do you think the idea was entirely his own?

I have no way of knowing. Now that we are aware that Sherry Thomas had bugged his mobile phone on his first visit to CSS it seems possible that she made some input. Certainly the tapes show her pushing him in that direction. And it wasn't to protect him. She just loved the idea of watching patients being examined in the surgery. She was sick. She was a pathological voyeur.

What about Alex? Was he not complicit? Wasn't he a 'pathological voyeur' too?

Not until he met her. Not even then. But he was in deeper than he knew how to deal with.

He bears no responsibility?

What he did was wrong. He knew it. The world knows it now. But he never meant any harm to anybody. And he came clean about it and decided to stop. For God's sake, his life had been falling apart. He thought I was having an affair, he thought his career was about to be ruined, he thought his daughter was having sex and his son stealing money. It was just a bad patch.

The General Medical Council viewed it differently.

85

That was just politics. Striking someone off posthumously is absurd. They were just trying to show that they were keeping their house in order – and if they want to do that, they should take some pressure off doctors. And change their complaints procedure so that it isn't all stacked in favour of the accuser. In fact, I think that CCTV cameras in surgeries would be an excellent idea.

Isn't that rather at odds with the aims of the Seymour Institute?

Not at all. What we stand against is coercive or secret taping. If it's fully consensual and optional – for instance, if patients are given the choice of having the camera switched off – then there's no objection. The Seymour Institute isn't anti-technology. It's pro-privacy.

Interview with Dr Toby Seymour

I don't have very long, I'm afraid. Samantha convinced me to do this, but I'm against it. We should let poor Alex rest in peace. Apart from anything else, I've got surgery in ten minutes.

I understand. I'll be as brief as possible. Dr Seymour, how long did you work with your brother?

More than twenty years. We set up the surgery together. Went to the same medical school. Both of us had wanted to be doctors since we were kids. We were very close.

What kind of a man was he?

This sounds rather ridiculous, but I don't really know. Not because he turned out to be someone different from whom we'd thought he was, but because he was a closed sort of person. Quite reticent, secretive. A good family man. But it was hard to get much out of him. I liked him, all the same. He was solid and reliable, responsible – hardly ever late, always worked longer than he strictly needed to. The patients mainly liked him – well, the good ones, anyway.

Good ones?

There are good patients as well as good doctors. I'm afraid in this practice we don't have that many good patients any more. Scum, some of them. Wastrels.

You think your patients are scum?

I'm too long in the tooth now to mince my words. I was never an idealist like Alex, but anyone who spends twenty years in a place like this is liable to learn some sharp lessons about human nature. But the good patients we do have seemed to like Alex well enough, although I'm not sure towards the end that it was reciprocated.

Meaning?

He was a very good doctor. I'm just not sure that he liked people any more. A practice like this – it's very testing. It's discouraging. I think the thing with Pamela Geale – someone who was meant to be on his side turning against him – was a turning point. He was just finding it harder and harder to sustain being a 'good' person, I think. I sometimes got the impression that he felt he'd chosen the wrong career. A job like this does end up as quite unrewarding. You pretty much know what's wrong with everybody who comes to see you. When you don't you refer them. It's not that challenging. It was getting him down. And, of course, he had family problems.

He told you about them?

Not in so many words. Like I say, he was a reticent man. But I could read between the lines. The odd comment here and there. It was obvious that he and Samantha hadn't been getting on too well. Of course, there was a new baby – that puts pressure on anyone. And he worried about Victoria. I expect you know all this. On top of everything else he felt – well, poor. Nowadays that matters much more than it did when we started out. His house needed work, there were the kids, the car was ten years old. He was at a bit of a low ebb.

Do you think he was having an affair with Pamela Geale?

No.

There was nothing between them at all?

Apart from the party. For once in his life, Alex got drunk. I knew perfectly well that Pamela had a thing about him. A lot of women did. But Alex was never that way inclined – he was uxorious, despite all the problems. Anyway, that night Pamela kept flirting with him. I saw it all. Alex didn't even find her attractive. She wasn't that attractive. But I think he felt it was rude to keep refusing her. He didn't want to hurt her feelings. So, after a few drinks – which, as I say, he wasn't used to – he kissed her. We all saw it.

It was innocent?

It wasn't just a peck on the cheek, if that's what you mean. It was a proper kiss. Quite passionate. But I don't think Alex ever lost control. I'm sure it didn't go any further.

What was your reaction when he sacked Pamela?

It didn't come as a surprise. She had been getting more and more lax. What can I say? Alex made a silly mistake, which he acknowledged and

*paid for. He had to let her go. He had no choice. She was becoming a
liability. Over-familiar, lazy.*

Did she complain that he was harassing her?

*Not formally. But she contacted me once or twice and implied certain
things. I had to take it seriously. The complaints procedure would have
been set in motion if she had spoken to the practice manager. But I didn't
believe her for a moment.*

And you have no doubt that Alex was innocent in the matter
of himself and Mrs Madoowbe?

*There's always room for doubt, but it would go against everything I
knew about him as a man and a doctor. And as my brother.*

Then I expect you would say that about this whole affair.

I suppose so.

Did you suspect at any point that Alex was installing cameras
in the surgery?

*Not at all. He probably came in and did it when the surgery was closed.
Did a neat job. Of course, it was wrong to spy on patients but, given his
situation, I can't say I blame him.*

But it went beyond that, didn't it?

If you believe what you read in the tabloids.

I can confirm that he took tapes to show Sherry Thomas at
Cyclops Surveillance.

*I have no comment to make, except that Alex was a good doctor and
a good man, and that we are beholden to show some respect for the dead.*

And for the truth.

As I say, I have no further comment to make.

Cyclops Surveillance Systems, Tape Two, Saturday, 5 May

Author's Note: It is exactly one week since Dr Seymour first visited the shop. The weather is much the same as it was on his first visit – hot and sunny.

Sherry Thomas is dressed differently from Dr Seymour's previous visit, though again she is smart and formal. However, instead of a grey suit, she is in a black dress, with a pale blue cardigan and strappy black shoes with high heels. Her hair is up, and she is wearing an expensive, glittering necklace. As before, her makeup is heavy. Her face seems pale, and her lips are a remarkably vivid shade of crimson.

Dr Seymour is wearing sandals, a pair of blue shorts and a faded white T-shirt bearing the insignia of a well-known pharmaceutical company. He is neat – Dr Seymour always dressed neatly, even on his rare days off – but observers wishing to infer that he was trying at this early stage to seduce Sherry Thomas would have to concur that he had made little effort with his appearance. Again, he has clearly been sweating profusely.

Sherry Thomas looks up and smiles when he enters the shop.

– *It's icy in here. Can't you adjust the air-conditioning?*

She begins to punch buttons on a desk calculator in front of her.

– *I won't be a moment. I'm in the middle of something. There are just some very important – Damn.*

It is apparent from viewing the section of the videotape preceding Dr Seymour's arrival that she was in the middle of nothing whatsoever – apart from medicating herself for her apparently frequent severe headaches, fidgeting and pacing up and down the shop. But now she makes a great show of punching buttons and making notes on a small pad in front of her. At one point she licks her pencil before she writes something. She does this slowly, almost theatrically, and there is a seductive element in it. However, if Dr Seymour notices, he gives no sign of it. He sits quietly while she feigns completing her work. Then, without looking up, she speaks.

– *I see you've decided to keep the equipment, then.*

– *Have I?*

– *Haven't you? Unless it's concealed about your person somewhere.*

– *I found it more useful than I expected.*

– *Was it interesting?*

– *Watching people talk rubbish is the opposite of interesting.*

– *Not your cup of tea, then?*

– *It had its moments, I suppose.*

– *Did you find out whether or not the nanny was stealing money from you?*

– *No. We sacked her anyway.*

– *If you didn't find out what you needed to find out, in what sense was the equipment of use to you?*

Dr Seymour seems uneasy with this question, and shifts uncomfortably in his chair, torn, perhaps, between keeping his counsel and sharing what he has learned with Sherry Thomas. She sits forward earnestly, as if she senses that a key moment in their fledgling relationship has arrived.

– *Just useful.*

She holds her gaze on Dr Seymour for several more seconds, then rises abruptly from her desk. Her dress has ridden up her thighs and he stares at them blatantly, then checks himself and turns away his gaze. She makes her way to the back room of the shop. As if to cover his embarrassment, Dr Seymour speaks, a little more loudly than is natural for him.

– *Where are you going?*

– *To turn down the air-conditioning. You're cold, aren't you?*

While she is out of the room, Dr Seymour examines her desk. He notices the pills she has recently taken, picks up the bottle and inspects it. Just as he replaces it, she enters the room. When she speaks her voice is neutral, brisk.

– That should be better. Warm things up a bit.

She sits down at her desk – again, apparently, being careful to expose the maximum amount of thigh. Then her gaze rests on the bottle of pills.

– I get headaches. The heat can make them worse.

– I'm sorry.

– I'm OK for the moment. My therapist says they're psychosomatic anyway.

– You need a therapist?

– Doesn't everyone? Anyway, you know I get headaches, don't you? You had a little snoop.

Dr Seymour makes no reply.

– Are you always so curious? Or just bored? But, then, boredom's a terrible thing, isn't it?

– I suppose.

– Most of the trouble in the world is caused by people not knowing what to do with themselves. Would you like a cigarette?

– Yes. But no.

Now she reaches into her desk, as on the first visit, and takes out a full packet of Marlboro Red. She has delicate, slender hands. The varnish on her fingernails matches the colour of the cigarette packet.

– Sure you don't want one?

– I do, but I'm not going to have one.

– Suit yourself. Though sometimes I think it's best to be who you are. Christ!

Now she touches her forehead, and screws up her face.

– I don't know what's wrong with me lately.

Dr Seymour looks concerned, reaches for the bottle of pills and inspects them again.

– These are pretty powerful beasts. You must have a real struggle with those headaches.

– I'm fine. It's like a kind of ice-cream headache. A brain-freeze. Agonizing for a couple of seconds, then it goes.

– You were saying that it's best to be who you are.

– It's one of the axioms of my philosophy.

– Why are you telling me your . . . philosophy?

– Why not? God, you English are so damn private. What's the payoff for putting all these walls up around you? You should open up a bit.

– This is the philosophy you want to tell me about?

– Not exactly.

– What, then?

– It's the idea that – well, we just spend so much time watching ourselves. Making sure we do the right thing. Whacking ourselves with an invisible stick every time we cross some line we've drawn in the sand. Maybe some people should just do whatever they want instead of spending a lifetime ruled by fear and guilt. Never really living because they're too afraid. But what are they really afraid of? The gun they're holding at their own head. And it's only their finger on the trigger. Is that a life? Is that your life? What did you do with the equipment, Alex?

There is a pause of several seconds before he speaks again.

– I watched.

Sherry Thomas shifts in her chair. Her lips are slightly parted. Her tongue is clearly visible, just touching the underside of her teeth.

– That's what it's for. Where did you put it?

– In the front room.

– Nobody noticed?

– It passed without comment.

– Where did you put the receiver?

– In the attic where I have a room. Nobody goes up there except me.

– What did you see?

Now Dr Seymour speaks almost pleadingly, as if he is uncomfortable at being drawn into this degree of intimacy, and lacks the power to resist.

– I don't see why it's any of your business.

Now there is a complete and sudden change in Sherry Thomas's demeanour. She sits up straight, picks up a pen and taps it furiously on the table. Again, she rubs her forehead.

– Maybe you should just go.

93

– But – hold on –

– I thought we had an arrangement, an understanding. It's impossible to conduct any proper business without a modicum of trust. Trust, Alex. I know it might seem odd talking about trust in a business that's primarily concerned with spying on people. But I know – from long experience in this game – that people who don't trust anybody at all . . . well, they go crazy. Now you have to decide who you're going to trust. Because I can help you find out what you need to know. But only if you have a little confidence in my integrity.

– Trust you? I don't even know you.

She waves away this comment as if it were patently absurd.

– You can bring me back my equipment immediately. **Today.** Or you can let me help you. Which is it to be? What did you see?

For a moment Dr Seymour does not move. Then he crumples. He purses his lips and gives a slight nod. At last he speaks, quietly at first, then with growing animation, as if the subject matter is drawing him in as he recounts it.

– Most of it was very boring. Nothing much happening. Yawning, empty spaces in conversations. Crushing, deadly banality. No one listening to anyone else. Pauses, silences, fidgeting. Meaningless, half-heard comments. It was . . . terrifying. You watch these tapes for a few hours, and you think, Is this all life is? Have you seen this film? What happened on Corrie? What's for dinner? I've lost this – do you know where it is? What did he say? What did she say? I mean, obviously, one lives life, so you should know what it's like. But seeing it on film, hour after hour, it was depressing. It's as if life is being squandered, and you suddenly have a window on how empty it is.

– That's what life looks like. That's the heart of it.

– But eventually I found something. A few . . . snippets.

Now he tells her about the cigarettes, about Victoria's assignation with Macy Calder on the sofa, about his wife's ambiguous conversation with Mark Pengelly. Sherry Thomas's body language and facial expression have changed. Now she seems engaged, fascinated. She leans forward, and Dr Seymour does too, conspiratorially. At one point their heads are only inches apart.

94

– *None of it is conclusive,* she says, very softly, when he has finished.

– *Except the cigarettes.*

– *Except the cigarettes. To make you give up and keep puffing away herself suggests a certain cynicism. A certain mendacity.*

– *I don't think so. I don't think Sam's like that. She's just being a bit silly.*

– *Do you think it's admirable always to put a positive slant on everything?*

– *There's no harm in giving people the benefit of the doubt.*

– *Isn't there?*

– *You can't just look for the worst in people.*

– *I'm a professional. I just look at the evidence. My conclusions aren't informed by prejudice or affection or even dislike. I'm just pointing out that she deceived you. And, as a consequence, it makes the conversation with Mr Pengelly more suspicious than it would otherwise have been. Have you noticed anything about her that's changed recently?*

– *She's – she's started to look after herself. For the first time since we had the baby.*

– *Look after herself how?*

– *Better clothes. New hairstyle. Working out at the gym from time to time.*

– *Really? Well, let's not jump to conclusions.*

– *I'm not jumping to conclusions. You are.*

– *Not at all. It's only evidence that interests me. Your daughter, for instance. I think the evidence there is inconclusive. She's a nice girl, yes?*

– *That's what I used to think. Now I'm not so sure.*

– *Do you think she's right?*

– *About what?*

– *About you being weak.*

– *No. She's very wrong.*

Sherry Thomas claps her hands and lets out a low, musical laugh.

– *She is. She **is** wrong. So, Alex, what are you going to do?*

– *I'm not sure.*

– *You'll be wanting to hold on to the equipment.*

– For a little while. Until I've got things cleared up a bit.

– Of course.

– And are you completely happy with it? Technically?

– As far is it goes, I suppose.

– And how far is that?

– Not that much happens in the front room. Nothing that anyone wants to keep hidden, anyway. I mean, if Guy or Victoria . . .

– You could have a second camera in their room for very little extra expenditure. Hooked up to the same receiver in your room.

– Really? That's interesting.

She gets up and goes to one of the glass cabinets that fill the wall space.

*– No. **This** is interesting.*

She takes out what looks like an ordinary Sony Handycam.

– They've withdrawn these now because of 'public outcry'. Corporate hypocrisy is more like it. They're amazing. All you have to do is fit an A35 filter on it, which I've done, and use the infrared night-shooting gizmo.

– Then what happens?

– Have a look.

She switches on the camera and passes it to Dr Seymour He takes it and puts the viewfinder to his eye.

– So what?

– You're pointing it at the wrong thing.

– I am?

– Point it at me.

Now she leans against the edge of the desk, legs crossed, a playful expression on her face. Dr Seymour aims the camera at her. He stares through the viewfinder, waits a moment, then puts it down almost immediately. He looks amused and faintly shocked.

– My God.

– Quite something, isn't it? Only works if you use it in daytime.

She giggles.

– You're a doctor so it's nothing you haven't seen before.

– It's impossible.

96

Author's Note: The Sony Handycam with the A35 filter was withdrawn in 1998 because it is capable of 'seeing through' clothes when the night filter is used in daylight conditions. The Sony Corporation apologized and discontinued the feature. Only a few models remain in existence.

— *Nothing's impossible any more. You're beginning to see that, aren't you?*

— *Perhaps.*

She replaces the camera and closes the cabinet.

— *It's not for sale. I keep it for my amusement. It's different for me.*

— *How is it different?*

— *You see people as bodies, don't you? They don't do anything for you.*

— *What do you mean?*

— *You don't get turned on every time a pretty woman comes into your surgery and takes her clothes off, do you?*

— *I don't think I know you well enough to answer that question honestly.*

Sherry Thomas laughs.

— *Perhaps that's wise. After all, you don't know who might be listening. Getting hot for one of your patients could get you into a lot of trouble.*

Author's Note: Sherry Thomas's bugging of Dr Seymour's mobile phone would explain how she seems to show prescience about the matter of Pamela Geale and Mrs Madoowbe, because Ms Geale has been making her threats through Dr Seymour's mobile phone. To Dr Seymour, however, this must have seemed uncanny, and quite possibly increased his identification with Sherry Thomas, making him feel that he was in some mysterious way 'understood'.

— *How is work, by the way?*

— *It's OK. There have been a few problems, I suppose. A bit of a situation.*

She does not respond. From the tapes, it is clear that she is adept at using silence to prompt others to speak. It is a technique much favoured by, among others, journalists and therapists. Clearly, Dr Seymour is vulnerable to this and seems to find long silences discomfiting.

– There was this woman. She came to see me. She was a Somali – a Muslim. Very young. She was in pain – said she'd fainted. I suspected an ectopic pregnancy, so I . . . She misunderstood me. Couldn't speak English very well. My initial brief examination suggested she'd been the victim of some kind of sexual violence. Anyway, she took all her clothes off. I didn't ask her to. I just asked her to get under the sheet and remove the lower part of her clothing. And at that moment my receptionist walked in. She drew the wrong conclusion. She made a big fuss about the patient being naked. I had to fire her.

– Because of her complaint about the patient?

– No, because she walked in without knocking.

– That seems a little extreme. Were any other factors at work?

Author's Note: Again, it would have been clear to Sherry Thomas from her telephone bug that other 'factors' were at work.

– We had a kind of . . . I don't know. Something stupid. I was drunk. She got the wrong idea.

– You slept with her.

– No! Good God, no. I didn't even find her attractive. I just . . . kissed her. That was all. But after that she changed. She became sloppy.

– I understand. I find sloppiness intolerable. It's lazy and selfish. I feel exactly the same.

– You do?

– Oh, yes. I feel the same as you in many ways.

– Such as?

– Well, for instance, I feel lonely sometimes. And . . . oh, God . . .

– What is it?

– My head.

She puts her head into her hands and gives a low moan. This time Dr Seymour gets up and moves to her side of the desk. She takes her hands from her face.

– What are you doing?

– You talked about trust. Just trust me for a moment.

– What are you going to do? Reiki? Acupressure? I've tried them all. They don't work.

– Someone once told me I had healing hands.

– *And do you?*

– *I don't know. I don't really know any more.*

She turns her head towards him and tries to force a smile through her grimace of pain.

– *Why don't we find out?*

At this, Dr Seymour stands behind her, places his hands on her head and begins to massage her temples and shoulders gently. She seems to stiffen, then relax. She leans back in her chair. For several minutes no words are spoken. Both Dr Seymour and Sherry Thomas have their eyes closed. There is nothing sexual about the massage, but it is tender. The longer it goes on, the more she seems to relax. After a few minutes he opens his eyes and stands back.

– *Anything?*

Now Sherry Thomas blinks and rubs her eyes.

– *It's gone, Alex. Completely gone.*

– *Has it? Has it really?*

– *That's amazing.*

– *I'm certainly amazed.*

– *You really do have healing hands.*

Dr Seymour holds them up to his face and regards them, first with puzzlement, then with a kind of fierce joy.

– *I knew it! I knew I did.*

As if he is a little dazed, he moves to the other side of Sherry Thomas's desk and sits down again.

– *Listen, Alex, do you want something for your surgery? As well as the kids' bedroom? Something that will make you feel safer?*

– *I don't know. It would be highly unethical.*

– *What would be unethical is if you were to have your career – your healing career – ruined for no good reason. Has the woman been back to the surgery since the incident?*

– *No.*

– *Do you think you could get her to come in again?*

– *Possibly.*

– *Then that's what you need to do. Obviously, if you've been abusing her she won't. But if she does you can talk about the previous consultation in terms that make it clear that nothing improper took place.*

– *Wouldn't it be enough just to get her back in to the surgery – without filming her, I mean?*

– *It might be. On the other hand, it might not. It might be thought that you threatened her, effectively forced her to come back. Perhaps she's an asylum-seeker or an illegal immigrant and you're threatening to have her deported.*

– *That's a rather far-fetched story.*

– *Perhaps. But are you willing to take the risk that any investigating agency wouldn't believe it – at least for long enough to ruin your career?*

– *I don't know. It would be a serious matter to tape a patient secretly.*

– *I don't offer any advice about the legality of one course or another. I just give out the equipment. But I would say this. Raping is worse than taping.*

– *That's an unpleasant way of putting it.*

– *It's an unpleasant business. The point is, no one is going to find out about the camera unless the worst comes to the absolute worst. It'll just be our secret.*

– *We have a different kind of smoke alarm at the surgery. The ones you sell would stand out like a sore thumb.*

– *There are plenty of other possibilities.*

Dr Seymour's eyes scan the room. His gaze falls on a large brown teddy bear with a dim-witted but convincingly lovable expression. Sherry Thomas follows his gaze.

– *The camera is mounted in one of his eyes.*

– *I have lots of soft toys in the surgery. For the kids. No one would notice another.*

– *That's a good idea. I'm sure it will make you feel much better. And I could give you a discount.*

– *What kind of discount?*

– *One hundred per cent.*

– *Why on earth would you give me the equipment for free?*

– *Because you healed me, Alex. And more than that – I like you. I like you because I can see that you're on – you're on a quest. You haven't just lain down and accepted it all like some kind of dumb animal. You're fighting back, Alex, in your own way. All those invisible worlds ranged against you. You've got the courage to do something about it. I respect that, I really do.*

– Is that all?

– No. There's one other thing. I'd like you to bring the tapes here.

– What on earth for?

– Because I can help you interpret them. It's a purely professional matter. You'd be surprised how easy it is to misread what you capture on a videotape. Also, if things aren't working technically, I can tell you how to improve them.

– Is this a service you provide for all your clients?

– To be honest, no. But I find your case interesting, and I think I can be of help.

Dr Seymour weighs the offer carefully before he replies.

– Can I think about it?

– Of course you can. No pressure.

Sherry Thomas gathers together the surveillance equipment – the teddy bear transmitter, an extra receiver and a new smoke-alarm transmitter for the children's bedroom – and places it in a plain white plastic carrier-bag. She hands it to Dr Seymour, who, without another word, takes it from her and leaves CSS.

Interview with Barbara Shilling

Author's Note: It was relatively straightforward to track down the therapist to whom Sherry Thomas referred in her second meeting with Dr Seymour. There were three listed in the local *Yellow Pages* within five miles of her home, and the second I rang, Barbara Shilling, confirmed that she had been a client.

The connection with Ms Shilling was invaluable, given how thin the available information is about Sherry Thomas. Even the tabloid press has been unable to unearth any more than a few scant details about her. Her name, or at least her surname, is fabricated. According to the story she told Ms Shilling, she had been in the UK for less than a year. She bought her shop lease and all her equipment with cash. She set up her bank accounts using false identification documents. A post-mortem revealed that she had had extensive plastic surgery. Attempts to discover traces of her on the other side of the Atlantic failed. According to Ms Shilling's limited knowledge of her, she lived a rootless life, moving from one place to another, living on her wits. There may be criminal records of her, but as it has proved impossible to unravel her numerous aliases no one knows for sure. One can only speculate as to the reasons for her arrival in Britain. Perhaps it was a desperate attempt to make a new start that failed. Certainly, what met her on this side of the Atlantic was still more loneliness and alienation. Whatever she was running away from pursued her.

Barbara Shilling runs a small practice in Ealing. She is not registered with any formal organization – the rules governing therapy in the UK are lax. She advertises herself as a specialist in psycho-sexual and relationship therapy. Her advertisement in the *Yellow Pages* suggests that she can alleviate or address problems of 'anxiety, hopelessness, phobias, abuse and compulsions'. She holds no formal qualifications in psychotherapy, but she is well read, and has an extensive knowledge of the various psychodynamic disciplines – Freudian, Kleinian, Personal Construct, Gestalt – as well as behavioural therapies.

Despite her lack of qualifications, my impression of Barbara Shilling was not that she was a quack. She is a small, serious-minded woman, who rarely smiles and peered at me through small, intense brown eyes that seem larger because of the powerful spectacles she wears. She speaks clearly and concisely, without gobbledegook. I found her an entirely credible witness. She seems anguished about the end her client met, and blames herself, to some extent, for failing to notice that Sherry Thomas was *in extremis*.

Thank you for agreeing to see me, Ms Shilling.

I'm grateful to be able to talk about it. It's been a burden. Poor Sherry.

Sympathy hasn't been the overriding response to what she did.

No, of course not. People fear understanding, lest it leaves them with no one to blame.

Are you saying you think Sherry Thomas bore no responsibility for what she did?

Certainly she did. I also know that she was an unhappy and abused woman who was doing everything she could to keep her head above water. In the end she destroyed the one person she thought might save her. Desperate people often take down with them those they care about, one way or another.

When did you first meet Ms Thomas?

Three months before this thing blew up. She picked me out of the local telephone directory. We had only six sessions so I don't have an immense amount of information, I'm afraid.

Why did she feel she needed a therapist?

The reason most people feel they need a therapist. Because she was unhappy.

What was your initial impression of her?

She put on a brave face. She came across as charming, positive and dynamic. That's not uncommon – particularly among Americans who consider it almost a moral duty to be happy. All the time she talked to me she was at pains to appear 'up', to put a positive spin on things.

What did you find out about her past?

I don't know. I'm not sure she was entirely honest about it. She told me she grew up in an institution in Salt Lake City, Utah, after being abandoned by her mother as a baby. Her memories of her childhood seemed rather vague – whether because she was falsifying them or because she had suppressed them, I couldn't be sure.

Author's Note: There is no record of any Sherry Thomas being brought up at any of the orphanages in the Salt Lake City area.

She claimed not to have had too bad a time in the institution, but she was very solitary and sometimes bullied. She said she was a plain-looking child, and that was why no one fostered her. She stayed there until she was sixteen, when she left and got a job at a local fast-food outlet. She started seeing boys at about this age, and claims to have remained a virgin until she was seventeen. Then she said that she met someone nice, and moved in with his family.

Did she mention his name?

I don't think so. She said he was a football player. 'Kinda sweet' was how she described him. 'Kinda sweet, but dumb.' Sherry had quite a high opinion of her own intellect, and a certain disdain for those she considered less intelligent than her. They broke up anyway, after a while.

And after that?

She was rather sketchy on the details. She told me she moved about a lot, getting involved with various men. She drifted, really. She was making jewellery in California at one time, then she claimed to have done a degree, and after that she started one of several retail operations.

To do with surveillance?

Not initially, although she said she had been interested in security from an early age.

Meaning what?

It's rather an odd thing to say, isn't it? But she told me she was obsessed with things like locks and keys. She always had the latest security bolts and installations on any apartment she lived in, she said, even if she wasn't earning much. She said she enjoyed going to security shops and choosing the latest innovations. It was a kind of hobby, she claimed. But she didn't get involved in surveillance until some time in her early thirties when she worked for a security firm in Oregon. That was where she picked up the know-how to start Cyclops.

Obviously she wasn't someone who felt particularly safe within herself.

Of course. The point wasn't lost on her. But to some extent she was in denial over it. She made out that her interest in security was rational, that the world was a dangerous place. Which, of course, it is.

When did she come to the UK?

I'm not sure. Quite recently, within the last nine or ten months.

What kind of life did she lead here?

She worked, mainly. She was very committed to making Cyclops a success, though I'm not sure how well she was doing. I know she went to the gym regularly. She would work out for exactly one hour, five days a week. But her social life, otherwise, was limited. She was fairly promiscuous, but made no lasting relationship. I'm not sure that she wanted one. She distrusted men, but she didn't find it easy to be alone.

Friends?

Not really. Always said she was too busy. But perhaps she wouldn't put herself into a situation where she might be rejected. She greatly feared rejection.

Anything else about her everyday life?

Not much. She watched a fair amount of TV.

Reality shows?

Funnily enough, no. She thought they were fake. Said they weren't 'hard core' enough. That they didn't get at the 'truth' about people. No, she liked old movies and weather reports. Said she found them calming. Other than that, she read celebrity magazines, and 'kept house', which took up a great deal of her time. She was fanatically houseproud. Cleanliness and tidiness were very important to her.

What did she tell you about the causes of her unhappiness?

First and foremost, it was loneliness. And anger. The loneliness came from the upbringing. Even by American standards, she was rootless, wandering from place to place, looking for something that always eluded her.

Was her unhappiness – how can I put this? – within the normal range of behaviour?

You mean, was she mentally ill?

Yes, I suppose so.

That's hard to say. Obviously, after what happened, it's easier, with hindsight, to make that diagnosis than it was at the time. From the little I saw of her, she seemed merely depressed.

She was described in the newspapers, of course, as a 'psycho'.

The word 'psychopath' has a precise clinical meaning. As many as twenty character traits help to define one. They would include, for instance, deceptive behaviour and lying, superficial charm, proneness to boredom, self-centredness, manipulativeness and, of course, lack of guilt or remorse. A psychopath is often promiscuous, has trouble maintaining relationships and tends to blame others for their actions.

And how many of these characteristics did you witness in Sherry Thomas?

It's hard for me to say. I saw her a total of six times. You don't find out a lot about people in five hours. Certainly, she was charming, but I never sensed that she was trying to manipulate me or that she was lying. On the other hand, I know that she suffered from acute boredom and, as I've said, that she was sexually promiscuous, often picking up men in bars for one-night stands.

Did she strike you as someone who was, not to put too fine a point on it, mad?

I object to the word 'mad'.

Deranged. Not in her normal mind.

Actually, no. She didn't strike me as being far beyond the pale. I liked her. She was trying hard to be honest with me, but it was clear that she had severe problems with living.

How did they manifest themselves?

She had a number of behaviours that might have qualified as compulsions. As I've said, she was extremely concerned with tidiness. Mess or clutter didn't merely irritate her, it infuriated her. She brushed her teeth about five times a day. Also, and more unusually, she was obsessed with the videotaping process. It was no coincidence that she set up a surveillance shop. She told me – and this was interesting – that she found the constant disappearance of time very disturbing.

Of time?

Yes. She said it was like moments were constantly being lost, that they were dying all the while. She felt she needed to capture them, to preserve them. Of course, it was really herself she was trying to preserve, her sense of reality, or self, which was fragile. I think she had a constant fear of disappearance, an immense dread of the evanescence of things. Many people do, in some form or another, but her fear was particularly acute. She had clocks everywhere, always set to exactly the right time. She hated lateness with a passion.

What else?

She was fanatically clean – hated all forms of dirt. She was – and this is not typical of psychopathic behaviour – extremely self-controlled most of the time. It was as if efficiency and organization were substitutes for life itself, which eluded her in some peculiar way. She was concerned to achieve, to keep on the move, but this always left her deeply unhappy. And her ability to connect emotionally with others was always sabotaged by her obsessions. Her emotional responses were ultimately very shallow. If she wasn't a psychopath, she was certainly borderline narcissistic.

Anything else?

Not that I can think of. She was superstitious – read the astrology columns, believed in destiny and that kind of thing. Thought it was all connected. Oh, yes, and she was fanatically patriotic. She believed America was the greatest country in the world.

If that's the definition of psychopathy, it's a lot more common than I realized.

[Ms Shilling does not laugh, and instead looks somewhat stern, reprimanding.]

We're talking about a terrible tragedy here. I don't think it's a time for levity.

I'm sorry. Did she talk about Dr Seymour?

Yes, she did. But we're going to have to leave that for another time.
I'm sorry to cut you short. I have a client now.

Thank you for talking to me.

You're welcome.

Dr Alex Seymour's Video Diary, Excerpt One, Sunday, 6 May, Time Code 02.03

Author's Note: Dr Seymour started recording a video diary on the night he returned home with the additional equipment. It does not amount to a great deal of tape – about thirty minutes in all. Perhaps the pressure he was under had led him to start recording himself as a kind of 'confessional' to assuage his guilt over his illicit activities. He was, after all, a lapsed Catholic. Samantha Seymour told me that in the past he had intermittently kept a written diary; this was just a new technology with which he had decided to experiment, presumably stimulated by his deployment of the other cameras in the house.

As it was recorded in the early hours of the morning in his loft room, the light is poor. He appears tired, but also quite energized, 'hyper'. Again, this may be the effect of the stimulants he was continuing to self-prescribe. He is wearing a blue cotton dressing-gown and speaking in a hushed voice – perhaps because the bedroom he shares with his wife is below and he fears being overheard.

I presume that red light means this thing is working. I feel a bit stupid. Right. So. Video diary entry Saturday – no, Sunday, the sixth of May. God, my mind's gone blank. Um. What's the first thing that comes into my head?

I don't know where this has come from. It's a memory. And it's a memory I don't think I've had before. A fresh memory. That's a rare thing. For so long my memories have been recycled things, a limited number of old tape loops that just keep playing. Memories are just recordings, after all. If this one really is fresh – and I may have forgotten having it before, so that's far from certain – it's still a recording. And since I'm now remembering the fresh memory, it's a recording of a recording. Which I'm putting on tape. Endlessly receding images. Mirrors facing mirrors.

Everything's in the past, when you think about it.

Anyway, anyway. The memory. The memory of the memory. We're all in the car. That old blue Volvo we had back in the nineties. Driving down some country road on the way to some cut-price holiday destination. I can't even remember where we were going. But we were bickering. That much I do remember. Disagreements with Samantha about directions, kids fighting, moaning that they were bored. Trees forming a green ceiling over us, light dappling through the branches. It was beautiful, but we couldn't see that it was beautiful because we were locked in our little box of conflict, love and anxiety. We were locked in the mind of a family. With all its jagged, hurtful edges.

Then the car started veering and juddering. The bickering stopped. Air of panic. I fought to keep it under control. We made it into a lay-by. Blown tyre. Lucky it hadn't happened on the motorway. This country road was deserted. We were safe.

Most times this would have been fuel to the fire. Stress upon stress. The children outraged, Samantha depressed, me infuriated at the random injustice of the gods. But instead I felt calm. We all got out. There was a patch of clear grass under the trees by the lay-by. The kids ran into it and began to play. The light was golden. Samantha helped me change the tyre. No other traffic, just us. We got mucky, me under the car, Sam working the jack, with the sound of the kids playing in the background, this canopy of branches. We had it fixed in no time. As we loaded the jack and the busted tyre, Samantha kissed me, touched my hand. Funny I should remember such a tiny detail.

There was something about that spot we had broken down at. It was . . . honeyed. Like someone had poured sweetness into the air. Sam had brought some sandwiches and juice and we sat down in the clearing together. The kids rushed over. They'd been picking flowers. I don't know the names of flowers but they were very blue – and they gave them to Sam. The kids must have been around four and five.

We all sat in that clearing together and ate the sandwiches. My hands were greasy. I got mess all over the kids, all over the food. Normally it would have been anathema to me, all that dirt, but this time it was on our faces, our clothes, and we just laughed. We laughed and laughed. Sandwiches in a patch of grass by a roadside. Not much of a memory. But there was something there in that copse. Perhaps it was there already, perhaps we conjured it ourselves. Yet it seems now like a momentary . . . Eden. Just the present. Just innocence and experience, side by side. Eating sandwiches. Loving one another, wordlessly, in the present. Victoria came and sat on my lap, and I gave her some water. That's it. That's the memory.

I wish I had a film of it. But a film could never express . . . the shape of those few moments. Perhaps it would have ruined them. Trying to hold things down. It can destroy everything.

And now those two children in that green, perfect copse . . . Guy stealing and Victoria trying to have sex, and Samantha . . . I don't know what Samantha's doing. I really don't. It's all unwound. Fast forward to . . . what? The everyday. The disappointments of the everyday.

What am I doing taping them all? Trying to turn the ephemeral into the concrete? Or am I just a snooper?

I suppose the first thing I want to say is that I fear I – I mean, if any of this was to come out I think I would be misunderstood. No one would appreciate why I was doing it. I'm not sure that I understand why I'm doing it. It feels wrong and right all at the same time. I know what I'm **telling** *myself is the reason. I'm telling myself that it's because I need to protect myself and my family. Pamela is turning into a nightmare. I just don't know how far she's prepared to go. Like Sherry says, I have to take precautions. As for Samantha – well, it's hard to believe. Impossible to believe. But she did lie about the cigarettes. And that tape of her and Pengelly . . . It's compromising, viewed in a certain light. A light I try not to bring to bear on it, but still . . .*

Sherry would say . . . Sherry. Sherry, Sherry, Sherry.

She bewilders me. Deep waters. What's going on? Again, I'm not sure. I feel I'm not myself just now. Nothing seems clear. I've had moments like this before in my life – when I couldn't see straight – but nothing like this. And, if I'm going to be honest, Sherry is helping me. She seems to understand. She seems to . . . know. It's very strange. I've not experienced anything like this before.

It isn't sexual. At least, not primarily. I love Samantha. Sam. I always have. So why am I betraying her? Am I betraying her? I'm watching her without her knowledge. But I'm not being unfaithful. I would never . . . Anyway, Sherry doesn't do it for me. Not all that much. Obviously she's a bit . . . with that trick camera . . . and all that . . . lipstick and her legs. But I don't think she means to be seductive, not in that way. She just wants me to come closer. Sees me as a kindred spirit, I suppose. And there's something in that. But it's not love. It's . . . it's fascination. And a shared view of things. That they have to be ordered. That they have to be watched. She understands that so well. I find her oddly compelling. But I don't think anything's going to happen – nothing sexual, I mean. It's a professional relationship.

*The point is, I'm responding to like with like. Samantha has secrets – I know that now. Victoria has secrets. I expect Guy does too. Can it be possible that he's stealing the money? Damn right it's possible. But I need to **know**. It helps me to be **fair**, if I know. And that's all I want. I want to be fair.*

OK, it's a dirty business. But what if I had the chance to come up with a cure for cancer by cutting a few corners? What if, say, a few dangerous experiments on drug addicts and some of those people who turn up at my surgery could result in a massive gain in the sum of human happiness? Doesn't the end sometimes justify the means?

*I have to know what's going on with Samantha and Mark. I need to clear that up in my mind. Then, maybe, the pain will stop. The fear will stop. Once I've found out that it's all OK, well, I can get rid of these stupid cameras, once and for all. It's just a temporary measure. I'm not some kind of weirdo. As Sherry says, half the country's at it. What matters is your intention. Mine isn't to **snoop**. No one's got anything to fear, so long as they're not doing anything wrong. That's what the government says when it puts up cameras on every street corner. When it bugs phones. Watching and listening everywhere. For our own protection, they say. What's the difference between that and what I'm doing? It's just a precaution. No harm is being done.*

God, I want a cigarette. And now I know where Samantha keeps hers. That's not nice. It's not right what she's doing. She'll say she was trying to protect me. I know her.

I thought I knew her.

If she says she was trying to protect me, we've both got the same defence.

I need to go to sleep. Can't, though. Can't sleep.

I'm going to switch this thing off now. Going 'live' tomorrow. I'm putting the new camera in the kids' room. They'll think I'm being paranoid about the fire risk. But I'm not paranoid. I'm just being careful, I'll tell them. And I am. I am being careful.

That's it. Goodnight. Goodnight, me.

Seymour Surveillance Tape, Week Two

Author's Note: These sequences were recorded during the week after Dr Seymour's second visit to Cyclops Surveillance on Saturday, 5 May. Unquestionably he installed the second camera at his home, in the children's bedroom, on the next day, Sunday, 6 May. It is less certain when he installed the camera at the surgery, but quite probably on the same day since the building would have been empty, providing him with the ideal opportunity.

Sequence One: Bedroom Camera, Sunday, 6 May, Time Code 14.29

Startlingly, the tape begins with Guy, who is staring at the camera in the ceiling. The viewer has the impression that he has immediately spotted it. He seems infuriated and, after a few seconds, calls his father.

– Dad. Dad! Come here. DAD!

Dr Seymour's voice can be heard faintly from downstairs.

– Guy, if you want to talk to me, come down here. Don't yell. I'm not your servant.

*– Dad. DAD! Come **here**!*

– Stop shouting.

– DAD!

After several seconds, Dr Seymour is visible at the bedroom door, looking flustered and annoyed.

– I've told you before, Guy. I'm not going to stand for this. I'm not at your beck and call.

– What's that?

Guy points directly at the camera on the ceiling.

– *You're not **listening** to me, Guy.*

– *I just don't see the point of me going all the way downstairs and coming all the way back up again. This way only one of us has to make one journey.*

– *It's just so rude. What would it cost you to show a bit of civility?*

– *What's that thing on the ceiling?*

– *What does it look like?*

– *It looks like a smoke-alarm.*

– *Bingo.*

– *What do we need one in the bedroom for? We've got one on the landing. We've got one downstairs. Are you freaking out?*

– *What's the matter with it?*

– *It looks stupid. There's no need for it.*

– *You can't be too careful about something like fire. It's for your protection, Guy, yours and Victoria's.*

– *Were you always like this? Or does it just happen when you get old?*

– *What are you talking about now?*

– *You're so scared all the time, Dad.*

– *When you do the job I do, you see how bad things can come out of nowhere. Then you start to realize –*

– *I'm not having it. It's my room and I don't want it.*

– *It's my house and it's staying.*

– *I'm taking it down.*

Guy reaches for a chair. Dr Seymour steps across to his son and grabs him roughly by the arm. Guy is clearly shocked.

– ***Dad!** What the hell. . . . ?*

– *You so much as **touch** that smoke-alarm, and you'll be in the biggest trouble you can ever remember.*

– *What's the big deal? It's just a –*

– *Just **shut up** and do as you're told for once. The smoke-alarm stays. If you tamper with it or try to get rid of it, I'll ground you for three months. I mean it, Guy. I know you think I'm weak, I know you think you can get away with anything, but I mean it, God help me.*

115

Dr Seymour is staring intensely at his son's face, which appears pale and shocked. Guy shakes off his father's hand. He is on the point of tears.

    – All right! Christ, Dad, it's only a smoke-alarm . . .

Dr Seymour stares up at the camera, then walks out as if he is furious. At the last moment he turns.

    – Guy, I'm sorry. I didn't mean to grab you like that.

    – Just go away.

    – I just . . . It's important to me. Your safety. Yours and Victoria's.

    – Get out. Get out, will you?

Dr Seymour leaves the room.

Sequence Two: Front-room Camera, Wednesday, 9 May, Time Code 17.30

Author's Note: This sequence shows Samantha Seymour with Polly. The room is messy. Polly is covered with food. Her mother is sitting on the sofa, feet up, reading a magazine, while Polly plays on the floor. After a while, Polly begins to cry. Barely looking up, Samantha Seymour reaches for the remote control and switches on a children's television programme. When this fails to distract Polly, she picks up a teddy bear from the cluttered sofa while continuing to read her magazine.

    – Say hello to Teddy! Say hello to Teddy!

    – Ga.

    – What's silly old Teddy doing? He's dancing. See? He's dancing.

She moves the teddy bear about rhythmically.

    – Da-da.

    *– Nooo. He's not your da-da. He's a big old silly teddy, not a big old silly daddy. He's furry and cute, not grumpy and wrinkly like Daddy. He's not. No, he's not. He's **shaped** a bit like your daddy, but that's about it.*

Polly quietens. Samantha Seymour has still not looked up from her magazine. Then there is the sound of footsteps on the stairs.

She looks puzzled. She puts the magazine under the sofa, gets up and starts playing actively with the baby. A few seconds later Dr Seymour appears at the door.

– *Alex. I didn't think you were home.*

– *Well, I am.*

– *I'm glad you're here. Can you take Polly for a while? I'm exhausted.*

Dr Seymour looks around the room.

– *You must be. Keeping this place spick and span must take it out of you.*

– *Oh, don't start, Alex. You have no idea what I do all day. It's a constant struggle. I don't have a moment to myself.*

– *Is that so?*

– *God, yes. You've no idea what it is to look after a baby on your own and keep house.*

– *Three days a week.*

– *That's it. Get the nails out. Climb up the cross.*

– *You're lazy. Look at the state of this room. Look at the state of Polly.*

– *Alex, I haven't **stopped**.*

– *Not for a moment?*

– *Not for a moment.*

Dr Seymour bends over, grabs the magazine from under the sofa and throws it next to her.

– *Do you know what I think?*

– *Oh, there's that magazine. I've been looking for it.*

– *I think you've spent the best part of the last hour loafing about. And I think that Polly slept for two hours while you watched TV with your feet up. And I think that you and Mark Pengelly had a very long lunch together.*

She looks taken aback.

– *What if we did have lunch together? For God's sake, Mark and I are friends.*

– *I'm sure you're very close.*

– *What do you mean?*

– *Things are going to change around here, Samantha. I promise you that. I've been played for a sucker much too long. I work all the hours that God sends and it's you who portrays yourself as the long-suffering one. Well, it's nonsense.*

– *Alex, calm down.*

– *Why don't you calm down? Lie back. Have a cigarette, perhaps.*

– *What are you talking about? You know I don't smoke any more.*

– *Oh, of course, that's right. You don't smoke. Listen, Samantha, I'm on to you. I'm on to you about **everything**. So you'd better shape up. Understand?*

– *What's come over you?*

– *The truth, that's what's come over me. Now I'm going out.*

– *Where?*

– *Down the pub. Where I intend to have a beer. And read a magazine.*

– *What about dinner?*

– *What about it?*

– *Well, aren't you making it?*

– *Tell you what, why don't you make it for once?*

– *But I've been with Polly all day!*

– *See you in an hour.*

Dr Seymour leaves the room. Samantha Seymour sits perfectly still for a moment, apparently transfixed. We hear the front door slam. Then she reaches for the phone and dials a number.

– *Mark. Yeah, it's me . . . No, I'm fine . . . No, it's just Alex. It's kind of weird. He's acting very strangely . . . I don't know . . . No, I don't think so . . . Yeah . . . Yeah . . . Are you OK? . . . Good . . . Good . . . OK, sweets, see you tomorrow . . . I'm looking forward to it too* [laughs] *. . . Yeah, definitely.*

She replaces the phone. Then, slowly, she begins to clear up the mess in the room.

Sequence Three: Bedroom Camera, Thursday, 10 May, Time Code 16.50

The children's room. Victoria and Guy are having a heated conversation. Guy is sitting on his bed, holding a mobile phone. Victoria is pleading with him, voice muted, as if she is afraid of being overheard.

   – *You **said** I could borrow it.*
   – *I've changed my mind.*
   – *It won't take a minute.*
   – *Want to call your boyfriend?*
   – *I haven't got a boyfriend.*
   – *Do you want to marry him?*
   – *Who?*
   – *Macy.*
   – *Don't be stupid! Anyway, he's not my boyfriend.*
   – *So who do you want to call?*
   – *None of your business.*
   – *If you won't tell me, you can't have the phone.*
   – *All right. I am going to call Macy. But he's not my boyfriend.*
   – *Why? Because he dumped you?*
   – *He didn't dump me.*
   – *Just because he's giving you a second chance doesn't mean he didn't dump you. Anyway, if you're saying he didn't dump you, you're admitting he's your boyfriend.*
   – *No, I'm not.*
   – *If you don't admit he's your boyfriend, you can't have it.*
   – *Guy! Give it me!*

Victoria snatches at the mobile, but Guy withdraws it.

   – *You give that to me or I'll tell Dad you've got it. And where you got it from.*
   – *No, you won't. And you don't know where I got it from.*
   – *I will. And I do.*
   – *If you tell anyone, you'll be sorry.*

– DAD! Guy's stolen a –

Guy slides the mobile into his pocket. Then, without warning, he jumps off the sofa, knocks Victoria on to her back and traps her under his knees. She cries out; Guy puts his hand over her mouth. Although he is younger than Victoria, he is clearly more physically powerful.

– Shut up. I'll spit on your face.

A thin line of saliva appears from Guy's mouth and hangs a few inches from Victoria's left cheek. At that moment Dr Seymour appears in the doorway.

– What's going on?

Guy looks up without changing his position.

– She hit me first!

– Get off her.

Dr Seymour, with some effort, drags his son off his daughter.

– You're a bully, Guy.

– I told you, she started it. She slapped me just because I said she had a boyfriend.

– I didn't, Dad.

– I know you didn't, sweetheart.

*– Shut **up**. You always take her side.*

– You shut up, Guy. And hand over that mobile phone.

Now Guy looks stunned.

– What are you talking about?

– You know what you're going to do, Guy? You're going to do two things. You're going to stop lying to me. And you're going to stop bullying your sister.

– I'm not lying to you! I haven't got a mobile phone, have I, Vick?

– Dunno. How would I know?

– Is that so?

Dr Seymour is looking pointedly at Guy's pocket.

*– Guy. I **know** you have a mobile phone. And I know you were bullying Victoria. You can't pull the wool over my eyes any more. And Victoria hasn't told me anything.*

*– What are you **talking** about? There's nothing to tell.*

– You've got half an hour to tell me the truth. If you do, I'm going to ground you for a week and I'm not going to ask you any questions about where you got the phone from. If you don't, I'm going to ground you for two weeks and I'm going to call the police about the phone if you can't show me a receipt for it. And if you can show me a receipt for it, I'm going to want to know where you got the money from. Is that clear?

– Dad!

– That's an end to the matter.

Dr Seymour walks out.

Sequence Four: Front-room Camera, Thursday, 10 May, Time Code 16.59

Samantha Seymour is feeding Polly on her lap. She doesn't look up when her husband walks into the room but concentrates on the baby while she speaks.

– What was all that fuss about upstairs, Alex?

– Guy was bullying Victoria.

– What were they fighting about?

– She wanted to borrow his mobile phone.

She stops feeding Polly and turns towards her husband.

– A mobile phone? He hasn't got one. You confiscated it.

– He's got another from somewhere.

– Where would he get the money?

– He stole the phone.

– Alex! Guy wouldn't do something like that.

– People can surprise you.

– Not that much.

– I'm sure we all have secrets. You have secrets, don't you, Samantha?

– Could you pass me Polly's beaker, please?

– I suppose no one knows anyone, really.

Dr Seymour passes the beaker to his wife, who hands it to the baby. Polly throws it on to the floor, then follows it with a handful of mush from her plate. Her mother sighs.

– *What are you talking about now, Alex?*

– *Secrets. Do you have any secrets from me?*

– *Of course not.*

Polly begins to cry. Samantha hands her to her father, who takes her gingerly to avoid transferring the glops of food from her clothes to his shirt. He holds her with one hand, reaches for a cloth and wipes her down. The crying continues.

– *For God's sake, give her a cuddle.*

– *In a moment. I don't want to stain this shirt.*

– *You hardly ever touch the child. Either you think she's going to give you some virus, or you think she's going to crap on you, or she's too messy. Do you even love her?*

– *How can you ask that?*

Samantha sits down wearily on the sofa.

– *What was the outcome with Victoria and Guy?*

Dr Seymour gives Polly a last wipe, then lets her rest her head on his shoulder. She quietens immediately. He pats her back.

– *I told Guy that if he could admit within half an hour that he had a mobile phone and that he'd been bullying Victoria I'd ground him for a week.*

– *And what if he doesn't?*

– *I'll ground him for two weeks and report him to the police.*

Samantha gives a brief dry laugh.

– *He'll call your bluff.*

– *What bluff?*

– *You haven't actually seen this mobile phone, right?*

– *Right.*

– *And you didn't actually see him bullying Victoria?*

– *No.*

– *He knows that. He knows you're not going to risk punishing him for something he might not have done. You shouldn't make threats that you can't follow through. Or won't follow through.*

– *Because I'm too weak.*

– *Don't start that again. Do you want me to take Polly now? I should give her a bath.*

Dr Seymour kisses Polly and hands her over. At that moment Guy appears at the door. He marches up to Dr Seymour, slams down his mobile phone on the coffee-table, and turns to walk out. Samantha stares at the phone, then at her husband, who allows himself the ghost of a smile. Then he turns towards Guy's receding, hunched figure. When he speaks, his voice sounds different from how it has on any tape before now. It is stronger, more assertive.

– *Guy. Come here.*

Instead of continuing to slouch out of the room, Guy hesitates. Then, slowly, he turns.

– *Would you mind sitting down with us for a moment?*

Guy addresses his mother, clearly expecting support to be forthcoming.

– *What's come over **him**?*

– *I think you should do as your father says.*

– *What? **Mum!***

Guy stares at her for several seconds as if appealing to her. Then, having realized that no support is forthcoming, he makes his way morosely to the chair next to his father and sits down.

– *Guy. I'm going to ask you a question, and I promise I won't be angry whatever answer you give. I just want to talk, that's all.*

– *Dad. I've given you the mobile. Let me go back to my room, OK? I don't want to **talk**.*

– *Just stop. For a minute, just stop. Sit still. Listen to what I'm trying to say to you.*

Guy gives a long, low sigh, but doesn't move. He throws an imploring glance at his mother, who looks away.

– *This is the question, Guy. Are you a thief?*

– *What?*

– *Do you steal things?*

– *No. Mum!*

– *Your father's worried, Guy. Money has gone missing. You know that's why we got rid of Miranda.*

– *You said she had to go back to New Zealand.*

– *We knew you liked her. We wanted to protect you.*

123

*– You **lied** to me. **Dad.***

– We didn't exactly lie. She has gone back to New Zealand. But partly because she lost her job. We didn't tell you everything because we thought you might be upset. We were only thinking of you. We got rid of Miranda because we thought she'd been stealing. If she hadn't been stealing, well, she's been unjustly treated. And I know she was someone you were fond of.

*– What are you **saying**?*

– I think you know what I'm saying.

Dr Seymour picks up the mobile phone and examines it.

– So, where did this come from?

*– I got it from a friend. Look. I've **said** I'm sorry.*

– You haven't, as a matter of fact.

– Don't shout at me.

– I'm not shouting.

– I'm going to my room.

– Guy.

Dr Seymour puts a hand on his son's shoulder, but Guy shrugs it off. Then, incredibly, he slumps and is racked by tears. Unexpectedly, he leans against his father in a childlike, almost infantile gesture. Dr Seymour puts his arms round him and holds him. The next few words are so low and distorted by tears as to be almost inaudible.

– I'm sorry.

– It's OK. We'll forget all about it, all right? Listen to me. I love you, Guy.

– Dad . . .

– I mean it. I know you find it embarrassing, but I mean it. I know you think I have some 'special relationship' with your sister, that's she's my favourite, but it's not true. Guy, I could never love anyone more than you.

– Dad! Stop it.

– All right. But you'll stop taking things, yes? If you need something, just come to me. OK?

Guy nods. Suddenly, as if he has realized what he's been doing, he pulls away. He wipes his eyes roughly. The hitherto ever-present expression of surliness and disappointment has been replaced by a raw, helpless look. Embarrassed by his loss of face, he walks out of the room. Dr Seymour calls after him, but with a certain lack of conviction.

– *Guy!*

The look on Samantha Seymour's face is hard to convey. It is one of astonishment, mixed with mild horror and a degree of admiration for her husband. When she speaks, her voice is low and almost humble.

– *Aren't you going to go after him?*

– *No.*

– *I thought you were going to ground him for a week.*

– *I don't want to humiliate him. If he's been stealing, I think he'll stop now.*

She gets up and sits next to him.

– *Why do you think that?*

– *Because he knows that I'll know.*

She lets her hand rest on Dr Seymour's knee.

– *Alex.*

– *Yes, Samantha?*

– *I'm impressed.*

Then she kisses her husband full of the mouth.

Dr Alex Seymour's Video Diary, Excerpt Two, Thursday, 10 May, Time Code 23.53

Dr Seymour stares at the camera for a few seconds as if it is hard for him to find the words for what he has to say. Then he begins to speak.

What an incredible day.

I never did much psychology at med school. I'm like a lot of doctors – good at looking at other people but not so good at examining myself. But now it's becoming clear why I'm doing this. Partly.

*I have always felt ineffectual. Not because I'm a . . . a **pussycat**, like they think, but because I can't bear to make the wrong decision. And my decisions are always wrong, because too much is hidden.*

*Now I have certainty, perhaps for the first time in my life. Or, at least, I'm moving towards it. Before I put in the cameras I was moving away from it at a terrifying rate. I'm still not sure what – if anything – Samantha is up to with Mark Pengelly. But I can find out. Then I can do what's right. As for Guy and Victoria – that was unbelievable today. Unbelievable. How many times have I heard a scuffle, gone up there and found one blaming the other? But this time I knew. I **knew**. And it felt good.*

Poor Guy. Yet I understand now that he was craving for me to act as a solid border to his life. That was why he cracked up. It was a kind of gratitude, mixed with shame.

This feels less wrong than it did a day or two ago. Then I felt guilty about it. I know that if I'm discovered they're not going to understand. But it's for the best, I'm sure it is. Now I can do what I need to do. Now I can be a man. A father, a husband. And the amazing thing is, they respect me for it. I can just tell. Sure they're angry, and sure they're upset. But on a deeper level they're reassured. Like they wanted to believe in God all along and now they've found out that He really exists.

OK, OK, I'm getting carried away. Obviously I'm not God. But a father – children want their father to look after them, despite themselves. Perhaps some women are the same. Very un-PC idea, I know. Samantha would be horrified. But it's a universal desire. I feel it too: the dream of someone to make the rules and take the rap.

I'll get rid of the whole set-up soon enough – once I've established a few basic understandings about the way the family works, about the things that are hidden that can be shown. I'm not in this for the long haul.

Like Sherry says, it's the most normal thing in the world. Everyone is going to feel a bit strange at first.

Sherry Thomas. She's the proverbial puzzle wrapped in an enigma. Why does she want to see tapes of my family? That **is** weird. But harmless enough, I suppose. And, if the truth be told, I find the idea of sharing them with her kind of interesting. No, not interesting – exciting. Yes. Let's try to be honest. That's what this whole exercise is about.

Sherry is . . . unusual. The paleness of her face. She's almost the opposite of my usual type – blonde instead of dark, all those business suits, thin lips. And American. Usually, there's something passionless and clinical about American sexuality. That thin reedy sound, that Midwest whine.

When I think of her – and I **do** think of her, as I sit in my surgery prodding joints, listening to coughs, probing abdomens, staring at raw red throats – it isn't in terms of . . . of sex. And it isn't her personality. She's not charming, or witty, or even particularly intelligent, although she has a weird insight. No. There's a kind of . . . corrosive blankness to her. As if she herself were a camera, and all the world the subject of her indifferent gaze.

And there's something else. Fearlessness. But why would that be attractive?

Perhaps . . . perhaps she's come to represent a sort of freedom in my mind. Not the freedom of youth, with its sudden imagined steps into perfection. Another kind of freedom. A compensating freedom. What is it?

A few seconds pass. Then he snaps his fingers.

Perhaps this is it. Sherry is unique, not because she's a voyeur, not because she wants to see the tapes.

She's unique because she's indifferent.

127

She's free because she doesn't care. And I've spent my whole life caring – about being a better man, a better husband, a better doctor. I've had these ideals as long as I can remember. I used to think they might liberate me. They were worthy. Purposeful. They would make me *feel* good. Virtue being its own reward, et cetera. But so often they feel like a series of chains and weights and harnesses. They chafe. All the time.

That's how I am. I can't do much about it. But none of those things means anything to Sherry. And . . . that's strangely wonderful. It's not that she's immoral. She's simply intensely – no, **violently** – curious. This emotion – it's so pure. It wipes out all other considerations. That's what's special about her. She's undifferentiated. She's absolutely pitiless.

I'm going to have to see her again. Not for more equipment – there's enough now. I'm not an **addict**. I just want to talk to her about how I feel. She's the only one who will understand. My friends will think I've gone wacko. Yet how can something that makes me feel so right be wrong? And I'm not doing any harm. It's no different from a CCTV camera watching for criminals on a street corner. If you do nothing wrong, you've got nothing to fear. That's right. That's **right**.

What about Samantha? How am I going to get to the bottom of this thing with Pengelly?

I think I have an answer. In the police force they call it entrapment. But in the household, there's no such thing. There's only what you can get away with. Sherry is teaching me that.

The kids are going away this weekend on that camping trip. If I arrange to go away too – a last-minute decision to be at that medical conference on Sunday that I told Sam I wasn't going to bother with – she and Pengelly will have the perfect opportunity to misbehave. When I get back I'll know all I need to know. I'll know if I still have a marriage.

And tomorrow Mrs Madoowbe is coming to the surgery. She has to say what I need her to say.

She has to.

Greenside Surgery, Tape One, Friday, 11 May, Time Code 12.04

Author's Note: The Greenside surgery is located in the middle of an extensive 1960s low-rise housing estate in Harlesden, north-west London. It is a small, functional building, not particularly attractive but clean and in reasonably good condition. Its waiting room has about thirty seats, and at consultation times it is usually packed.

Dr Seymour's room is a fairly typical doctor's surgery. There is a wall of box files, a desk, a set of scales, a sink, an examination couch and three chairs, including Dr Seymour's. There are windows, but there is not much of a view – just the surgery car park. The walls are painted cream. There is a goldfish bowl on Dr Seymour's desk with three fish in it. A pile of soft toys is arranged against the east wall. We cannot see all these toys on camera, because the camera is located in the eye of a large brown teddy bear. However, the wide-angle lens gives a good view of the room: all who enter and leave can be seen clearly.

Dr Seymour switches on the camera about thirty seconds before Mrs Thibo Madoowbe appears through the surgery door. She is strikingly attractive, apparently in her teens, wearing Western clothing – jeans and T-shirt – but with a Muslim headscarf. Her sister appears considerably older and is dressed in a more traditional style – a full-length Somali *guntiino*, similar to an Indian sari but made of red cotton. She also wears a headscarf. Dr Seymour has on a white coat over his suit and appears ill at ease.

Throughout the exchanges that take place, Mrs Madoowbe's older sister, Yasmin Farah, translates for her.

– *Good afternoon, Mrs Madoowbe. How are you feeling?*
– *She says she is well.*
– *Any more pain?*

– No. The pain has gone away now.

– Good. That's good.

– She wants to know if you have had the test results.

– Tell her that before we get on to that, I would like to talk to her about something else.

– I don't understand.

– Let me explain. She may remember a woman coming in from Reception when I was examining her.

– She says she does, yes.

– Tell her I would like to apologize once again for any embarrassment it may have caused her.

– She understands. The examination – it was difficult for her.

– Difficult? In what way?

– In our culture it is not normal for men who are not our husbands to touch women intimately, even if they are doctors.

– But she was in some danger. Until I examined her properly I couldn't be sure whether or not she had an ectopic pregnancy. There was no woman doctor available.

– She understands. Nevertheless . . .

– I mean – has Miss Geale, the receptionist, tried to get in touch with her?

– Who?

– The last time she came – the woman who came in. Has she phoned you?

– Why would she be in touch? Can she speak Somali?

– Well, she might not have known . . . Look, could you just ask Mrs Madoowbe?

– She says no one has been in touch.

– I see. And last time she came . . . forgive me, I have to ask this. Last time she came to see me, well, your sister seemed distressed. I wanted to ask her . . . did she feel I behaved improperly?

Author's Note: There is a long conversation in Somali here

130

between the two sisters, sometimes rather heated. Finally Yasmin Farah speaks again to Dr Seymour.

– *She was distressed.*

– *I understand that. I know she was distressed. But does she have any complaint to make?*

– *She does not want to make trouble. She does not want any authorities involved.*

– *Nothing will go further than this room.*

– *Why are you asking? What is the importance of this?*

– *It's a precaution.*

– *Please, Dr Seymour, what kind of precaution? This conversation is embarrassing for her. For us.*

– *The woman . . . The receptionist, Miss Geale, is under the impression . . . Because Mrs Madoowbe took off her clothes when I did not **ask** her to . . . Miss Geale thinks . . . She formed the impression that I may have been acting – improperly. It's complicated. But there is a danger that Miss Geale may make a complaint.*

– *We do not want the authorities involved. We do not want a fuss.*

– *I know. But it's important for me, you see.*

– *We don't really see. She doesn't really see.*

– *Look, can I ask your sister a direct question?*

– *Can we please talk about the results of the test?*

– *I just want to know . . . those injuries she had. Mrs Madoowbe, those bruises you had when you last came to see me. On your thighs. On the inside of your legs. How did you get them? What happened to you?*

– *Bruises? She said nothing to me about bruises.*

– *She had them. Contusions, scratches, bruises. Ask her about them. Please.*

Again, Yasmin Farah addresses her sister. This time, the atmosphere becomes extremely tense. Yasmin Farah becomes animated, even angry, while Mrs Madoowbe becomes quieter and quieter, nodding and shaking her head. Eventually she starts to cry, and Yasmin Farah, clearly upset, turns back to Dr Seymour.

– *I think we should go now. This is not good. It is not right.*

– *This is completely confidential. I will not –*

– We cannot afford to have problems with the authorities, do you see?

– Of course, but . . .

The women get up as if to go. Dr Seymour also rises from his chair.

– What were the test results?

– Mrs Madoowbe is absolutely fine. She just had an infection, which was nothing serious. I am sure that the antibiotics I gave her will have cleared it up.

Yasmin Farah talks to her sister in urgent, hushed tones. Mrs Madoowbe looks relieved.

– Thank you. Yes, she is fine. Now we must go.

– Hold on. Look. Please ask your sister. I want no trouble either. Just ask her if she felt I behaved properly towards her. If she was offended.

– She was very upset. In our culture –

– Yes, yes, I know you are not meant to be examined by men. But did she think . . . that I made . . . Did she believe I made any kind of sexual advance? Because, you see, this is what the receptionist, Miss Geale, is trying to pretend, to say, for her own reasons. I need you to tell me that this is false. That I treated her with respect.

Once again, Yasmin Farah appears shocked. They seem about to leave, but Dr Seymour looks pleadingly at them. They have another brief conversation. Yasmin Farah speaks.

– My sister is a good woman. Her situation at home is very difficult. Without her husband, she says, there is no future for her. There is no money without him. She has to be a good wife. It is difficult for her. He gets . . . What is your expression? Carried away. He is a passionate man. He has fire in his belly.

– Miss Farah, please ask your sister if I made any sexual advance towards her when she visited me in my surgery recently. Please. Ask her that question directly. I would be very grateful.

There is a long pause. The three people in the surgery stand still for what seems a long time. Eventually Yasmin Farah speaks once more to her sister. The exchange is brief. This time, after the translation of the question, Mrs Madoowbe looks puzzled. Then she shakes her head, looks directly at Dr Seymour and answers for herself, in English.

– *No. There was not nothing.*

– *You mean there was nothing? You mean, nothing happened?*

– *No. Nothing happened. Yes.*

One can almost hear Dr Seymour's relieved exhalation. He allows himself a brief smile.

– *Thank you, Mrs Madoowbe, Miss Farah. Thank you so much. You have been very helpful.*

– *We must go now.*

– *Goodbye. And thank you, both.*

The women leave. Now Dr Seymour gazes at the camera, smiles and speaks directly to the lens.

*And thank **you**. I feel . . . just like you said I'd feel. Like you always knew.*

Dr Alex Seymour's Video Diary, Excerpt Three, Saturday, 12 May, Time Code 00.07

Author's Note: Dr Seymour looks tired but otherwise seems happy and relaxed. As before, he is in his blue dressing-gown. He is holding a half-filled glass in his left hand, and visible on the table behind him is a bottle of Laphroaig whisky. His words are slightly slurred, but he is not obviously drunk. Again, he keeps his voice low.

Good evening. Good evening, me. It's been a good day. A good, good day. For the first time in as long as I can remember I feel . . . Ah. I don't know how I feel. But it's wonderful. And what with all the things that happened on Thursday . . . A revolution. That's what it feels like. I'm rising, rising.

Is it down to Sherry? After all, she talked me into it. It helped me. I hate to admit it, but I'm excited about seeing her tomorrow. Later today. Whatever you want to call it. Really looking forward to it. To share the triumph that I can't share with anyone – except this tiny red blinking eye in front of me.

It's a great weight off my mind. There's a whole secret world out there, isn't there? That just drifts away. That you can't see or hear. People continue to exist when you're not there. You forget that sometimes.

But you know who I really have to thank? God, this is embarrassing. God. See, I don't think it's Sherry, not really. It's because . . . I can't say it. Sam would think I was off my head.

*Oh, this is absurd. I'm only talking to me. To **me**. So why hold back? I mean, the whole reason I'm making this tape is to have a record. An honest record.*

*In this last week I **prayed** for the first time in so many years. Which is stupid, because I haven't believed in God – not properly, not really – since . . . since I don't know when. Very hard to believe in God when you're a doctor. You see the randomness, the pain. Anyway, you can take* the boy out of the Church but maybe not the Church out of the boy. The habits – the mental habits – persist.

I suppose it's just coincidence. But when I'd got to the end of my tether, with the family, my life, the boredom, the meaninglessness of it all . . . that was when I reached out. I got on my knees, and I reached out. Felt completely stupid. But the next day – the next **day** – I went to Hamid Ali's and got that card. And then Sherry, and then this, a problem that has been eating at me, solved. In the most unlikely fashion.

It **is** coincidence. I know that. Or, at least, the rational part of me knows it. There is no God. No one is watching us. No one is looking at us, twenty-four hours a day, checking what we do, how we feel. We are the only gods now.

But perhaps there is something in prayer. Not to God, not to the old man with the beard. Jesus and Mary. The rosary beads, the relics, all the gobbledegook. But if we're the only gods, maybe we need to pray to ourselves.

There's all this stuff, isn't there, in your subconscious, that you can't get at, that you can't know about? A huge well, a vast ocean of it. That's God, isn't it? That's God.

This is good whisky. A bit too good. Getting tired.

As . . . I . . . was . . . saying, if we're God, we can do it. We can pray to ourselves. Of course, it won't make things happen – not out there, not in the world, not directly. Winning the pools. Making the cancer go away. But praying to yourself – it's like diving into the ocean for pearls. It's talking to the bits of you that you can't quite apprehend. So the part of you that is unconscious can help the part of you that is conscious. Help you to be strong, to be good, to do the right thing, to make the right decision, to forgive yourself, to forgive others, to have willpower. All these things, they are not something you can **muster**. They come by grace. They are something you have to accept, to open your heart to. That is why you are like God – your subconscious is like God.

I'm pissed. I'm talking absolute shit. Except there's something in it. Somewhere.

I've got an idea. A prayer. A **video** prayer. Because if I pray out loud, into the lens, I'm putting it out there, not just talking in my head. It's *making it more real, it's making it penetrate more. My subconscious will listen to me. Because it is being **addressed**.*

What am I talking about? I want to go to bed.

I'm going to do it, though. I'm going to pray.

Dr Seymour drains the remainder of his Scotch, closes his eyes, puts his hands together, giggles, then composes himself. After about thirty seconds of silence he begins to speak.

*Dear God. Dear **me**.*

I'm not sure what to say. I feel foolish.

Help me . . . help me to do the right thing. Help me overcome my fear and anger. Help me to know the difference between right and wrong.

I am confused. Can it be right for me to watch, as you watch? As you are said to watch? Is it a sin? What is a sin? No one seems to know any more, God. We have to make up our own minds. We have to take the burden ourselves. It is a terrible responsibility. To face consequences without you.

Help me to look after my family. Help me to be strong with them. Show me how not to be weak. For I know they think I'm a fool. Help me to show them I'm someone they might respect.

Help me not to hate my patients. For some of them, truly, I do hate. That fat bloody woman from the block round the corner who comes in every week because she wants to pull a sickie. Her stupid, useless husband who pushes drugs and hits his kid. The Russian hustler who looks at me like I'm nothing. That old Polish guy, that old Nazi.

People are terrible. When I started out as a doctor I thought they were good. But people are terrible.

Please help me, God. Help me to see the good in people again. Help me to see the good in myself.

For thine is the kingdom. The power and the . . .

Dr Seymour opens his eyes.

This is stupid. Ridiculous.

Cyclops Surveillance Systems, Tape Three, Saturday, 12 May

Dr Seymour arrives as Sherry Thomas appears to be closing the shop. She is switching off the lights, collecting her bags. When Dr Seymour comes in, he is breathless, anxious. She seems professional, regretful, and gives no sign at first of the degree of intimacy that has been developing between them.

– *Sherry. Sorry I'm late.*

– *I'm just closing.*

– *Yes, I know. The train, it was a nightmare. Broke down, stuck in a tunnel for half an hour. Look, can we talk?*

– *Like I say, Dr Seymour, the shop is . . .*

She looks at one of the two synchronized clocks on the wall.

– *. . . closed. Why don't you come back next week?*

– *Sherry, don't be annoyed with me, it really isn't – Just because I was late didn't mean that I'm not –*

– *I'm not annoyed with you, Dr Seymour. Why should I be? Now, if you could just leave the premises, I need to set the alarms.*

– *Don't be like this. Don't you want to know how much you've helped me? What a difference you've made to my life? It's worked, Sherry. Or, at least, it's working. Everything is beginning to turn round. And it's thanks to you.*

– *That's excellent news. However, I'm late for an appointment . . .*

– *Look, I really am sorry I'm late. I know somewhere near here that does a pretty decent lunch. Why don't we just sit down and talk for a while? I have to talk. There's no one else I can share this with. And I know we don't know each other very well, and I'm sorry to assume, but, please, aren't you just a bit hungry?*

Sherry Thomas does up her coat, picks up her bag and takes a final glance in a mirror situated by the shop door.

– *I think lateness is very rude. It's unacceptable.*

– *I've said I'm sorry.*

– *Anyway, I don't think there's anywhere decent around here.*

– *No. But you've got a car, and we could go somewhere. Just so we can talk a bit.*

She seems to consider this for several seconds. Clearly she is genuinely annoyed about his unpunctuality. Then she unbends.

– *I'm not a cheap date, Alex. I hope you're not thinking of a Happy Meal.*

– *Do you know anywhere?*

– *How about the Belvedere in Holland Park? Ten minutes away down the A40.*

Dr Seymour looks taken aback. (The state of the Seymours' finances made fancy meals a rare occurrence.)

– *Doesn't Michael Winner go there?*

– *I'm sure we won't bump into him.*

– *In that case, why not?*

– *Excellent.*

– *And, Sherry, one last thing.*

– *This is getting like a Colombo movie. There's always one last thing. What is it? House wine only?*

– *This isn't a date. It's lunch. A business lunch.*

– *I know that, Alex. What I'm not sure about is what the business at hand is.*

The camera watches both parties leave the shop. The external camera shows them climbing into Sherry Thomas's BMW, which is parked outside. They drive away.

Author's Note: Obviously we have no direct way of knowing what passed between Sherry Thomas and Dr Seymour at the restaurant. She did not talk about their conversation to Barbara Shilling. However, Dr Seymour, in his final 'confession' to his wife, shortly before his death, mentioned this meeting. What follows is a transcript of my conversation with Samantha Seymour on the subject of the lunch at the Belvedere.

Interview with Samantha Seymour

What did Alex tell you about that lunch?

Not much. Nothing at all when it actually happened. But at the end I insisted he tell me everything, and he mentioned that they had lunch together.

You must have been pretty annoyed.

I was mainly annoyed that they had lunch at the Belvedere. The best we can manage – could manage – was the local Indian. He was clearly out to impress her – or, at least, keep her on board. And that hurt.

Nevertheless, he seemed to be at pains to point out that it wasn't a date.

He also claimed to me that there was nothing romantic about it. That he just wanted to talk, that the whole thing was too big a burden for him and she was the only person he could talk to about it. So that was what he did. That was all he did. Or so he said.

Did he give you any details about what they said to each other?

He said it was all very innocent. That they talked about his job as a doctor, how she got into the surveillance business, that kind of thing. Pretty routine, really.

But what about the tapes? Did he talk about them?

He started to. She said she wasn't interested.

Really? That's surprising.

*She wasn't interested in **hearing** about them. She wanted to see them. The tapes from his home. She wanted him to bring them to CSS. She said it was purely a professional thing, that by seeing the tapes she could help him interpret the information properly.*

What did he tell her?

At the time he said no. But then, he told me, he felt it would be harmless enough. He didn't think it mattered. She was just trying to help. So he decided at some point in the following week to take them to her.

Did he tell you anything else?

Yes.

And . . .

He said that Michael Winner looks much older than he does on TV.

Seymour Surveillance Tape, Week Three

Sequence One: Front-room Camera, Monday, 14 May, Time Code 08.31

Samantha Seymour is dangling a teddy bear rather apathetically in front of a complaining Polly when her husband walks in.

– *Are you going to the shops today?*

– *Probably.*

– *Can you pick me up a few things?*

– *OK.*

– *I need some dental floss, a new toothbrush head, some razor blades and some deodorant.*

– *Sure.*

– *Can you remember that?*

– *Of course.*

– *Don't you think you should write it down?*

– *I don't need to write it down. I can remember.*

– *It's easy to miss one of the items when you're in the middle of a supermarket.*

– *Alex, stop fussing. It'll be fine.*

– *I'll trust you, then. But I still think you should write it down.*

There is the sound of yelling from upstairs.

– *You'd better go and sort that out, Alex.*

– *Don't forget.*

– *I won't.*

Sequence Two: Front-room Camera,
Tuesday, 15 May, Time Code 08.20

Again Samantha Seymour is in the front room with Polly, this time watching *Tellytubbies* on TV. Dr Seymour comes in wearing his bathrobe.

– *Samantha, did you get me the shaving foam?*

– *You didn't ask for any.*

– *I most definitely did. I knew you'd forget.*

– *I didn't forget, Alex. You asked me for floss, a toothbrush head, deodorant and some razor blades.*

– *And shaving foam. I remember specifically. You're such a shambles sometimes, Samantha. Well, it doesn't matter, really. I can use soap. But could you remember today, please?*

– *You didn't ask me last time. I didn't forget. You're always so sure that what you remember is true, but nobody's memory is perfect.*

– *You know how absentminded you are, Sam. It doesn't matter. Forget it.*

– *Sure. That's what I'm good at, apparently. Shouldn't you be getting to work?*

– *Just a minute. Just a minute.*

– *What?*

– *Nothing. I'll be back in a minute.*

Dr Seymour leaves the room. Samantha mutters to the oblivious Polly on her knee.

– *You know what your daddy is, darling? You're daddy is a bighead. A big fat bighead.*

Sequence Three: Front-room Camera,
Tuesday, 15 May, Time Code 08.29

Samantha Seymour is still in front of the TV with Polly. Dr Seymour walks in.

– *Sam, I'm sorry.*

– *What?*

– *I never asked you for shaving foam.*

– *I'm right? You're telling me I'm right?*

– *Yes, I am. I've thought about it, and I'm sure I never asked you for shaving foam.*

– *What's come over **you**?*

– *Could you get me some today, please? The gel type. I'm sorry I was so unfair.*

– *Are you?*

– *Yes, I am. See you later.*

He kisses her tenderly.

– *See you later, Alex.*

He leaves the room. She stares after him, astonished.

– *Daddy's gone crazy, Polly.*

Sequence Four: Front-room Camera, Wednesday, 16 May, Time Code 18.00

This is simply a recording of Victoria watching *The Simpsons*. The tape shows nothing but her, giggling, for twenty minutes. It reveals nothing hidden. I can only speculate that Dr Seymour retained it for the pleasure of watching his daughter laugh.

Sequence Five: Bedroom Camera, Thursday, 17 May, Time Code 18.33

This shows Guy Seymour alone in the bedroom he shares with Victoria. He is sitting on the floor with some pieces of coloured card, sticky-tape and scissors. As he works, his tongue protrudes. Music is playing at considerable volume in the background, some kind of rap. Guy has one shoe on and one shoe off; a chair is wedged against the door knob to stop anyone coming in. He gets up, goes to his computer and connects to the Internet.

Given the chair wedged up against the door, it is tempting to assume that he is about to access something illicit on the web, perhaps pornography. The camera does not show the screen, however. After a while there is a jump cut in the tape. The time code shows that some twenty minutes have passed and now Guy is printing something out. Still we can't make out what it is, but then he takes it on to the floor and begins to cut it up and stick it on to the pieces of card we saw earlier. In the gaps between the loud music we can hear him humming to himself.

Here there is another jump cut, this time of ten or so minutes. Now, finally, it becomes clear what Guy is doing. He lifts the assembly from the floor and examines it. The camera can pick up the detail. In carefully drawn multicoloured letters made from downloaded images of flowers, the card reads, 'Happy Birthday to the Best Mum in the World'.

Sequence Six: Front-room Camera,
Friday, 18 May, Time Code 09.09

The camera is activated when Samantha Seymour walks into the front room. She hesitates, then moves to the sofa, feels under the cushion, and fishes out a packet of Silk Cut Ultra. She takes one out, puts it into her mouth and leaves it there. Then she removes it, without lighting it, and replaces it in the packet, crushes it, and throws it out of the open window into the street. She gives a small nod, then leaves.

Cyclops Surveillance Systems, Tape Four, Saturday, 19 May

Author's Note: Dr Seymour is dressed smartly: pressed cream slacks, a blue shirt, polished shoes. His hair is combed, and there is a spring in his step. He is carrying a white plastic shopping bag in his left hand. He stares up at the camera, then at the shop. Then his face registers puzzlement and anxiety.

The shop is closed. He rattles the security grille on the front. He speaks in a low voice but loud enough for the microphone to pick up. (Although it is unusual for external CCTV to have a sound facility, in this case it is on a loop with the internal system.)

– Sherry?

He retreats a few paces and examines the shop façade, as if a secret opening or portal might be revealed to him. Then he stares directly at the camera.

It is unlikely that Dr Seymour could have known for certain that Sherry Thomas had a video link from the shop to her home a mile away – a basement flat somewhere in the no man's land between Park Royal and the A40 junction known as Gypsy Corner. But it seems that he guesses it's a possibility, because he addresses the camera directly.

– Sherry, are you there?

There is a long pause, as if he is harvesting his next words from thickets of confusion.

– You like playing games, I know that. You live to watch. To move pieces round the board. I understand that. I know you're watching.

Another pause. Then he reaches into the white plastic bag and brings out two videotapes. He holds them up to the camera for more than a minute. The trill of a mobile phone breaks the silence. He fumbles and locates it eventually in his inside jacket pocket.

– Hello? Sherry?

144

It seems that no one answers him.

– *I know you're there. Please answer me.*

He grows more agitated, pacing up and down in front of the camera.

– *I've got the tapes. I need to see you.*

He punches the grille in front of the shop.

– *Look. OK. I know what you're doing. It's OK. But it has to stop now. Or I'll walk away. And, Sherry, I won't come back. In five seconds I'm going to switch the phone off. If you don't answer me by then, this is the last time you'll see me. All right? Five, four . . .*

The camera, as if listening, pans up and down in a kind of symbolic bow. Now Dr Seymour reacts. His face registers urgency and concentration. Presumably Sherry Thomas has broken her silence.

– *Where are you? . . . Right . . . Thirty-one A Adams Street . . . left, then right, then right again . . . OK . . . I'll find it . . . How do you know I've got an A–Z? . . . I'd never venture into strange territory without a map. Right.*

He clicks off the phone, face flushed. He takes out a London A–Z from the white plastic bag, and consults it. Then he begins to run, and is out of the sight-line of the camera in seconds.

Adams Street, Tape One,
Saturday, 19 May, Time Code 12.48

Author's Note: Adams Street is a stretch of run-down, large Edwardian terraced houses. All the façades are a dirty cream. Unlike similar terraces in more gentrified parts of town, no one has attempted to brighten it with Mediterranean blues and yellows. Some of the houses seem derelict. Others are inhabited, but have blankets for curtains, or no curtains at all. The whole street is bleak and depressing, even in the bright sunshine.

The entrance to 31 A is down a flight of concrete stairs to a small yard, which, although tidy and neat, has no flowers or decorations. The windows of the basement flat are protected with iron bars. A metal grille, with flaking yellow paint, covers the front door. Closed Venetian blinds block any view of the interior. The camera that was originally fixed above the door has since been removed by the police. It is the footage from this camera that we see first.

Dr Seymour makes his way down the concrete stairs and apparently becomes aware of the camera following his progress. Almost sheepishly, he waves at the lens. Then there is the click of a latch – the internal door – opening. Dr Seymour smiles. In the following dialogue, we see only him: the hall, where Sherry Thomas is standing, is out of the range of any camera.

– *I've not been well, Alex. My head . . .*
– *I can help.*
– *Are you going to come in and examine me, then?*
– *Not if you don't unlock the security gate.*

There is the sound of a lever being turned inside, and the gate can be seen swinging outwards. Dr Seymour disappears and is picked up, moments later, on the internal camera, as is Sherry Thomas. She is wearing loose pink cotton pyjama trousers and a long-sleeved baggy white cotton shirt. Both look cheap, but are carefully pressed. Her feet are bare. Her hair is brushed. Her face is pallid, and she is trembling slightly. Her right hand frequently rubs her temples. She appears unlike she has on any other occasion in the shop – vulnerable, softer, casual. They do not touch in any kind of romantic or suggestive fashion, but Dr Seymour puts his hand on her forehead.

– *You have a slight temperature.*

– *Why don't you come in?*

The interior is murky, almost lightless. The camera just about picks out a cheap three-piece suite, a coffee-table, a sideboard and a rack of what look like technical magazines. There are no pictures on the walls, only a large analogue clock above the fireplace. There is also, on an opposite wall, a large digital clock. Both show precisely, to the second, the same time.

There is no carpet on the polished wooden floor. The room is plain but immaculately clean and tidy. The only thing that looks remotely luxurious is the television, which is an enormous flat-screen home cinema. A daytime TV chat show is running. The image of the presenters is sharp, vivid and clear.

Dr Seymour sits down on a sofa facing the TV. A bottle of wine, with a glass poured, stands on the coffee-table. To the left, a set of shelves is filled with what looks like a hundred or so video-tapes. There are a few books, whose bulk and colouring suggest airport blockbusters. There is a Bible, and a set of encyclopedias that look pristine and unused.

The walls are taupe, the doors are painted white. Everything is neutral to the point of dullness. A door to the left leads directly into a bedroom: the headboard of a single bed is visible, with an unframed mirror hanging over it. There is another clock on the bedside table.

– *Nice place.*

– *No, it isn't, but it's all I can afford to rent in this overpriced hell-hole. It costs more than New York. When I lived there I did better than this. I'm going back some day. Some day soon.*

Sherry Thomas sits down on the armchair facing the sofa.

– I thought the surveillance business was booming. BMW. The shop.

– Appearances are everything. The BMW is leased. Shop's in hock. But, like I told you, I'm not in it for the money. It's more a hobby that got out of hand.

– Out of hand? Or out of control?

– I don't really care if it's both or neither. The point is, it absorbs me. Very little in life can do that for me any more. Do you know what I mean, Alex?

– I think so.

Dr Seymour fidgets with his bag of tapes. Sherry Thomas runs her fingers through her hair and grimaces.

– Can you help me? It feels like I've got a pile of sharp rocks in my head. Last time – what you did, it was amazing. Like you conjured the pain away into thin air.

– Maybe you should just take some of your painkillers.

– They don't work. Please try. You really do have a special gift.

He gets up slowly and adopts a position behind her chair. He places his hands on her head, and begins to massage her temples gently.

– Aaah, God. There it is. Right away. Like someone's opened a channel for all the poison to sluice away.

– Really?

– I'm not kidding. Your talent is extraordinary.

– It's good to hear you say that. I stopped believing I had a gift a long time ago. Now I just hand out pills to people looking for perpetual erections, slim hips, thicker hair. I give out sick notes, I refer people to hospitals with six-month waiting lists. I'm not a healer any more. I'm an administrator, a patsy, a slot machine.

– You're a healer, Alex. You can take away pain. You just have to believe in yourself.

– Whether I believe in myself or not is neither here nor there.

– Perhaps. But I know you can do it. Because you're doing it.

Despite his protestations, Dr Seymour looks pleased. He continues to massage Sherry Thomas's head for several minutes.

She sits silently, eyes closed, in an attitude of perfect relaxation. As he massages, Dr Seymour surveys the room. Eventually his eyes settle on the shelves of tapes.

– *You've got an awful lot of videos.*

– *They pass the time.*

Dr Seymour stops massaging, walks over to the shelves and inspects the contents. He nods, then returns to his patient. Sherry Thomas opens her eyes, then closes them again almost immediately as she speaks.

– *From* Awakenings *to* Zabriskie Point. *All my favourite movies. What were you expecting?*

– *I'm not sure.*

– *Listen, Alex . . .*

– *Yes?*

– *Thanks for coming over. I appreciate it. Really I do. It's very . . . caring of you.*

– *Not really. I didn't know you were ill.*

– *All the same, thanks. You can stop now. The pain has gone.*

– *Really?*

– *Pretty much. Still a bit of an edge. But bearable. Would you like a drink?*

– *No, thanks.*

Dr Seymour returns to his seat on the sofa.

– *How about a smoke?*

– *You know I've given up cigarettes.*

– *I wasn't talking about a cigarette.*

Sherry Thomas reaches across to an enamel-inlaid wooden box positioned exactly in the centre of an occasional table adjacent to her chair. She takes out some cigarette papers and a small package of greenish leaf, compressed into what looks like clingfilm. She unwraps it.

– *This helps to remove that last edge. The other great healer.*

She holds the leaf towards Dr Seymour.

– *I know that smell.*

– *User?*

– No. Some of my patients reek of it. They must go about with great lumps in their pockets. I've never used any kind of illegal drug.

– Do you object?

– Not in principle. But are you sure you ought to? You're unwell, after all.

– It helps me. Anyway, suddenly I feel a great deal better.

She rips open a cigarette with the point of a nail, and spreads the marijuana on an outsize Rizla paper.

– Do you want to get high?

– It's not really my thing.

– Yes, it is, Alex. You just don't know it yet.

She adds some more marijuana leaf, rolls deftly, licks the paper and produces a perfect cylinder, then inserts a rolled-up piece of card – a 'roach' – into one end, and twists the other. She throws her legs casually over the side of the chair. She lights the joint and blows smoke towards Dr Seymour.

– I don't want to get hooked on smoking again.

– Again? You're still hooked on it. That's your trouble. You deny yourself pleasure. All you think about is duty. You need to loosen up a little bit. I find this helps me a lot.

– In what way?

– I told you. I'm like you, Alex. I like to have everything a certain way. A particular arrangement of things. Everything in its place. I've got no problem with that. I'm glad I'm that way. Even though I suspect it contributes to the headaches. But there are other ways of being. You can afford to experiment a bit. Slip in and out, this way and that. Not too much. Just enough. Sure you don't want a toke?

Dr Seymour smiles.

– This is highly unusual. And rather immoral. Above all, it's . . . strange.

– Is it?

– I **like** the strangeness of it.

– Why?

– Because in my life I always seem to know what's going to happen next. But at the moment I don't have a clue.

– Is that good?

– It frightens me. But yes. It's good.

– So, then, in that spirit, do you want some?

– No.

– Are you sure?

– I'm not sure, no. In fact, to tell you the truth, I'm rather tempted.

– I know you are.

– You won't take advantage of me, will you?

– Is that what we're here for?

– I've no idea.

– I expect we'll find out. Here you are.

– Just one puff, then.

Dr Seymour takes the joint and draws deeply on the smoke. He coughs and sinks a little further into the sofa. Sherry Thomas grins widely, showing very white, small teeth. Her face has gained colour. The paleness of her lips has been replaced by a coral pink.

– What are we going to do now?

Dr Seymour holds the smouldering joint out towards Sherry Thomas. Languorously, she rises from the chair and takes a step to where he is lounging. As she takes the joint, her hand brushes against his.

– We could talk.

There is a long silence while they regard each other through the mist of smoke that separates them. Dr Seymour breaks it.

– Are we going to have sex?

– Do you want to?

– I don't think so.

– It's not exactly what I had in mind either.

– What are we here for, then?

The expression on her face changes to one of faint puzzlement, as if even the posing of the question betrays some fundamental misunderstanding by Dr Seymour about the nature of their relationship.

– You know that. We're here to watch.

– You want to see these tapes?

He indicates the plastic bag lying at his feet.

– *Not yet.*

– *What, then?*

– *Would you like to see some of **my** tapes?*

– *An X-rated movie?*

Dr Seymour giggles. The marijuana is taking effect.

– *Not exactly X-rated. More family viewing.*

Sherry Thomas rises, unsteadily, from her chair and moves across to her bedroom door. She disappears from view. Dr Seymour watches after her, drowsily. She returns holding a videotape. He stares at the spine on which a single word appears to be written in black felt-tip pen.

– *'Carl'. Who's Carl?*

– *He was my first boyfriend. In Salt Lake City. He's married with kids now.*

She feeds the tape into a VCR on the floor beneath the giant TV screen, and presses play.

An athletic young man with wide shoulders – footballer's shoulders – concealed under a baggy T-shirt appears on the screen. Sherry Thomas sits down in the chair, and takes another puff of the joint. In the video, Carl has a basketball; the camera pans back to reveal a hoop on a backboard in the front yard of a large wooden house.

– *He lived there with his parents, Ned and Francine. Ned was an a-hole. He tried to make a move on me. I slapped his face. He still tried. The gimp.*

Carl is aiming the basketball at the hoop. It sails into the air and drops through the hoop. He lets out a whoop, does a little dance. The sound of what is recognizably Sherry's laugh can be heard off shot.

Now the picture cuts to an interior scene – a dining-room table in a large, vulgarly furnished room. It is laid with an immense turkey and steaming bowls of vegetables. Four people are seated round it, smiling and holding up glasses to the camera. One is Carl, the other a boy who looks about fifteen, weedy with glasses.

At either end of the table are two middle-aged adults, an over-weight, red-faced man with an untidy moustache and receding hair, and a petite, tidy woman in a homely pastel pink woollen sweater. She is smiling uncertainly; the man is grinning broadly. The two teenagers look as if they just want to get through it. There is an empty chair in front of a laid place – presumably for Sherry Thomas.

– *Happy Thanksgiving!*

Now she leans forward and puts the image on freeze-frame.

– *The perfect American family. You know, at that time, I really thought I was going to be able to cut it.*

– *Cut what?*

– *Fit in. Join the monkeys in the zoo. That was what I wanted. Still want, I guess. But I'm outside the cage now.*

– *How does that feel?*

– *Cold. Clear. Limitless. Look at that woman. Carl's mother.*

– *What was she like?*

– *She was scared. Have you ever seen such fear?*

She presses a button on the remote, and the picture zooms in on the woman's face. The smile is tight, absolutely controlled. Her eyes, as Sherry Thomas has suggested, hold a faint yellow light that seems to conjure the idea of quiet, domestic terror.

When Dr Seymour speaks, it is more slowly and deliberately than usual, as if he's having to concentrate very hard.

– *I feel strange.*

Sherry Thomas steadies her gaze on him.

– *Watch this.*

She presses play again. The shot pulls back from the mother's face to take in the whole scene. There is a clunking sound as the video camera is put down on some flat surface within the room and arranged so that the entire table is visible. Then Sherry Thomas appears in the frame, grinning. She looks about seventeen. Her blonde hair is highlighted and teased, Farrah Fawcett-style. She is wearing a smart red skirt and a crisp blouse. Her cheeks glow.

The videotape continues. She dances round the table in a pastiche of a high-school cheerleader. Instead of pompoms, she uses cushions from the sofa. Then she puts them down, and plants a kiss on Carl's cheek. Carl's father speaks.

– *Don't give it all to him. Leave some for me.*

– *I hated him with all my heart*, says Sherry Thomas, her eyes fixed to the screen.

Dr Seymour doesn't look at her. On screen, the younger Sherry is disentangling herself from her boyfriend's embrace and making her way along the table to where Ned is sitting, holding out his arms to her. But she avoids them and instead, playfully, reaches for his cutlery and feeds him some turkey. The rest of the diners laugh as Sherry shovels in the food. At first Ned is playing along, joshing and laughing with the rest of them. But Sherry won't stop. After he's swallowed five large forkfuls, the laughter has died down and Ned is holding up his hands in supplication.

– *Enough, enough. You'll make me fat.*

– *You already are fat, you big gorilla.*

Now she picks up another pile of sliced turkey in her hand and tries to stuff it into his mouth. The laughter from the rest of the table is intermittent now, uncertain. Ned seems unsure of what is going on. He opens his mouth as if to continue playing, although it is clear he has had enough. Sherry, seizing her opportunity, stuffs the huge handful into his maw, and presses it home so that he begins to choke. Suddenly, roughly, he pushes her away.

Carl's mother freezes with shock. The two teenagers are laughing again, as Ned's face turns red, and he tries to swallow the mess, then to spit it out.

The teenage Sherry picks up a glass and raises it to the camera.

– *Happy Thanksgiving.*

The scene changes. A different room, smaller, darker. Now a naked male body can be seen reclining on a bed.

Dr Seymour takes another deep toke of the joint, examines it, sees that it is finished and stubs it out. During the sequence his eyes hardly leave the screen. Sherry Thomas, on the other hand, watches his face rather than the footage, as if captivated by the possibility of his reactions.

Onscreen, the camera pans so that the face can be taken in: Carl's. Then it sweeps down his body to his groin. His penis, rising from an undergrowth of coppery hair, is erect.

Now Dr Seymour glances at Sherry Thomas. She seems unconcerned. She gives him a sideways glance that is an odd mixture of absolute coolness and tightly controlled excitement. He shifts in his chair.

The young Sherry now appears in the frame of the TV screen. She has set the camera on a tripod, perhaps, or a piece of furniture. She is naked. The heavy breathing of the young man, Carl, is audible. The seventeen-year-old Sherry's eyes are fixed on the bedroom camera. She straddles the young man, facing the camera, takes hold of his penis and pushes it into her.

Dr Seymour looks uncertainly at her: she speaks softly but matter-of-factly.

– *Do what you like. It's OK.*

Dr Seymour looks puzzled. He watches as Sherry and Carl have sex, at first slowly, then urgently, noisily, almost violently. Sherry stares at the camera, never engaging with Carl.

Then, slowly, clumsily, Dr Seymour unzips his trousers and begins to masturbate. All the time, he watches the giant TV image. Sherry Thomas ignores the screen and gazes at him, but otherwise does not move. Dr Seymour climaxes quickly. Sherry Thomas, as distant as if she were a doctor observing an operation, speaks in a low voice.

– *There are some tissues to the left of you on the floor. This is the last segment coming up. Watch.*

He picks up some tissues and cleans himself.

– *I thought I couldn't do that any more. That I had become incapable.*

– *Watch. Watch the video.*

Now the setting is different again – an exterior shot in a park somewhere. Carl is sitting on a bench, his head down.

– *What's happening?*

Carl looks up at the camera. It is immediately apparent that he has been crying. His eyes are red, his mouth distended in a grimace of misery.

– *Put that away, Sherry.*

– *Pictures aren't just about happy Thanksgivings, Carl. Pictures need to cover it all.*

The sound of weeping echoes from the speakers. Carl puts his head into his hands again.

– *Please, Sherry, We can work this out.*

– *There isn't anything to work out. I don't want you any more.*

– *But why not?*

– *Does it matter?*

– *I need to know.*

– *OK, then. Because you're clumsy and lazy in bed. Because I don't like the way you're happy with so little. Because you have hair on your back. Because I hate the spluttering noise you make when you laugh. But, above all, because you bore me.*

The camera remains trained on Carl. His face, contorted with pain and fury, stares into it. Then he turns and walks swiftly away. The camera remains trained on his back, as the sobbing becomes indistinct, and the image recedes to a blur.

Then the screen goes blank. Dr Seymour stares at it, as if in shock. Sherry gets up, removes the tape from the VCR, and replaces it in its box on the shelf.

– *Would you like a cup of coffee, Alex?*

– *OK.*

There is a clatter of crockery from the kitchen. Dr Seymour looks sleepy and confused. He tries to stand, but staggers and sits down again. She returns with two steaming mugs. She sits down next to him with a brisk, businesslike smile.

– *So much for pleasure. This will clear your head a little. Then we need to discuss what's happening in your work situation.*

– *That situation has been resolated . . . resoltified . . . resolved.*

His eyes are bleary and red. He sips the coffee carefully.

– *So quickly? You've heard nothing from Pamela?*

– *No, it's not that, it's . . . How did you know her name?*

– *You told me. The first time you came into the shop.*

– *I don't think so.*

He says these last words in a playful, singsong voice.

– *Does it matter?*

– *Probably not. Nothing does much.*

– *Have you got anything to show me from the surgery?*

– *No.* Nada. Nix.

A shadow of puzzlement, even irritation, crosses her face.

– *That's disappointing.*

Dr Seymour responds with a long, idiotic grin.

– *Don't get **uptight**, Sherry. It really wasn't very interesting. Just a discussion between Mrs Madoowbe, her sister and me. Mrs Madoowbe confirmed that I behaved properly when I examined her. That was all I needed. The camera has served its purpose.*

– *Has it?*

– *Yes. I was going to return it next week.*

– *I don't think you should do that.*

– *Why the dickens not? The 'dickens'. Where do you think that expression came from?*

– *Security. Are you telling me that something similar couldn't happen again?*

There is a pause. Then Dr Seymour, still under the influence of the marijuana, giggles. Sherry Thomas smiles at him.

– *I must say, I've been missing out. All my life. This stuff is top-hole. Now, that's another odd expression.*

Dr Seymour seems profoundly disoriented and intoxicated, while Sherry Thomas is entirely in control of herself.

– *You certainly have been missing out, Alex.*

– *I **definitely** have.*

– *Can I see the tapes from your home at least?*

– *No, you can't.*

– *Why?*

– *Because they're behind . . . they're behind . . . Oh, my God, I can't stand it.*

Dr Seymour collapses into giggles once more. Sherry Thomas joins in, somewhat artificially.

– *You can't see them because they're behind the sofa!*

While he is doubled up with laughter, she gets up calmly, walks behind the sofa, retrieves the videotapes and loads one in to the VCR. After a few moments, all the scenes recorded in the Seymour household, over the past three weeks, are played back. Dr Seymour and Sherry Thomas watch them in silence, apart from his occasional inane giggles. Sherry Thomas is straight-faced but fascinated: at no time do her eyes leave the screen. She freezes the tape on the final frame, a second after Samantha Seymour turns to her husband and says, 'I'm impressed.'

– *So am I.*

– *Are you?*

– *Your wife is very pretty.*

– *I suppose she is. I haven't thought about it for a long time.*

– *Do you think she's having an affair with this – Mark Pengelly?*

– *I don't know. 'Affair'. That's a strange . . .*

Sherry Thomas, impatient, cuts him off.

– *Speaking professionally, I wouldn't say there was enough evidence. Speaking as a woman . . . well, perhaps it's none of my business.*

– *Now that **is** funny. You've just watched recordings of my family in their home and you suddenly think it's none of your business. God, I'm hungry. Have you got any chocolate?*

She ignores him.

– *Speaking as a professional, I think there's not enough evidence. But speaking as a woman . . . there's something between them. Some bond. I don't know yet whether it's sexual or not. But there are indicators. For instance, does she usually wear makeup during the day when she's looking after Polly?*

– *I'm not sure. I haven't noticed.*

– *In the tape, when you're just at home with the family, she's isn't wearing any makeup. But when she's with Pengelly she is.*

– *Could be coincidence.*

– *Could be. I'm just saying. And their body language.*

– What about it?

– They stand a few centimetres closer than they need to.

– Oh, Sam's always been a close talker. Gets right up to people as if they were deaf. Whoever it is.

– This is different. Look at the way she holds her body.

– God, I feel sleepy. It comes in waves, doesn't it? I need some fresh air. Are you sure you don't have any choccy?

Sherry Thomas rewinds to the scene with Mark Pengelly and freeze-frames half-way through.

– Look at that. See the way she leans towards him. And this . . .

She runs the tape thirty seconds on.

– See how she brushes against him?

– That mightn't mean anything at all.

– It might not. It might. We'll have to keep watching.

– We?

– You are coming back again, aren't you?

– Am I?

– Yes.

– Yes.

They exchange a glance. Then she replaces the tape with the other and presses play. They watch the initial sequence where Victoria is fooling around with Macy.

– This must be painful for you.

Now Dr Seymour seems close to tears.

– God, yes. My little Victoria. I can't believe that she's . . .

– Girls mature pretty early nowadays.

– She's my Victoria. She's acting like a – like a whore.

– She's just experimenting. I'm sure she's a good girl. Now, Guy, on the other hand . . .

She winds to the section where he bullies Victoria.

– He's just a teenager.

– He's turning into a man. He's developing a man's cruelty. He needs to be watched. Carefully.

– Samantha always says –

– Let's talk about Samantha.

– *We already have.*

– *How's your head?*

– *Clearing a little.*

– *Do you trust your wife?*

There is a long pause before Dr Seymour answers.

– *Yes. I trust her.*

– *Good. That's good. So we won't need to watch her any more.*

– *Won't we?*

– *What do you think?*

– *I don't know. I'm going to a medical conference tomorrow. I'm going to be gone the whole day. The kids are away on a school trip. There's a chance for her to misbehave.*

– *Perhaps she won't take it. But it does seem like a good opportunity to find out.*

– *Can we talk more generally?*

– *In what respect?*

– *The whole thing. The . . . thing. It's having a kind of positive effect, isn't it?*

Sherry Thomas reaches over and pats Dr Seymour's hand in a sisterly fashion.

– *Of course it is. You see, the thing is, Alex, they're beginning to respect you. They took you for a weak man. And you're not a weak man, are you?*

– *No.*

– *You're a strong man. A strong man, rendered weak by trying to be good.*

– *That's right.*

– *And I can help you.*

– *You already have.*

– *But I can help you more. Right?*

– *How?*

– *We need to find out some more things. You can get stronger and stronger. They will love you the more. They will respect you the more. You will be safe.*

– *Yes.*

Sherry Thomas looks, rather theatrically, at her watch.

– I think we need to wrap this up now, Alex. It's one fifty-eight. I have an appointment with my therapist in an hour.

– Do we have to?

– Don't you have to be home?

– Not especially. Victoria and Guy are away. Samantha's gone with Pengelly to some baby gym or other.

– So after this Sunday – after the conference – you'll probably know about her and Mark Pengelly. Once you've watched the tape.

– Yes.

– Are you scared?

– I'm very scared, Sherry. I love Samantha.

– I know you do. We'll watch the tape together, then decide what to do.

– All right. If it's all for the good.

– Can I ask you something, Alex?

– Of course.

– Just one thing.

– Go ahead.

– Why did you bring me these tapes?

– What?

– You seem puzzled. It's a simple question. Why did you bring me these tapes?

– Because – because you asked me to.

– Do you do everything that strange women in shops ask you to do? Including bringing them videos of your family?

– Of course not.

– Then why did you?

Dr Seymour stands up and paces uncertainly round the room. He shakes his head as if to clear it.

– Don't start this.

– Don't start what?

– This. **Grilling** me.

– I'm not grilling you, Alex. I'm just asking you.

– Why has everything got to have a reason? I just did it. I just wanted things to be a little less predictable, is all.

– Is that it?

– What are you suggesting? That I'm some kind of weirdo like –

– Like me?

– I didn't say that.

– I don't think you're a weirdo, Alex. But I do think you're lonely. I understand that.

– I'm not lonely. I've got a wife, a family, friends.

– That's fine, then. How could you be lonely with all that?

– Exactly.

– You should go home now, Alex.

Dr Seymour stares at her blankly, then gets shakily to his feet, swaying.

– OK. I'll go. It's been . . . peculiar.

– Come back next Saturday. I'll be in the shop. OK?

– Sherry, I –

– Goodbye, Alex. And one thing before you go . . .

Dr Seymour stands up uncertainly and moves towards the door. She reaches into a drawer under the table she is sitting next to.

– Would you like a cigarette? A lovely full-strength Marlboro Red.

She takes out the packet, withdraws one, lights it and inhales deeply. Dr Seymour hesitates, then smiles.

– No thanks.

She nods, as if it is the answer she expected.

– No pressure. Maybe next time.

– Maybe.

Dr Seymour gives a small wave, and the camera watches him leave the apartment. Then Sherry Thomas reaches for a switch. The recording cuts off.

Interview with Barbara Shilling

You have observed that Sherry Thomas had psychopathic tendencies . . .

I pointed out that she has some of the characteristic personality traits of psychopaths, which is not quite the same thing.

Was she a voyeur, then?

Again, this has a specific psychological meaning. And although her behaviour displayed aspects of voyeurism it was not necessarily typical. Voyeurs are typically male and younger than her. Like most voyeurs, she was deficient in her relationships with the opposite sex. Voyeuristic activity fulfils a sense of adventure and participation missing in 'real' life. The subject is usually introverted, timid, over-controlled and socially isolated. Again, Sherry only partly fitted the bill. But she did have a fear of failure and of losing control, which was typical. She often told me that she had a sense of being unable to control events in the real world.

Are there people who study this?

Certainly. Simpson and Weiner, for instance, contend that voyeurism is not simply about sex. Voyeurs, they say, are stimulated or satisfied by covert observation of many kinds. The main thing is that people are being watched in secret. It gives the voyeur a sense of power. But at the same time, like any compulsion, it leaves the sufferer feeling empty and hopeless. As an alcoholic needs more and more alcohol, the voyeur needs to witness deeper and deeper secrets, you might say.

It's almost a national trait, now.

Yes, or a national sickness.

At an individual level, is it treatable?

That much is dubious. Some have tried to treat it with anti-obsessive-compulsive disorder medication, such as fluoxetine or paroxetine, and have reported limited success.

Did you try these out with Sherry?

I am not a psychiatrist. I cannot write prescriptions.

Of course. Tell me . . . Last time I came to see you, you said that Sherry talked to you about Dr Seymour.

I can't be sure it was Dr Seymour, but she did say that someone had come into her life who was very special. She never used his name.

Was she in love with him?

It's hard to say. Sherry, typically, was always having crushes that ended in disappointment. It seems that Dr Seymour was just one disappointment too many. Clearly she was excited that she'd found someone else to share her obsessions, although she didn't talk to me about it in specific terms.

What did she say?

Only that a man had come into her shop who seemed kind, and who seemed to understand her. She mentioned that he had helped her with her headaches, which were a constant source of suffering for her.

Were they rooted in any physical ailment?

I don't think so. I would feel pretty sure that they were entirely psychosomatic, although that didn't make them any the less painful. She seemed to find Dr Seymour a soothing presence. At the same time, she was also irrationally infuriated by him.

Why?

I think the simple fact that he had a family, a life that was at least superficially successful, tormented her. All the things he had and she had never had and felt she never could have. I think she came to hate his wife, for no other reason than that she was his wife. Underneath all her charm, she was deeply angry.

Was she angry with Dr Seymour?

She seems to have been at the very end. Or, rather, she was angry with everything – herself, her past, her abusers, those she thought of as having abandoned her – and Dr Seymour provided a conduit, a symbol, if you like, for that anger.

How did you try to help her during your sessions together?

By listening, mainly. By being non-judgemental. By helping her to clarify her thoughts. I never tried to suggest solutions to her. One of the first things you learn as a therapist is that you can't solve people's problems for them, but you can persuade them to look at them more honestly, and perhaps help to break destructive patterns of habitual thought.

Did you have any success?

[Drily] *Apparently not.*

OK. I put that badly. Did she feel you were helping her?

I don't know. To be honest, I think therapy was simply another of her addictions, and a strategy for assuaging her loneliness. I don't know if she changed her thinking as a result of coming to see me.

Was there any part of you that was unsurprised when you read what had happened with her and Dr Seymour in the newspapers?

Hindsight is distorting. Now it's happened, I can imagine I must have seen it coming a long way off. But before it happened, I thought she was just another unhappy person, trying to survive in a world she found unfriendly and bewildering.

Did she have any insight into her own condition, if condition it was?

Again, hard to say. But she did say to me once that she felt as if she was always in a speeding motor-car. She knew she was going to crash but she was frightened to stop the car. Or perhaps she said she didn't know where the brake was.

Interview with Samantha Seymour

How did viewing the video of your husband at Sherry Thomas's flat make you feel?

Sick.

Because of the sex?

There wasn't any sex. There was only masturbation. And that's what this whole thing is about, isn't it? Watching from a distance and getting off on it.

So that part didn't bother you?

I found it absurd. Amusing. Pathetic.

But it wasn't that which made you feel sick?

If they had had sex, it would almost have been better. But to sit there in front of him . . . It's so cold. It wasn't even sexual – at least, not for her. Her pleasure was in his humiliation. Although, of course, poor Alex didn't realize he was being humiliated. He would have thought it was erotic. Because he didn't understand.

What was it that he 'didn't understand'?

I know what went through Alex's head while this was going on. He would have thought that he hadn't betrayed me because they hadn't kissed, hadn't touched, hadn't had sex. He didn't understand betrayal. He didn't understand power. She did. And that was what excited her.

What was the betrayal, then?

The secrets, of course. So much more intimate than sex. Secret film from the inside of our house. Conversations between us. Family secrets, bonds, codes. Our problems and challenges, our negotiations. The fabric of our lives. She stole those. She came into our house and we didn't even know it. It's so foul.

But you said before that you didn't blame Alex.

Not in the same way I blame her. Because Alex was just foolish. He thought that this was a kind of innocent fun that would spice up his middle-aged life. *He didn't understand that when someone has an affair it isn't the sex that hurts most but the secrets. It's the idea that someone is alone with the person you thought was yours and giving them knowledge that you thought belonged to you alone. The exclusion in that is terrible. Far more terrible than the sex. She knew that. She got off on it.*

What do you think of their discussion about you and Mark Pengelly?

Unbelievably insulting.

Because nothing happened between you and Mark?

You've seen the rest of the tapes. Why do you need to ask me that? We've had this conversation anyway.

I know. I had to pay for it. With my own confession.

So that and the rest of the tapes don't convince you?

Up to a point. All the same, it would be helpful in laying this matter to rest if Mr Pengelly would talk to me. But he won't.

That's his decision.

You haven't discussed it with him, then?

Whether I have or not, I can't control him. If he chooses not to speak to you that's his affair. You've seen the tapes. I've answered your question about Mark and me. The matter is at an end.

All right. Let me ask you something else. What was your sex life like with Alex? I mean, before it dried up.

In what respect?

Was it normal? Regular? Satisfactory?

Mind your own business.

It's relevant.

I don't see how.

Because I need to understand what drove Alex towards Sherry Thomas. And there was obviously a sexual element to their relationship, even though they didn't make contact.

You would think that.

I just want to know if –

You want this so you can sell the tabloid rights – because you get the fees from newspaper serializations. It's a commercial decision. All that 'understanding' line. It's a ruse.

There's something in what you say. It is somewhat prurient. It does increase the value of the serialization. But it's not only that. I do want to know. It may be key. It may not. But I can't tell unless you speak to me about it.

OK.

Just like that?

With a little more quid pro quo. Yes.

Oh, come on. I've paid that price. I've done what you asked.

You keep asking for more. Why shouldn't I?

No. No, I won't do it.

Then I won't answer your question. If you want me to be a whore for the tabloids, you can sign up to the brothel.

The tabloids wouldn't be interested in me.

No. But the broadsheets might. And I'm interested, which is the main thing. I'm interested in you being authentic. You give me all this about being honest, about the truth, about opening up, but you guard yourself ferociously, like all writers.

You wanting me to humiliate myself isn't about *quid pro quo.* It's about cruelty.

Isn't this whole matter about cruelty of one kind or another?

Why should you punish me? You asked me to do the book, after all.

I don't see why my family should be the only ones who suffer for this project, do you?

Is there a limit to the suffering you demand?

*Is there a limit to the suffering **you** demand?*

What do you want me to talk about? I haven't got a limitless supply of dirty secrets.

I don't know. Why don't you think about it?

Author's Note: I realized, at this point, that the further down the road I went with the book the more I was putting myself into Samantha Seymour's power. The more time and effort I invested in it, the harder it was to deny any requests to put myself on the line. It had not occurred to me that she would ask me to reveal myself again, especially as I had told her the first time how excruciating I had found the experience. This was naïve – in fact, it was dawning on me that I had been naïve about my subject all along.

I was beginning to suspect that my pain in telling the story about my uncle had encouraged her desire to push me in the 'confessional' direction rather than the reverse. After all, asking her about her sex life with Alex was not such a terrible intrusion on her privacy – not in comparison to all the other humiliations she had suffered. Or perhaps that was the point: it was the last corner of her life that she wished to remain private.

But I suspected that there was something not merely symbolic in forcing me to dredge up painful secrets but retributional. It occurred to me that Samantha Seymour wanted revenge for something she had openly solicited in the first place – the book. Although she accepted that it was necessary, both to raise funds for the Seymour Institute and to set the record straight about her husband, she disliked the whole process, and had decided to use me, her collaborator, as a scapegoat.

Whether or not my analysis was correct hardly matters. The fact was that she had me over a barrel – even more so than before. The further I went with the project, the more time and effort I expended on it, the higher the price she could extract from me for its continuance. I tried to explain to her that she was exposing other, innocent people. She pointed out that the exposure of innocents was what all this was about.

So I agreed, reluctantly, to recount something else I found shameful – and not only shameful; the telling would almost certainly destroy an existing and rather fragile family relationship. But even as I spun the narrative, my mind worked to find some way out of the dilemma into which she had cast me. Apart from anything else, it damaged the style of the book. Who, when buying a volume about the Seymour Tapes, would want to read the confessions of a minor writer? Samantha Seymour was not only hanging my dirty laundry out to dry, she was compromising the integrity of the final product.

Nevertheless, for the time being I acceded to her request. I simply hoped that she wouldn't continue to push the stakes higher – but I also worried that the game, like Dr Seymour and Sherry Thomas's game of spying, was addictive for her.

If you read *The Scent of Dried Roses* then you'll know I once had a difficult relationship with my older brother.

I do remember that, yes. You hated him.

Well, the way I saw it, Jeff hated me.

Because when you were born you were sick and your mother spent three months in hospital with you and didn't see your brother at all.

That's my take on it. Jeff thought, and still thinks, differently. In his memory there was never a problem between us. Anyway, the hostility between us, for a long time it never went away. He moved abroad when he was in his late teens, first to France, then Québec.

Where did he end up?

In America, in Louisiana. He married a woman much younger than him. She was very pretty. The first time I saw her I was very attracted to her.

When was that?

In the mid-1980s. I was chronically depressed at the time. It was 1984, I think. I spent the summer touring America by myself, thinking it was going to be romantic and exciting, but I was lonely and homesick. Anyway, after a few weeks I ended up going to visit Jeff and his wife.

Although he was welcoming, things were bad between them. The air was thick with tension. It felt like things were always about to topple over into an argument. They divorced eventually, but at this point the marriage was in its death throes. It was sad to watch. I felt bad for him. And yet, in my depression, an ugly part of me was pleased that things weren't going too well. The melancholic secretly hates the happiness of others. Also, we've always been terribly competitive. Anyway, I stayed for about ten days.

The thing is, Monique and I got on well. We had a rapport, a shared sense of humour, and sometimes, it seemed to me – at least in my deranged state – that we were more like a couple than her and Jeff. This, I sensed, was painful for him, yet I did nothing to discourage it. In fact, I sometimes think we were in a conspiracy to hurt him. She was routinely cruel and dismissive about him, and when we were alone together, she used to make snide remarks about him, and criticize him. I didn't join in, but I didn't defend him either. I was secretly pleased that we were forming a bond. It felt like a kind of triumph over Jeff. Even as I felt this, I was ashamed too.

Author's Note: There is now a long pause.

That's it? That's your story? You're going to have to do better . . .

Just give me a minute. I'm fighting a strong impulse to get up and walk out of here.

That makes two of us.

OK. The two nights before I left, well, Jeff was busy doing something, and Monique and I went down to the local music club, Tipitinas. We danced and drank and had a great time. When we left, it was a hot night and we couldn't find a cab so we started walking back together. We were leaning against each other, giggling and flirting, I guess. Then we found a cab and fell into the back. The driver was kind of wild and swung round corners, and every time he did it, we fell across each other. About the third time it happened, I felt that she wanted me to kiss her. So I did.

And?

She kissed me back. Then, suddenly, we were in this passionate embrace. By the time the car was approaching where they lived we were all over each other. Monique got the car to stop a block away and we found a park bench and carried on.

Did you have sex?

No. But it was unquestionably sexual. We – touched each other. Intimately. This went on for about twenty minutes. Then I sobered up enough to realize that Jeff must be wondering when we'd get home. We walked the block or so back to their house. When we got there, I could see him through the window. And I could see that he'd been crying, that he was in a desperate condition. Not because he dreamed that anything had happened between me and Monique, but because his marriage was ending. I had never seen my brother cry before, and it came as a tremendous shock. I felt such love for him, and such bottomless shame for what I had done.

And then?

We just walked into the house as if nothing had happened. Jeff pretended he was fine, we sat up watching TV, and thirty-six hours later I had gone. Jeff and Monique divorced a few months later. I never said anything to him, and I never spoke to Monique again. But the betrayal of that night has been with me always.

How are things with your brother now?

Much better. He's married again, got two kids. We're pretty good friends.

Think you'll stay pretty good friends after he finds out about this?

I doubt it. Satisfied?

I think so. Yes.

Author's Note: The telling of the story of my brother and Monique turned out, if anything, to be more painful than recounting the secrets about my uncle. I thought it would almost certainly smash up Jeff's and my long-standing truce, and even our friendship. This left me feeling furious. And it meant that something I had never experienced before in writing was developing between Samantha Seymour and me – at least on my side. Genuine enmity.

Just as she had felt herself raped by the media, by Sherry Thomas and, finally, by me, I felt violated by her. Although an intellectual part of me recognized the force of her arguments, a deeper part felt that she was bringing non-combatants into the arena, and that this was fundamentally unfair.

Still, I could see no way to right the balance. For the time being I had to keep playing along – at least until I'd got all my material on file. Then I could try to find some way of excising the confessional dilemma I had been manipulated into – either by Samantha Seymour's vengefulness or by my own determination to finish the project.

Interview with Samantha Seymour (resumed)

So, Samantha, I've paid my price. Time for you to pay yours. What was your sex life like with Alex?

I'm sorry to disappoint you but it was pretty normal. Better than normal, in fact.

What's normal?

Two point three times a week, so I understand.

You had an active sex life, then?

Yes, until the baby was born. I found Alex very attractive. He was an attractive man. When we first met, we were at it like rabbits – at least once a day. When you've been married as long as we had, it usually drizzles down to once or twice a month – at least, from what my friends tell me – but Alex and I were always quite sexual beings. I think it was the only place he could let go. Lose himself. He was a good lover. Very passionate, very caring. Tough, masculine, energetic. He took me to places I would never admit to myself that I wanted to go. A few months after Polly was born, I was starting to be interested again, but he had a problem, as we've already discussed.

What was he into?

I can't believe you're asking me that.

Quid pro quo, right? I've told you my secret, now you have to answer my questions.

Do you mean was he into anything weird?

Specifically, voyeurism.

I think he used porn.

You think.

I know he used porn. But not regularly. Just from time to time. It's not unusual, is it, among men? Have you used porn? You know, did your session at your uncle's establish a lifelong dependency?

It's still your turn. What did you feel about it?

Relatively liberal. It didn't do anything for me, although I sometimes pretended that it did, for his sake.

So voyeurism wasn't an alien concept to him.

Everyone's a voyeur, more or less. Look at all the gossip magazines, chat programmes. Look at Big Brother, look at reality TV. Everyone watches everyone else. It's the great unifying passion.

But did it go beyond a few porn movies? Did he ever want to watch in real life, or be watched?

No. He never suggested that. Perhaps he was too scared. I mean, I can imagine him being into me and another woman. But that's just bog-standard male fantasy, isn't it? Nothing especially pathological there.

Do you think he was attracted to Sherry Thomas?

Not sexually, no, but he was attracted to something about her.

Do you think she had something you didn't?

Rather the reverse. She lacked something that I — Alex and I — had.

Which was?

Any sense of limits.

Seymour Surveillance Tape, Week Four

Author's Note: This sequence takes place on the day that Dr Seymour attended a medical conference in Birmingham. Both Victoria and Guy Seymour were away on a school trip.

Mark Pengelly, Samantha Seymour, Polly and Theo appear on the tape. In contrast to her previous appearances with Mark Pengelly, Samantha Seymour is wearing no makeup, and is dressed in baggy, unflattering clothes. Theo and Polly are on the floor, playing with a selection of brightly coloured plastic toys. Pengelly and Samantha are sitting some distance apart, he on the sofa and she on the adjacent armchair. Both are drinking tea and eating chocolate biscuits.

Sequence One: Front-room Camera, Sunday, 20 May, Time Code 11.55

– *Polly's such a pretty girl.*

   – *Yes, she is, isn't she? Aren't you, darling? You're a pretty girl, aren't you? A gorgeous little sausage.*

   – *It's not surprising, with you as her mother.*

   – *Do you think she takes after me?*

   – *Absolutely. She's got your eyes. Those flecks of bottle green mixed with the richest, brownest . . .*

   – *It's sweet of you to say so, but I think they're more her father's eyes.*

   – *Where is he this weekend?*

   – *Some boring bloody conference.*

   – *Come on, I know about those conferences. All they do is get pissed and flirt.*

   – *Not Alex. He's far too moral to do anything like that.*

– I thought you said he –

– A momentary aberration. It was all that stupid receptionist's fault. Well, mostly. Anyway, once in all these years isn't so bad.

– Behaving yourself can be a bit of a bore, though, don't you think?

– Without rules, people would find the world unbearable.

– We make it all up. It's all in our heads.

– That doesn't matter. Without a sense of good and bad, well, it would be unbearable. Would you pass me Polly's beaker, please?

– Here you are. It's just fear of being found out, isn't it?

The camera shows Polly hitting Theo Pengelly on the head with a plastic toy.

– Polly! Stop that.

Mark Pengelly picks up Theo and calms him down. Then he returns him to the floor beside Polly.

– We should be mature enough to take responsibility for our own lives and live with the consequences. It's the twenty-first century. Everything's biddable, isn't it?

– Is that what you're going to teach Theo?

– Well, no. I'll teach him the rules of the game. But they're not absolutes.

– Give me an example of a non-absolute.

– Well . . . fidelity, for instance.

– So, you think that if you can get away with it, you should do it?

– Sometimes, in some circumstances. No one gets hurt if no one knows.

– But the participants know.

– So what?

– Do you believe in God, Mark?

– Of course not.

– Neither do I.

– So, there's nothing to stop you doing whatever you want, except fear of the consequences.

Now Samantha stops what she's doing, which is searching for a book to read to Polly, and turns, almost angrily, towards Mark Pengelly.

*– But that's not **true**. Because in the absence of anything else you can only imagine yourself into being yourself. You are only what you **believe***

you are. And if you stop acting and thinking and behaving like that thing, you stop **being** it.

    – *I'm not really with you, Sam. Speak slowly, I'm an actor.*

    – *Once you start abandoning standards, your boundaries dissolve.*

    – *Can I get a translator?*

    – *It's like if you keep making resolutions and breaking them. After a while, you become weak, incapable of action. In not believing that you have the capability any more, you lose it. And the same with doing the right thing. If you wriggle out of your own morality often enough, if you* **cheat**, *it ceases to have any meaning for you. Thus it stops existing – not objectively, because it was never there in the first place, but it stops existing as far as you're concerned. And you're faced with a world that has no limits, and that is terrifying.*

    – *I wasn't expecting a philosophy lecture.*

    – *Let me put it a different way for you, then, in a way that you'll be able to grasp. Then I'm going to change Polly's nappy.*

    – *Please do.*

    – *I'm not going to sleep with you, Mark.*

    – *What?*

Mark Pengelly looks bewildered and shocked, while Samantha Seymour is calm and collected. She begins to change the baby's nappy. During this process, she occasionally shoots Pengelly a glance, but stays focused mainly on her task. She is impeccably blasé.

    – *I know that you're attracted to me. I know that you've been low since your wife left you. I know we've kissed, once. Can you pass me those Wet Ones? Thanks. Look. I know you think there's something special between us, and there is. There's friendship – a tender, special friendship. But nothing more. There never was.*

    – *Who said I thought there was anything more?*

    – *I'm a woman, Mark. Not a moron. You've been manoeuvring for months.*

    – *I did think that perhaps – I mean . . . Your marriage . . . it's unhappy, isn't it?*

    – *Marriages like mine and Alex's aren't happy or unhappy. They're beyond that. I'm sad you never got the chance to find that out with Catrina.*

– But . . . do you love him?

– Things are not good at the moment. I have loved him and I will love him again. Love comes and goes. The marriage remains. The respect remains. The children remain. We're going through a difficult period. Alex, particularly, is suffering. But he's trying very hard. I'm not going to smash everything apart just because everything isn't twenty-four-hour roses. I owe him more than that. And myself.

– I thought you said he was weak – that you'd stopped respecting him because of it.

– I did say that, but I was wrong. There you are, Polly darling. Clean as a pin, you stinky thing.

– You think you were wrong? What? Suddenly he's changed? Suddenly he's a different man?

– Perhaps. Or perhaps I just wasn't able to see it before. There's something about him at the moment. Like he's turned a corner. Seen some kind of light. Though I can't imagine what that corner might be or where that light might have come from.

– But surely, between us, there's been some kind of . . .

– I won't say I'm not attracted to you, Mark. You're a good-looking man. But you know that, don't you? And I like you. You're a good father, you're kind and attentive. But I have to make this as clear as I possibly can. We're just friends. We can only ever be friends.

– But, Samantha, Sam . . .

– And if you want us to keep on being friends, you need to respect that. Thank God we never did anything. Because now we can carry on with the relationship that we've had. Don't you think?

– Yes . . . I suppose . . .

– Be an adult about this, Mark. We're neighbours, our children are friends. We get on very well, we're support for each other. It would be crazy to mess that up for a bit of – I don't know . . . for a cheap thrill.

– Right.

– OK?

– If you say so.

Samantha Seymour gets up and plants a small kiss on Mark Pengelly's cheek. He does not move.

– *You'll be fine, Mark.*

– *I'll be fine.*

– *I know you will. Now, let's sort out some lunch for the kids, shall we?*

She picks up Polly and moves briskly out of the room. Slowly, as if suffering from some sudden bout of cramp, Mark Pengelly rises and follows. A single tear falls from his left eye, and he wipes it away with his sleeve. Then he gathers himself, smiles carefully, as if testing that the necessary muscles still work, and follows Samantha into the kitchen with Theo.

Dr Alex Seymour's Video Diary, Excerpt Four, Monday, 21 May, Time Code 02.03

Dr Seymour is in his underpants, no dressing-gown, presumably because of the heat – the loft room, at the top of the house, gets very warm even on relatively mild days. His hair is ruffled, but otherwise he seems relaxed. Clearly he has grown used to making his video diary. There is no hint of the embarrassment he exhibited when he began it.

There goes the self-justification for what I am doing. Kaput. The strange thing is, part of me almost wanted Sam to be having an affair with Mark because, obviously, it would get me off the hook. It would ease my conscience. But now what I've been doing looks uglier than it did before I knew she was innocent.

*Even so . . . even so. Can anyone really judge me? Since I caught Guy out, he's begun to change. I know that he's stopped bullying Victoria – I don't guess it, I **know** it. Because I can see what he's doing. Admittedly I had to confront him a few more times, but this time I had the evidence, and even though I couldn't show it to him, he knew that I knew. He sensed it. And it's made him manageable, respectful. This has been a wholly positive result. Victoria is protected. She must have picked up something from the change in Guy because she's made no more attempts to sneak Macy into the house. Guy has learned an important lesson. There's more peace and order. And, obviously, the change has even registered with Samantha. There's even a part of me that believes she **would** have had an affair with Mark Pengelly if she hadn't sensed the transformation within me, whatever she comes up with about 'imagining yourself into being' and 'abandoning boundaries', and all that fancy talk she threw at Pengelly. But the fact is, she held back. Because she said I'd changed. And I have.*

But where does that leave me now? What am I to do? One of the central pillars of the justification I'd made to myself about why I was doing this with Sherry has now disappeared. No, two have. No. All of them. Because I've protected myself against Pamela Geale now. The tape of Mrs Madoowbe and her sister does it. I'm safe. Victoria and Guy are behaving themselves. Samantha's loyal. So why don't I just return all the equipment and never see Sherry again?

It's not that I'm in love with her. I'm not. I'm really not. But she does fascinate me. She's made a change in me. She's taken me this far. How much further could she take me?

I'm going to have to go back, of course. I promised her I would. She said she wanted to show me some more of her tapes. And, of course, she wanted me to bring more of mine. But I'm beginning to think this has gone far enough.

Perhaps it will be enough for me to sit and watch her tapes with her. She's lonely and a bit strange. I've spent my life trying to help people. Why shouldn't I help her?

All the same, keeping it secret from Samantha – especially now that it's plain she's not being disloyal – feels less and less right. I enjoy it, yes. It's interesting, for God's sake, and my life has been so bloody dull for so long.

OK. I **will** go and see Sherry Thomas again. We arranged to meet at the shop this Saturday, and I'll do it. Apart from anything else, I wouldn't mind some more marijuana. It really is rather fun. But at heart I'm a moderate man. A sensible man. I know there have to be limits to this thing.

Polly's quietened down at night. The stress is off at work. I'm sleeping better. I'm getting past my moment of crisis. I'm sure of it. Soon I'll be able to put Sherry Thomas behind me. I think I already could. But I don't think it would be fair on her. I can't just abandon her. Not after she's helped me. Not yet, anyway.

I'll give it a few more weeks. Then we'll have to have a talk.

Now Dr Seymour bows his head towards the camera.

Dear Lord, thank you for saving me. Thank you for giving me once more the gift of healing. Thank you for showing me the way that may lead to my salvation. Thank you for my wife, Samantha, and for the love that keeps her faithful. I dearly want to know how to make her happy, *for only if I can make her happy can I make myself happy. But I think, like she says herself, that our marriage is beyond these things of happiness and unhappiness. We are what we are.*

Thank you for my beautiful Victoria, and thank you for showing me a way to protect her from Macy Calder and Guy. I know Guy's not a bad boy, whatever Sherry says. He's just going through a difficult time and, with your help, I know that he'll grow into a good man. Because that's what I want for him. And now he's learning about the way you work, God, he's discovering that there's no cause without effect, that there's no transgression without punishment, because he is watched, Lord, by his father, as you, our father, watch over us. He may resent the justice that falls on him now out of a clear blue sky, but how much more must he have hated it when there was no justice other than what he could get away with? Now there is order. Now there is structure. So now there can be peace.

Please help Sherry Thomas, because I know that the woman needs help, and I will only be able to help her so much by sharing in her pain, in her obsessions. I know the time will come soon when I have to walk away from her, but we must all learn to live on our own, mustn't we, God? Mustn't we? All we have in the end is ourselves and you. And you are we.

I'm tired, now, God, tired, and I want to go to sleep.

Please help me go to sleep.

Author's Note: The only surveillance tapes extant from the days that follow this are a video diary scene and a confessional sequence. Either Dr Seymour made the decision to cease taping, having assured himself that his wife was not having an affair, or he deleted any subsequent footage. Either way, there is a gap in time here until his next visit to Cyclops Surveillance the following Saturday.

Cyclops Surveillance Systems, Tape Five, Saturday, 26 May

Dr Seymour arrives at the entrance to CSS to discover, once again, that it is closed. He rattles the security grille, then looks up at the external camera and speaks directly to it.

– *Sherry, what the hell are you doing? I thought we had an appointment.*

His phone rings. He answers.

*What are you doing? . . . Right . . . You've been ill **all** this week? . . . So why didn't you let me know?*

He checks his watch.

– *I don't know – I don't know, Sherry. I'm a bit pushed for time, to tell you the truth.*

The tone of his voice, unlike on his last visit to Cyclops, sounds tetchy rather than needy.

– *OK. All right, then.*

Adams Street, Tape Two, Saturday, 26 May, Time Code 12.30

Dr Seymour enters the flat dressed much as he was before. Sherry Thomas is dressed radically differently from any previous occasion. Her face is well scrubbed, glowing, clear of makeup. She is wearing carefully pressed jeans, immaculate new-looking sneakers, a demure white long-sleeved blouse, buttoned at the wrists. Her hair is tied back in a girlish ponytail. For the first time, she seems innocent, almost vulnerable.

We do not know what access she had to Dr Seymour's state of mind, other than the bug in his mobile phone, and no records exist of any conversations she might have picked up. Samantha Seymour says Alex told her, in his final confession, that now he was clear of any suggestion of impropriety with Mrs Madoowbe, and had 'cleared' his wife of infidelity, he was already moving away from Sherry Thomas. He admitted to her that he was still fascinated with Ms Thomas as a character, but said that he had no wish to carry on with the surveillance. His distancing of himself from her is apparent in the following exchanges. Dr Seymour seems more impatient with her than on his previous visit, as if regretful, especially in the light of his wife's innocence, that he has allowed things to go so far. According to Samantha, he was planing to finish the relationship with Sherry Thomas, but had decided that she was psychologically fragile and needed handling carefully. He suspected that to 'dump' her might lead to unpredictable, even dangerous consequences – though doubtless he imagined the danger to be to herself rather than him.

    – You don't look very unwell to me.
    – You have no idea.
    – What's all this in aid of, Sherry?

– *Come in, Alex. Please.*

He sits down, as before, on the sofa facing the large TV screen.

– *I'm sorry, Alex. I understand that you might be angry with me for dragging you out here again but I need to show you something.*

– *Why didn't you just say that?*

– *I thought you wouldn't come because you'd decided I was weird or something.*

– *I don't think you're weird. But I don't think the way you're behaving – that either of us has been behaving – is particularly healthy.*

– *Perhaps I need to see a doctor.*

– *Let's not flirt. I want to talk.*

– *What about?*

– *Look. What happened last time. It was – I don't regret it. It was special.*

– *But?*

– *You've really helped me, Sherry. The cameras – they've shown me things about my life I could never have known. They've changed me. You've changed me. In this short time.*

– *How have they changed you?*

– *I've learned, for one thing, that my wife loves me.*

– *Did you bring the tape? Of her and Pengelly?*

– *No, I didn't, but it exonerates her. And this changes everything. I was sure you were right. I thought that she was having an affair. That she was betraying me. Now I know she would never do anything like that. So it makes me . . . it makes my betrayal more unjustifiable, do you see?*

– *Betrayal? What betrayal? We haven't done anything.*

– *I've shown you secrets, Sherry.*

– *For the best of reasons.*

– *I don't think Samantha would see it like that.*

– *So what? You're just going to stop?*

– *I don't know. This could go too far, if it hasn't already.*

– *You don't understand, Alex. You're in a position of power but only because of the cameras. You know what's going on. Once you've lost this power your family will sense it. Your wife and children will lose respect*

185

for you again. They will see what happened, your momentary rebirth, as a sham, a trick, a fluke. You'll be back at square one. Believe me.

The couple sit in silence for a while, as if in stalemate. Sherry Thomas takes out a Marlboro Red, offers it to Dr Seymour, who, as usual, refuses. She lights it.

– *Can I show you something?*

– *Another tape?*

– *Yes.*

– *From your life?*

– *Yes.*

– *How many have you got?*

There is a long pause.

– *Alex, I trust you. You know that, don't you?*

– *I don't know why. But yes, I do know that.*

– *Will you come into the next room with me for a moment?*

– *The bedroom?*

– *Don't worry. I've not got designs on you. Not this week, anyway. No pressure. Just come for a moment. You can leave the door open, if you like. I won't try anything.*

Dr Seymour gets up from the couch, and Sherry Thomas from her chair. She moves to the doorway to the left, glances at Dr Seymour once more, then opens it. She walks in, and Dr Seymour follows tentatively.

The room is not wired up for vision, but the microphones from the front room still pick up the conversation that ensues.

– *What is this?*

– *It's my life.*

– *What do you mean?*

– *Exactly that. My life. Since I was seventeen, I've been taping. Every chance I can get.*

– *But there's – there's thousands.*

– *Yes. I've taped more or less every day. For the last twenty or so years.*

– *You tape every **day**? That's . . . crazy.*

– *Don't say that, Alex. Please. Even if it's true. Anyway, even if it's true . . . I can be healed, can't I? You can heal me. You have a gift.*

186

– Can we get out of here? This room gives me the creeps.

The camera shows Dr Seymour retreating slowly. Sherry Thomas follows him, holding a videotape.

– I know it seems a little odd.

– Odd? Is that what you call it? Look, I'm sorry I called you crazy. But you need help. I can put you in touch with some good people.

– It's all there. My graduation. My stepfather's funeral. My first day at college. My last day at college. All the days in between. All the endless days.

– Sherry, why do you want to show me this stuff?

– Ever since I was a child I've had this thing in my head. It's hard to explain. It's just that – moments are always ending, aren't they? Somehow that seems like a billion little deaths. A moment's there – and it's gone. All the time, disappearing, disappearing. But with videotape there is no death. Do you see?

– Sherry, I have to be honest. I have no idea what you're talking about.

– But I can explain. You'll understand. I just want you to watch one of the tapes.

– Right.

– I need you to know, Alex. Then maybe you can help me. I know you can help me. Just to share with you will help me. I've been so alone.

– I don't know, Sherry. I'm really not sure this is a good idea.

– It won't take long, Alex. I promise.

Dr Seymour sits down on the sofa, looking shaken. Sherry Thomas joins him, still holding the videotape. She points at it and looks at Dr Seymour.

– Number one.

– In a series of?

– Six thousand, one hundred and seventeen.

– Oh, my Lord.

– This one has a different directorial style from all the others. More crude, I think.

– Why is that?

– Because I didn't make it. But it started me making them.

– Who did make it?

– You'll see.

She gets up, loads the videotape into the VCR, switches on the TV and goes to sit down. But as she passes Dr Seymour he gets up and grabs her arm.

– Alex, you're hurting me.

– I have one more question.

– Sit down a minute.

– What?

– Just sit down. Then you can ask the question. And we can watch the tape.

Slowly, Sherry Thomas sits next to Dr Seymour. She turns to him. He is still holding her arm.

– What do you want to ask me, then?

– Just this. Why do you always wear long-sleeved shirts?

– You're kidding me.

– However hot it is, you always wear long-sleeved shirts, jackets or sweaters.

– So what?

– I have a patient who does that.

– Let go of me, please.

– Not yet. Do you want to know why my patient always wears long-sleeved shirts?

– Not particularly.

Now Dr Seymour roughly pushes up the cuff of Sherry Thomas's shirt. The camera is not close enough to show what it reveals, but she screams and pulls away her arm.

– Fuck off!

– When did you do that?

– Does it matter?

– You need help.

– Do I?

– Those scars are old, aren't they?

– I guess.

– How old?

She pauses, then holds up the tape.

– Shortly after this.

Dr Seymour examines the box and reads aloud.

– 'Me and Ned. Salt Lake City'.

Sherry Thomas wipes her face with the back of her hand and pulls down her sleeve. She slides the tape into the machine and reaches across for the videotape remote control. She hits play, and an image appears on the screen – herself, much younger, and in much the same incarnation in which she appeared in the earlier Thanksgiving tape.

– I had just turned seventeen, Alex. Just a kid, really.

She is wearing a simple pink summer dress and looks little more than a child. She appears surprised – part amused, part annoyed. Whoever is pointing the camera appears to have come into her room uninvited. Sherry stares blankly at it.

– Ned, stop fooling around.

– Hi, Sherry. How's my pretty daughter-in-law-to-be?

– She was pretty good until you turned up. Now, will you get out of here, please?

– That's not very nice. Come on, Sherry, don't play-act with me. I've been getting your signals.

– Signals?

– How about letting me get a look at those cute little dugs?

– Get out, Ned. Get out right now or I'll get Carl.

– Come on. You didn't mind at the swimming-pool. Where's the difference?

– Carl!

– Carl's gone out for the day. You know, I listen to you and my son. You're quite a noisy girl. Yeah. A real screamer.

– I'm leaving.

Sherry Thomas reaches for her jacket and makes for the door. Then she speaks directly to the video camera.

– That thing gives me the creeps, Ned. Really. Cut it out.

– A camera gives you the creeps? Nothing scary about a camera. Wait till you see what I got here.

Sherry Thomas's face registers extreme shock.

– No, Ned.

– Take your dress off. Or I'll stick this right up your cooze. And – bang! Six times.

Dr Seymour speaks very quietly.

– He has a gun?

Sherry Thomas nods.

– Smith and Wesson .44.

The seventeen-year-old Sherry Thomas looks terrified. The present-day Sherry Thomas mirrors her expression, as if she is reliving the whole experience. She clutches Dr Seymour's arm. He covers her hand with his. Then, suddenly, Dr Seymour reaches across, grabs the remote control and switches it off. The screen registers a grey electronic fuzz.

– I don't want to see this, Sherry.

*– What? Why not? It happened. It **happened**.*

– I don't need to see it, for God's sake.

– Of course you do!

She scrambles for the remote control, but Dr Seymour holds it away from her.

– You have to see it! You have to see it!

– I can't. It's not right.

– But if you don't see it you won't believe what happened. Nobody would believe what happened. They wouldn't believe a word of it. Not even Carl would believe it. That's why I had to leave him, even though I had nowhere else to go. Ned would have got away scot-free. If I hadn't – if I didn't –

– What? What, Sherry?

– Never mind. The point is, I couldn't go to the police because they wouldn't have believed me. Because Ned had the tape showing me 'enjoying' myself.

– Enjoying yourself? How did you get this videotape off him?

– I stole it.

– But couldn't you go to the police then?

– It was too late.

– What do you mean?

– *Please watch the tape. Then you'll understand everything.*

– *It would be obscene, Sherry. I won't watch it. You can just tell me. I'll believe you.*

– *No one believes me. No one.*

– *I'll believe you. I don't need to see the tape. Just tell me what happened.*

Sherry Thomas cries for several more minutes. Then she stops, composes herself and begins to speak in a low, urgent voice.

– *He raped me. Not once, but time and again. He set the camera up on a tripod and videoed it.*

– *My God.*

– *But he was clever. Made sure I wouldn't go to the police.*

– *How?*

– *He made me act stuff out on camera. I had a gun pointed at me, of course, but you couldn't see it. All you could see was me. He reshot, so it appeared like when he walked into the room I was topless. Then he made me come on to him, like I was some kind of Lolita. He even filmed the rape, Alex. Filmed it, and made me look like I was enjoying it. Because if I didn't he'd kill me. Then he took away the tape and laughed. Said that if I tried to start anything he'd show the world what a slut I really was.*

– *So what did you do?*

– *What could I do? I couldn't go to the police. They wouldn't have believed me. Ned was a very respected guy locally. A real hot shot. Order of the Buffaloes, Rotarians, you name it. I was some kind of low-life whore, as far as most people in that swamp were concerned. I was an orphan, trailer-park scum. None of the family thought I was good enough for their Carl. I can just see the trial. 'White-trash tramp tries to frame respected local citizen'. Then the tape – can you imagine the shame of it?*

– *But you got hold of the tape showing him threatening you. After that, couldn't you –*

– *How do you think I got hold of the tape, Alex?*

– *I don't think I want to know.*

– *I don't see what choice I had. It was him or me. I recovered after this . . .*

She holds up her wrists, showing visible old scars.

– . . . *but I knew that next time I would get it right. But I didn't want to die. I just needed to. So long as he was around, life hurt too much. There was only one way to make it bearable again. Not liveable. Just bearable.*

– *What are you saying?*

– *You **know** what I'm saying. Surely you don't blame me. Say you don't blame me, Alex.*

– *I think I should go.*

– *All right. OK. But you will come again, won't you? Next Saturday, as usual?*

– *I'm not coming here again.*

– *Fine. To the shop, then. OK? I'll be there. I realize now I've gone too far. There are so many things I haven't understood. Please come to the shop.*

– *I'll think about it.*

– *Don't think about it. Promise me.*

There is a long pause.

– *OK.*

Dr Alex Seymour's Video Diary, Excerpt Five, Sunday, 27 May, Time Code 13.00

Unlike Dr Seymour's other video diaries, this is recorded in daylight. He looks brisk, businesslike and back to normal. He seems healthy and alert.

This is the last time I'm going to do this. It's gone far enough. What the hell have I been playing at?

I can sleep again. My job is secure. My marriage is secure. My life is in order. Enough is enough.

Two things.

One. My wife has not been unfaithful to me. What an enormous relief. I feel so grateful to her and for her.

Two. Sherry Thomas is obviously a very sick woman. I understood that she was strange, but I didn't know how strange. She is clearly a danger to herself, and quite possibly to others. I believe her story that she murdered 'Ned'. I'm sure now that she's capable of it. Should I go to the police? But if she was guilty – and she was extradited . . .

It's unthinkable. She could be executed, for God's sake. And it was all such a long time ago now. Besides, the man was clearly a monster.

*And that bedroom full of tapes. Her whole **life** recorded on tape.*

She needs help, but I can't help her any more. I'll send the equipment back to her with a full remittance. I'll urge her to see a psychiatrist. This 'therapist' of hers is probably just another fantasy. But I'm never going to see her again. Promise or no promise.

Poor woman. Her being raped – did that take place? I suspect it did. This is sick. Sick. It's got to stop. And I've got to make amends.

Which means I've got to face the hardest part of all. I've got to tell Samantha what I've been doing. I'll do it later this week. Once I've considered all the options, worked everything out in my own head. What to say. How to stop her divorcing me. How to apologize enough.

I don't know where to start. But after she's shown such faith in me,

I can't keep secret something as big as this. I wouldn't be able to live with myself.

Perhaps she can forgive me. I don't know. I hope so.

I'll talk to her. Then we'll decide – together – what to do about Sherry.

Interview with Barbara Shilling

Did Sherry Thomas ever talk to you about being raped?

Not directly. She told me that something like that had happened, but that she didn't feel ready to talk about it.

Did she tell you about her collection of videotapes? She had more than six thousand. Apparently she taped more or less every day of her life.

Good Lord. That's . . . She never told me that.

Did she allude to it at all?

I knew she liked watching people without their knowledge and I knew she drew a certain comfort out of videoing sometimes quite banal everyday events. But I had no idea that it went that far.

What does it tell you about her state of mind?

That she was obviously far more deeply disturbed than she ever let me know. I think I've read about a similar case, funnily enough. In Japan, five or six years ago. A compulsive voyeur was virtually incapacitated unless he could record his experiences. It was almost as if nothing was real for him unless it was transferred into a spectacle, unless it was stored in some way.

Almost a throwback to this primitive belief about a camera stealing your soul.

Only in this version it's the watcher, not the subject, whose soul is stolen.

Yes. Did Sherry Thomas lose her soul?

I don't really understand what that question means. But if she did, I think it was stolen from her a long time ago.

Did she ever say anything to you about committing murder?

No. Although she did talk sometimes in a very ruthless way. She had these absolute views about right and wrong – or good and evil, as she would have termed it. She believed the only way to eradicate evil was to destroy it. *She was a strong believer in capital punishment, for instance, and in retribution. I wouldn't find it too hard to believe, particularly after what she did to poor Dr Seymour. This Manichean view of the universe was comforting to her in some respects. It provided her with a kind of solidity that her moral universe lacked. At the same time it tormented her.*

Why?

*Because she couldn't make up her mind at which pole she stood. It was almost a child's view of the world. Either people were completely good or completely bad. And she couldn't decide which **she** was.*

Was that the meaning of her final act?

*No one knows in the end what such things mean. They are always mysteries. But her rage at her abandonment and at herself for **being** abandoned was boundless. What happened to her, as much as what happened to Dr Seymour, was an act of vengeance as much as an act of despair.*

Did she ever talk about suicide?

She fantasized about it, but that's not uncommon, even in mildly depressed people. Even in people who aren't depressed.

What was the appeal – other than escape from an existence that she clearly found unbearable?

To show the world how much she'd been hurt.

'Look what you made me do'?

Something like that. But every suicide is both universal and at the same time unique.

Is there anything else you can tell me about Sherry Thomas?

She had bad dreams.

What were they like?

One kept coming back to her. She was naked in a vast, dark sea. It was always freezing cold and the water was flowing away. The sea was getting lower and the sky was getting darker. The more it flowed away the more frightened she became. She dived, searching for the hole, as if she might be able to plug it. If she could do that the light in the sky would come back and she could keep swimming. But if the sea ran dry, she would end. Everything would end. She found a plug, and she found a hole at the bottom of the ocean. But she just couldn't get the plug into the hole. *It was the wrong shape, or she couldn't hold her breath any longer, or a current took her away, or the hole grew as she reached for it. The water kept sluicing away, and she couldn't stem the flow.*

What happened when all the water had gone?

She always woke before it did.

What did the dream represent?

The crude interpretation would be that the water was the passage of time. I don't really know. In fact, I think I've told you everything I do know now. In conclusion, all I can say is this. I wish I'd been a better therapist. I feel I should have known. Perhaps I could have done something.

As you implied, hindsight is both cruel and misleading. You can't take responsibility. It's irrational.

Ms Shilling gives a low, bitter laugh.

Did I say something funny?

*It always interests me that people talk as if the rational part of the mind controls us. The world is out of control because **we**'re out of control. Because we cannot stand against the darkness any more. It's too big – the anger, the cry for vengeance, for atonement. Too deep within us now.*

Ms Shilling, thank you. I won't trouble you any more.

I'm sorry I couldn't be of more help.

Seymour Surveillance Tape, Week Five

This is the final tape from the interior of Dr Seymour's house. The scene is the front room. The date is Tuesday, 29 May. The time code shows 6 p.m. Samantha is reading a book on the sofa. Dr Seymour is sitting, fidgeting. He looks nervous and unsettled. Occasionally he throws a glance at the hidden video camera on the ceiling. Samantha looks up from her book.

     – Are you all right, Alex?

     – What?

     – You seem uncomfortable.

     – Do I?

     – Is anything the matter?

     – Samantha.

     – What? What is it?

Shockingly, Dr Seymour begins to cry. She puts down the book and takes her husband's hand.

     – You look pale, Alex. What's wrong?

     – Samantha, do you love me?

     *– Of course I love you. What are you **talking** about?*

     – There's something I need to tell you.

     – What?

     – It's very hard . . .

     – Alex . . .

     – I just don't know how . . .

     – Oh. I see.

     – Do you?

     – I think so.

     *– I don't know how you **could** . . .*

Angrily Samantha pushes his hand away from her.

     – Right. Right.

– What?

– It's Pamela Geale, isn't it? You're having an affair with her.

– Pamela Geale? For God's sake, Samantha, of course not.

– Who is it, then? Who are you sleeping with?

– No one. I'm not sleeping with anyone.

– Well, then, what is this? Are you leaving me?

– Of course I'm not leaving you. I love you, Samantha.

– Alex, I don't understand. What have you done that can have been so terrible?

– It's hard to explain.

– Is it?

– Well. No. It's not hard to explain. It's easy to explain. What's hard to explain is why I did it.

– Why you did **what**?

– Samantha – I have something to confess to you . . .

– So you've said. What is it? Spit it out.

– This conversation . . . the conversation we're having now . . . it's being taped.

– What?

– On videotape.

Samantha suddenly goes from appearing irritated and impatient to being concerned, even sad. She gets up and puts an arm round her husband's shoulders.

– Oh, Alex. Poor Alex.

– I've done a terrible thing.

– No one's watching you, Alex. It's OK. It's all in your head. I know that you've been under a lot of pressure. With the trouble at work. With everything. But . . . look. You need to see someone.

– I know, Samantha. I know no one's watching me. But someone's been watching you.

– Right. OK, darling. Who's been watching me? Tell me.

– I have.

– You have.

– That's right.

Dr Seymour pulls up a chair, balances on it, then reaches up for the smoke-alarm, which covers the camera, and rips it away. The camera remains operative but is now exposed to view. His wife's expression is of puzzlement.

– *What on earth. . . . ?*

Dr Seymour gets down off the chair.

– *It's a surveillance camera. There's one in the kids' room, too.*

– *Alex?*

– *I put it there. I put them both there. I've been watching you while you didn't know it. I'm so sorry, Samantha. I just felt . . . I think I was losing my grip on things. But it's over. I had to confess it to you. I could have shut up about it, just got rid of the equipment, but I . . .*

– *You what?*

– *I wanted you to know. So that you could trust me again.*

– *I . . . I . . .*

– *But I'm the one who's guilty of not trusting you. I thought . . . I thought you were having an affair with Mark Pengelly.*

– *That's ridiculous!*

– *I know it is. I know it is now. Because I've seen you talk to him on tape.*

– *I don't fucking believe this.*

She hits him in the face. It is not a slap but a punch with a bunched fist. He clutches his cheek.

– *You stupid bloody* **idiot**, *Alex.*

– *Sorry, Samantha. Sorry. It was this woman, Sherry Thomas.*

– *Woman? There's a woman?*

– *Sherry Thomas. She runs a surveillance shop. I'll tell you everything. Everything. I'm so sorry, Samantha.*

– *Hold on a minute. Is that thing taping* **now**?

– *Um . . . I suppose so . . . yes.*

– *You unbelievable fool. And what have you been doing with these tapes?*

– *Watching them, of course.*

– *Shut that thing off. Shut it off immediately. SHUT IT OFF!*

Interview with Samantha Seymour

How did you feel when Dr Seymour told you what he had been doing with Sherry Thomas?

I felt violated, of course. Sad. Furious. Deeply bewildered and shocked. But in a way, underneath, I understood. I knew that Alex had been in a bad way. Confused. I felt I had failed as a wife. There was a sense in which I felt I deserved it.

Did you tell the children anything about it?

Not at that time. Alex and I saw no reason to. Guy, particularly, we knew would be incandescent with rage. He is intensely private. Of course, in the end I had no choice but to tell them the whole story.

How did they react?

Very differently, I think, from how they would have reacted had they not lost their father. The general sense of intrusion, of betrayal, it all got lost in their grief for their father. I'm not sure they have ever really reacted. Never mourned the fact that their father was not, in the end, someone they could trust.

How did Alex end up going round to Sherry Thomas's home again?

I didn't want him to. But when he rang her – in front of me, after he'd confessed everything – she threatened suicide. It was painful for me to agree to it, but in the end I supported his decision. I came round, momentarily at least, to seeing her in the same light he did. As a kind of patient, a victim, someone who needed help. I believed him when he said he hadn't had an affair. He had no need to tell me about the hidden cameras. He could have removed them without me ever knowing anything about them. That he did tell me convinced me of his essential integrity. He'd had a lapse, that was all.

Another lapse. After Pamela Geale.

The whole thing with both women amounted to a kiss and a wank. It hardly amounts to a grand passion.

Did he show you the tapes he had made?

Yes, he did.

What did you do when you saw them?

I thought very seriously about divorcing him. Especially when he told me he'd shown them to Sherry Thomas. I just couldn't believe that part.

But . . .

But I loved him. I've always loved him.

Did you have any desire to meet Sherry Thomas?

None whatsoever.

Do you feel guilty about what happened?

Of course I do. I feel terrible. If only I had stopped him going back. I tried, God knows I tried, but he wouldn't listen. Also, in letting him return, I thought I was being grown-up. I thought I was being tolerant, understanding, making him see that he could be forgiven.

What do you remember about the last time you saw Alex?

He'd removed all the recording equipment from the front room, the kids' bedroom and his attic. He packed it all up, said he was sending it back to that woman. He rang her, there and then, and put the conversation on speakerphone so I could listen. They had an arrangement to meet the following week but he told her he wasn't coming. That he'd told me everything. He was very insistent about that. Everything. That any secrets he possessed were in future for his wife alone. That what existed between them was over for ever. He even asked her if she wanted to talk to me.

What was her reaction?

She was hysterical. That was why he decided he needed to go over to her after all.

Because she was so upset?

*Because she was threatening to kill herself. She took it badly that Alex had told me all about him and her, and especially about her personal history. He was frank with her about everything that had passed between us on that subject – I suppose to compensate for the betrayal he'd visited upon **me**. He made it clear to her that he had told me everything. About her rape. About the suicide attempts. The 'murder'. That crazy room full of videotapes. Sherry Thomas considered this a terrible violation – for him to have shared that information with me. Ridiculous that she had* the temerity to be upset after what she had done to me and my family. But there you have it. You're dealing with a lunatic here. Also, it meant she'd lost her power. She couldn't bear it. I think in some way she had come to see Alex as her saviour – someone who understood her, who could take away her pain. A man she could finally trust. And when it all came apart she was devastated.

What did he say to you before he left?

I begged him not to go. But him and his famous conscience! He said he wouldn't be able to live with himself if anything happened. He said he was sorry. He promised it would be the . . . He promised it would be the last time. So I gave in. I let him go.

[Samantha buries her head in her hands and sits silently for about thirty seconds. Finally she sits up straight, and regards me neutrally.]

Can we continue?

I want this to be over. Soon.

It will be. I promise. Did Sherry Thomas actually say she was going to do something to herself?

She said that she would if he didn't go round. He knew about the scars on her wrists. I told him it was blackmail. I thought if she manipulated him this time, she'd do it again. He agreed, but he said he owed her this visit.

Couldn't he have simply rung the police?

She said that if he rang the police, she'd kill herself there and then.

Did he leave immediately?

Yes.

What time approximately?

About nine thirty p.m. He drove. His car was still there when they found him.

How did you find out about what had happened to Alex in the end?

I started to get worried about two hours later. He wasn't answering his mobile. I called the police and gave them the address. I was worried, but not seriously so. Then, another hour later, there was a knock on the door. It was a policeman. What he said was stupid. He said there had been an accident.

But, of course, it was as far from an accident as it could have been. As premeditated, as cruel, as insane as you can imagine any act to be.

Terrible . . . Although one or two positive things must have come out of it.

Such as?

At least you don't have so many money worries any more.

That was an unbelievably tasteless remark.

I'm only doing responsibly what the tabloids did irresponsibly. And I'm acknowledging the fundamental truth that even out of the worse circumstances some good can emerge.

It's true Alex left us well provided for. He was keen on insurance. He liked the idea of a 'safety net'. Now at least I will be able to pay for all the kids to go to good private schools, and afford a house where they can have their own rooms. But I would live in a hovel and educate the children in a ditch if I could have Alex back.

I'm sure you would. I'm sorry if I've caused offence. I can see this has been painful for you.

Yes, it has. Do you think we could take a break now?

Author's Note: There is a break of around ten minutes before taping begins again.

Let's finish with you telling me a little more about the Seymour Institute. You set it up last year. Is that correct?

I'm the founder and managing director. There are so many organizations that deal with freedom of information and so forth, but there seemed to be nothing that dealt with what you might call the opposite, the maintenance of privacy. A case like Alex's demonstrates clearly – luridly, even – what the spy culture, at its extreme, can lead to.

I know we dealt with this at the beginning of our interviews, but tell me exactly what the Institute does.

It campaigns for our right to exist unobserved. Currently, for instance, what Alex did in this household was legal. Bugging is loosely regulated. That seems unacceptable.

The Institute also works to turn the tide of 'reality' TV shows, which we believe are inappropriate entertainment even when the participants give their consent. We all know how Big Brother *was cancelled after the last series, when Michael Parker threw himself off a bridge after being voted off. That was when society realized how disgusting and dangerous this constant . . . feeding off each other can be. Now Alex has died, the pressure is even greater and the support we have is terrific and growing every day.*

We campaign for heavy penalties for any individual or group, professional or amateur, who tapes people secretly and without their permission for whatever purpose. We are fighting to have CCTV cameras removed from the streets of Britain to stop this turning into an Orwellian state. We are working to rebuild a half-forgotten world – the world of privacy.

Can I ask you one more question? How much do you pay yourself as managing director of the Seymour Institute?

What?

What's your salary?

A modest amount – not that it's any of your concern.

More or less than you were earning as a PR?

That's an offensive question, but I'll answer it since we're about to wrap up these interviews. So long as you give up something in return.

The *quid pro quo.*

That's right.

Author's Note: This was a battle that need not have happened. But I was not quick enough on my feet. Had I been an investigative journalist, rather than a novelist, I would certainly have known that any company has to publish its figures and that Samantha Seymour's salary, sooner or later, would have been in the public domain anyway. A little research further down the line would have revealed that she received a six-figure sum from the Seymour Institute – £117,500, a considerable amount, which did not include any expense allowance. However public-spirited the principles of the Seymour Institute were, the private rewards for Samantha Seymour were clearly considerable.

During the interview, however, this simple piece of research did not, absurdly, occur to me. I had frequently felt myself out-manoeuvred by her during the course of our conversations, and once again I felt she had put me in a situation that left me no option but to comply with her request. Also, she had made it clear that this was our last interview. There was nothing else to add. So I knew that this was the last time I would have to offer myself up for sacrifice.

But what could I tell her? Any individual has only so many dirty secrets – or, at least, only so many that they can remember. Something that was going to satisfy her voracious appetite for raw, bloody lumps of my private history seemed out of reach.

Finally something occurred to me – something that had happened a long time ago and that I had succeeded in driving into the most distant recesses of my memory. When it surfaced, I tried to force it back again but it kept bubbling up. I could think of nothing else. She was looking at her watch and, it seemed to me at the time, was about to wind up our last interview without giving me what I considered a vital piece of information. I was beginning to sense by then that Samantha Seymour was not merely disingenuous but manipulative and, quite possibly, blatantly dishonest. In short, I thought I had missed something important about my subject but at that point I had not been able to work out what it was. All I knew was that the more parts of the puzzle I put together the more appeared to be missing.

Interview with Samantha Seymour (resumed)

So. What have you got?

I was a teenager. An immature one. And I did what teenagers in my area did. I joined a gang.

What area was that?

Southall, in West London.

I know it, of course. We used to call it Little India.

It was white when my family first moved there. Then the first waves of Asians came – from Uganda, I think. The character of the place began to change. Well – you've read *The Scent of Dried Roses.*

Presumably what you're about to tell me is something you've left out.

Yes.

And I thought that memoir was so searingly honest.

But of course it was censored. By me – or, at least, my subconscious. Some things don't bear remembering, let alone repeating, or publishing.

I'm intrigued. Please continue.

I was in this gang. Well, I call it a gang. There were about ten of us. We just wandered the streets looking for something to do. It was so damn boring. We were vandals, loafers, street-corner cider-drinkers. Reasonably harmless, or so I had always thought. Not the worst kids in the district by any stretch of the imagination. You wouldn't have been scared of us. A bunch of spotty four-teen-, fifteen-year-olds, sprawled on the pavements, smoking low-grade resin, giggling. When it happened, it was hard to believe. Still is.

I don't remember what month or year it was, only that it was very cold. The streets were empty, there had been snow. I do remember that sometimes we would find cars with the doors unlocked, then fill them with snow and run away. That was about the extent of our hooliganism.

I don't know if we'd been doing it that night. Mainly we'd been drinking wine – cherry wine, from the off-licence on Allenby Road. Anyway, we were pretty drunk. We used to have competitions to see who could drink the quickest, see, and the wine was rough. We could hardly see straight.

We were just hanging out on the corner of Somerset Road, just a few blocks from where I lived with my parents. Most of the Asians lived in what we called Old Southall, around the railway station. But they were gradually buying up houses towards Greenford, near where we were. It didn't bother us much – although some of the parents were angry, felt it would threaten property prices and all that tripe.

So there we were, hanging around on the corner. The road was icy, there was nothing to do. We were drunk and bored, raging with hormones and frustration. And this Sikh kid appeared from an alleyway and started walking towards us.

I want to make something clear. We were not a violent gang. We'd never got into any trouble. We weren't skinheads or thugs, just bored kids. And this Sikh, there wasn't anything provocative about him. Except that he was scared as he walked towards us. We could all see it – we could all see him hanging back. He needed to walk past us to get to where he wanted to go and he didn't want to do it. But eventually he reached us, ten of us, raucous, stupid, drunken kids. Then . . .

Then?

Then he slipped over. On the ice, right in front of us. He was lying down in front of us. As if . . .

As if what?

As if he'd wanted it to happen. I don't know.

You attacked him?

That's too simple a word. One of the kids we hung around with, he was a bit backward, a year behind everyone else. We let him hang with us because he got us blow – you know, grass – from time to time. Anyway, none of us moved to help the Sikh kid up. I don't know why. He just lay there, looking more terrified than ever. That was it, see? His fear. It triggered something in us, some kind of pack instinct. Then the backward kid, he just sort of aimed a kick at the Sikh. On the behind. Nothing vicious, just a joke, really. We all kind of laughed nervously, but then he started screaming as if we'd really attacked him or something. We started to panic, telling him to shut up, but he was screaming more and it – it was infuriating. Then someone else – I can't remember who – kicked him, this time in the stomach, and he grunted, but kept on screaming. We just wanted to shut him up. We just wanted him to stop so we wouldn't get into trouble. Then, suddenly, we

208

were all on top of him, kicking and punching and scratching and it was – it was horrible.

You too? You joined in?

And the reason it was so horrible was that we were enjoying it. It was like a fucking orgasm, you know, all this hate and anger coming out of us, being exorcized, on the head of this poor little scapegoat. I can still hear him – I can hear him when he stopped screaming at last and there was just this funny little whimper, like a little animal, a cat or something, and all the ice was brown with blood, and we all stopped at the same time and stood in perfect silence, and then we ran away. I'm finishing now – I will not continue.

What happened to him?

Will not continue. You have your pound of flesh.

Did he die?

He didn't die. I can't talk about this any more. Just leave me alone now.

Author's Note: At this point Samantha Seymour gets up to leave.

Thank you for sharing. It's OK to cry. I understand.

You have to answer my question, Samantha.

What?

About the Seymour Institute.

I'm sorry . . .

Samantha, you agreed to answer the question about your salary.

Oh, yes. I earn more than I did.

Yes, but how much? I've heard it's a very large sum. How much do you earn?

I couldn't possibly tell you that.

But you said – we agreed –

What I agreed was that I would tell you whether it was less or more.

No. You said you'd tell me how much.

I think if you check the transcript, that's not the case.

What?

Here's a tissue. Wipe your eyes. I can't say I've enjoyed this, but it's been necessary.

Why? To keep paying your salary at the Seymour Institute?

Good luck with the book. I'm sure it will be a big success. If you want any other information you can get in touch with my lawyers.

We have the final tape to discuss, of your husband's last hours with Sherry Thomas.

I don't think so. I've done enough.

Samantha.

Yes.

I wish I'd never started this fucking book.

That makes two of us.

Don't go. Not yet.

Goodbye.

Adams Street, Tape Three,
Tuesday, 29 May, Time Code 21.57

The location is Sherry Thomas's flat in Adams Street. The external camera shows Dr Seymour arriving, slightly out of breath. He is carrying a bag that contains all the equipment he had taken from Cyclops Surveillance. He rings the bell, but there is no answer. However, apparently the door has been left open because the camera shows him disappearing into the flat.

The internal camera shows a disturbing scene. Sherry Thomas is splayed on the floor, face down, fully dressed. As usual, the flat is immaculately tidy. There is an empty pill bottle just out of reach of her fingertips. She does not move.

– *Oh, my God. Sherry! Jesus Christ.*

He rolls her over, takes her pulse. Then he reaches for the telephone, presumably to call for an ambulance, his back to Sherry Thomas, who remains prostrate on the floor. The moment his back is turned, Sherry Thomas rises from the floor, apparently silently, and almost in one movement. She is holding a large claw hammer that has been concealed under the adjacent sofa. She strikes Dr Seymour on the back of his head. With a puzzled look on his face, he drops the phone, but remains standing. Slowly, deliberately, Sherry Thomas takes careful aim and strikes him again on the left temple. Blood can be seen on his skull. Gradually, he collapses to the floor. She stands over him, breathing heavily.

– *Alex? Alex?*

Dr Seymour does not respond. He is apparently unconscious. Now Sherry Thomas pulls off his shoes, and drags him, with considerable effort, across the floor into her bedroom.

The internal camera from the front room shows us nothing else for several minutes. Then she returns to the room to pick up the bloodstained hammer with which she bludgeoned Dr Seymour.

Handheld Video Camera Tape, Sequence One, Tuesday, 29 May, Time Code 22.08

This tape was nicknamed the Skin Tape after sections of it were posted on the Internet. A large number of people – many thousands according to some estimates – have seen part of it, although the total footage posted seems to be no more than a minute in length. Thus it represents only a fraction of the complete footage.

I was not merely unwilling to watch it: I felt I would be unable to. It does not interest me, except as a brutal symbol of the extent to which voyeurism has the power to extinguish every decent emotional response to tragedy, replacing it with curiosity of the most life-negating and morbid variety.

I will describe the tape, but the action that preceded it, recorded on Adams Street, Tape Three, is, to me, far more interesting – and, quite possibly, a great deal more frightening in what it reveals about the pathology of an empty soul.

Dr Seymour has been stripped naked. He is tied to the bed. Behind the lens, Sherry Thomas is out of shot. Dr Seymour is coming round.

There is a closeup of his face. His eyes flicker open, and he tries to take in his surroundings. Throughout most of the following sequence he is unable to speak, and seems to drift in and out of consciousness.

– *Sorry, Alex. I'm so sorry. I'm sorry if I hurt you. But you hurt me too. Once again I feel I am forced to make . . . restitution. Would you like a drink of water?*

Dr Seymour manages to incline his head enough to indicate in the affirmative.

– *Here you are.*

Her hand appears in shot holding a glass of water to his lips. He drinks, and coughs.

– Sorry. Has it gone down the wrong way? Sorry. Lord, I can't help apologizing. It's hard to explain but I really don't want to do this. It's like when I cut my wrists. It wasn't really that I wanted to – I was terrified of dying – I just felt I had to. Don't you ever feel like that? That you have to do something, even though it's awful? I know what's happening here is vile, disgusting and unfair. But sometimes things are out of control. That's the way it feels to me right now. Like some kind of destiny – stupid word, I know, but I can't think of anything more appropriate – has got hold of me. It feels very wrong, Alex, but also inevitable. I'm in the grip of that inevitability. It's just cogs turning.

Dr Seymour struggles weakly against the ropes that keep him tied to the bed.

– I can't untie you. I'm not lying when I say that I'd really like to. But there's a larger part of me that won't let me. I'm sorry. This is like a bad TV movie, isn't it? And I'm stuck with having to watch it. You probably think I'm crazy. I can tell you do. I find it very upsetting when you think that of me. Although I can also see that in a way it's true. But I'm not raving, am I? I'm not dribbling and twitching.

Dr Seymour makes an attempt to talk but all that emerges is a series of splutters and gurgles.

*– Also, though, it's a misogynist way of marginalizing my needs and desires. Ned was the same. I was 'crazy' because I didn't want to have sex with him. I'm not saying all men are the same. Of course not. That's just a cliché. But **some** men are. And I thought you – I thought you were someone I could trust. I genuinely thought you cared about me. But then you go and tell Samantha everything about me. You tell her all our secrets. You tell her about me and Ned.*

Again, Dr Seymour tries to speak. This time he manages a few mangled syllables.

– My . . . wife . . .

– I just don't see what she has to do with anything. That she's your wife didn't stop you watching her secretly. And it didn't stop you watching me and Carl and doing . . . well, you know. I don't need to spell it out. You can't play it both ways. Either she's the keeper of the secrets or I

am. 'Wife' means little here. 'Trustee' would be a better word. That person whom you trust.

Dr Seymour makes another attempt to speak, but fails.

– Please be quiet now, Alex, or I'll need to hit you again. God, this is horrible. I wish it would stop. Time just never does, though. Tick, tick, tick.

She puts down the camera on a table where it takes in most of the room. Dr Seymour's face is bloodied, bruised and swollen. She moves into shot and stands next to the bed.

– I'm so sorry I hurt you. I didn't want to. But things have a way of happening of their own accord. It's an awful thing to do, but I'm so very tired of people like you – almost as tired as I am of myself. People who can't remain consistent. Who I think are on my side, then turn against me.

Suddenly Sherry grabs her temples and moans.

– Jesus, my head.

She rocks back and forth, apparently in extreme pain.

– These headaches – they got better for a while with you. With your hands. Now they're back and they're worse than ever. Why did you have to go and do that? Why make them worse than ever when I thought you were trying to help? People make no sense to me. That's what makes me so furious. They're perverse. They're inconceivable.

Sherry Thomas shakes her head now, as if to clear it. She looks up, blinks, as if seeing Dr Seymour for the first time.

– What on earth are you doing here? You're hurt.

She reaches across and tenderly wipes away the blood from his eyes with a tissue she has taken from a box on the bedside table.

– I wish I could make it all OK again. I can't explain. Stop asking me questions.

Now she looks at him directly, unmoving, for maybe ten seconds. Finally, Dr Seymour speaks, his voice so shaky and tearful that it's hard to understand what he's saying.

– I'm scared.

Sherry Thomas nods.

– First I want you to explain. Why did you do what you did? We had

214

*things so good. It was so nice in here, watching the world. Safe. In control. You liked it. Don't say you didn't. It changed your world. So . . . why did you go and **do** that thing? That bad thing. Calling me up like that. Saying those things. When I gave you so much. You think the tape showed that she still loved you. That Samantha still loved you. And I'm going to let you go on believing that. Because I care about you. I'm going to let you go to . . . wherever you have to go to with a clear mind. With your faith. With everything you took away from me.*

Dr Seymour appears to drift into unconsciousness again, but she continues.

– You see, despite everything else – despite this ludicrous, B-movie situation – I have my integrity. Dishonesty is just too untidy. Untidy in the head.

Dr Seymour opens his eyes and moves against the ropes. Sherry Thomas is still standing rigidly at the end of the bed, but now moves down the side, sniffing.

– What's that smell? God, Alex. You've made a mess.

Her face contorts. Then she seems to bring herself back under control, but when she speaks again her voice is tight with fury.

– Have a cigarette, Alex. Want a cigarette? No pressure.

She takes out a packet of Marlboro Red and puts one between his lips. He shakes his head. She slams the video camera straight into his face. His nose, apparently broken, starts to bleed profusely.

– Have a cigarette, Alex. You want one. Just be honest for once in your life.

She lights the cigarette, and this time a clearly terrified Dr Seymour inhales deeply. Then she continues to feed him the cigarette.

– How is that? I know you were a smoker, Alex. You'll always be a smoker.

There is silence while he attempts to finishes the cigarette, coughing and spluttering incessantly. Then he begins to mutter inaudibly. She leans over and listens carefully.

– Speak up. I can't quite make it out. What is it? Oh. The Confitor.

I recognize that. In fact, I know it by heart. Nuns took me in for a while when I was a kid. You're still a religious man at heart. That's why you don't get it, I suppose. The fact that we're fucked and abandoned. That's the thing. That's the essential thing. You smell the shit, Alex? That's the smell of life.

Now she gets down on her knees next to the bed. She puts her hands together.

– *Shall we confess, then? It's got to be worth a try. I'll do it with you. OK. Come on. It might work. It might work on me. I don't want to go through with this. I want someone to stop me. I want the door to burst open and someone to throw me to the ground and bludgeon me. I want an angel to appear and take away my power. That could happen. It might happen.*

Dr Seymour screws up his face in a grimace. He starts to cough blood, and wheeze. Then Sherry Thomas speaks in a clear, distinct, slightly ironic voice.

– *I confess to Almighty God, to blessed Mary ever Virgin, to blessed Alex the Archangel, to blessed John the Baptist, to the holy apostles Peter and Paul, and to all the saints, that I have sinned exceedingly in thought, word and deed, through my fault, through my most grievous fault. Therefore I beseech blessed Mary ever Virgin . . . I'm bored now. This goes on for hours. Will you do something for me? Will you close your eyes? Close your eyes. Go to sleep. You must be so tired. We'll talk again when you wake up. It'll be all right. Just be quiet now for a while.*

Dr Seymour's eyes are already closed and he is still. It seems that he is unconscious once more.

– *Just go to sleep. I'll make everything all right. It'll be fine. Sleep now.*

Sherry Thomas stands by the bed, watching the inert figure of Dr Seymour for several minutes. His breathing becomes slow and regular.

Then she produces the bloodstained hammer and strikes Dr Seymour two or three times on the head. It is over very quickly. At the end we can hear no more than her heavy breathing and a few words.

– I loved you, Alex.

It is now that the flaying of Dr Seymour takes place.

Some newspaper reports have suggested that Dr Seymour was flayed alive. The electronically doctored tape, with dubbed-on sound effects of groaning and screaming, is what led to the establishment of this myth. The actual tape proves conclusively that this was not the case. However full of anger and madness Sherry Thomas was on Alex Seymour's last visit, she was not a torturer.

The question remains, why did she try to remove the skin from the cadaver of Alex Seymour?

Clearly, it was not something to which she had given serious consideration before she began. Flaying, as a cursory inspection of the admittedly limited literature on the subject has shown me, is a reasonably skilled job. From as much of the tape as I can bear to watch Sherry Thomas had little idea of what she was doing, and attempted it with a sharp kitchen knife rather than the precision surgical instrument that would have been necessary. She abandoned her efforts after about ten minutes, leaving exposed little more than part of Dr Seymour's chest.

It is obvious that she was now severely deranged, but even in the minds of the most deranged, some kind of logic operates. What that logic was can only be guessed at.

Clearly Sherry Thomas was obsessed by seeing what was secret, taboo, hidden from view. It was one reason among several that she was attracted to, indeed compelled by, Dr Seymour – the fact of his profession, which was to see what most people thought of as private, forbidden. All that was normally unseen and unrecorded gave her some kind of charge, sexual or otherwise.

In the end, her attempt to 'look inside' Alex Seymour was the logical conclusion of her lifelong torturous reasoning. In the way a cruel or disturbed child pulls the wings off the butterfly out of random curiosity unlimited by empathy, Sherry Thomas was fascinated by interiors. To look inside a body was perhaps the last taboo for her. Maybe an even greater taboo would have been to look inside a living one, but, in the end, she was not a sadist. Just someone in great pain, searching to fulfil a compulsion that was rotting her from the inside. What she found – mere flesh, mere bones, mere blood – did not satisfy her. Nothing could. It was the pornography of existence that she sought to uncover: hidden life, hidden death. And, like all pornography, it left her feeling empty, unsatisfied, self-disgusted.

This seems to have been what triggered the final episode on the tape: Sherry Thomas had now explored every last border of her obsession and it had left her only with despair.

Watched by the camera, on film that would later be watched by others, she watched the inside of Dr Alex Seymour; she was caught inside a terrible hall of mirrors when she suddenly glimpsed herself.

There is a moment during this unbearable sequence when she drops the knife, and turns to the camera. It stares back at her, perpetually disinterested. And Sherry Thomas gives it a look of such desolation that I have to turn away, although until then I have managed to witness the flaying from beginning to end.

Then she switches off the camera.

Handheld Video Camera Tape, Sequence Two, Tuesday, 29 May, Time Code 22.49

According to the time code, it is about seven minutes since the previous sequence ended. Now the camera appears to have been set on a tripod or rested on a flat surface.

Sherry Thomas stands in front of the camera. She is now wearing a simple pink summer dress that seems several sizes too small for her.

The dress is familiar. Then it registers with me that she wore it in the video of her immediately before she was allegedly raped by 'Ned' twenty or so years ago.

Sherry Thomas speaks to the camera. She seems unspeakably weary. In her right hand she holds a large gun – a Smith and Wesson .44 revolver. It is clearly the weapon to which Ned referred when he appeared to threaten her with rape.

She stands about three feet from the camera and addresses the lens directly.

– *This isn't really going to be like dying. That happened a long time ago. The thing no one says about loneliness is how boring it is. Boring. An innocent word. Innocuous, even. Doesn't sound such a disaster. But it's the worst thing in the world. Still – to my surprise, I'm scared. Perhaps there are worse things than the awfulness of monotony.*

Now, for the first time, on a face that was otherwise blank, Sherry Thomas gives an almost-smile that dies at the moment it is born. I have the impression that she is addressing somebody in particular, rather than the anonymity of the camera, but if she is, it is impossible to say who.

– *Goodbye, then. Even though, of course, we never met.*

Very quickly she puts the gun to her temple and pulls the trigger. Her head appears to explode. She collapses slowly, below the field of the camera. It carries on taping, for the next hour, a wall that was once taupe but is now painted with blood, bone and brain.

Author's Note: In my first draft of this book, the narrative wound up at this point, apart from a brief postscript that contained a number of fairly unconvincing amateur psychological theories about Sherry Thomas, which I eventually discarded. Contemplating insanity, I concluded, is fruitless. Why? Because madness is like a star so distant that its light can never reach us. Madness is what it is: the submersion of reason in the great oceans of mystery that it surmounts. That vast body of the unconscious is unmappable, unknowable, and its logic must always remain an impenetrable secret to the sane. I was not prepared to embark on a quest that I had no hope of finishing.

Also, my attempts to find out more of Sherry Thomas's personal history ran up against an endless succession of dead ends. Tidy-minded as ever, she had taken the precaution of destroying, or dumping, her collection of videotapes before her last meeting with Dr Seymour, along with any remaining papers or documents that might have led to her identification.

The conclusion, therefore, focused mainly on the mind and actions of Dr Seymour, who, although clearly in danger at times of losing his reason, seemed to have returned more or less to sanity by the time he arrived that night at Sherry Thomas's flat.

I summed up my conclusions thus: that, variously, under the pressures of encroaching age, sexual-impropriety allegations, fear of his wife's infidelity, anxiety about his children, and the weariness caused by a new child, Dr Seymour sought out Sherry Thomas as a desperate measure for taking back control of his life at a time when he felt himself to be losing all semblance of autonomy and, therefore, hope. Clearly he was going through a period of disturbance in his life and Sherry Thomas was, finally and inarguably, insane. I believed that all other parties in the story had essentially been innocent – with the possible exception of Pamela Geale, whose motives, then and now, remain questionable.

I wound up what was to be the final chapter with a terse homily about the dangers of surveillance and voyeurism, and decided to put the project to bed. Samantha Seymour had persisted in refusing my requests for another interview, as had Mark Pengelly. There seemed to be no other channel of inquiry worth pursuing. Samantha Seymour, through her lawyers, approved my manuscript for publication with surprisingly few amendments.

I had fulfilled my brief – to be as honest I knew how – my contractual obligations and my unwelcome, extra-contractual compacts with Samantha Seymour to expose myself in the way that she felt she and her family had been exposed. I returned the Seymour videotapes to her for removal to a vault, and the other tapes to the Metropolitan Police.

So convinced was I that the story was now told that I handed the manuscript to my publishers, Viking. They informed me that they were delighted with the results, and intended to begin the production process with the aim of publishing some time in the late summer of the following year.

It was some three months after I had delivered the book to Viking that I received an unexpected phone call.

It was from Victoria Seymour, asking if I could meet her and her brother, Guy, at the earliest opportunity. She said they had something important to tell me.

To say the least, I was surprised. From the beginning Samantha Seymour had vetoed my speaking to them: she said, reasonably, that it was exploitative to involve children. I had accepted her point of view, although I would have been interested to hear their take on events.

When Victoria rang me the first question I asked was whether or not their mother knew about them making contact with me. She said she did not. I pointed out that I would need her consent, but she said that it was unlikely to be forthcoming. She asked me to bear with them, talk to them, and that there was no need to commit myself to using the material they would give me until after we had met. This seemed innocent enough, and I felt less morally bound to Samantha Seymour than I once had since she had effectively blackmailed me into delivering confessions from which I recoiled.

They visited me in my office two days after Victoria's phone call, on 14 September last year, six months after I had last spoken to their mother. As the videotapes and interviews with Samantha Seymour suggest, Guy is emotional and fiery. He is wiry-looking and highly strung, while Victoria seems depressed and fragile. She has lost weight since her appearance on the video footage, and the tattoo of the phoenix on her upper right arm looks unattractive, and unconvincing as a symbol of her current state of mind. Their father's death hangs heavily over them: they look several years older than the fourteen and fifteen that they are respectively.

Interview with Guy and Victoria Seymour

Victoria Seymour: Thank you for agreeing to see us.

I'm happy to talk to you, but you must recognize that, for legal reasons, I may not be able to use what you tell me.

Guy Seymour [rather cynically]: *I'm sure you'll find a way.*

So, what do you want to talk to me about?

VS: First, we want to talk about Dad. We feel very upset that we were excluded from this book. He was our father. We wanted to say something.

Your mother said that you . . .

GS: Mum's been lying.

VS: We always wanted to talk to you. But she wouldn't let us.

Perhaps she thought it would be too traumatic for you – it has been very painful for her to relive the whole thing.

GS [again cynically]: *Terribly painful.*

VS: Guy. Please. Let's just keep it simple. Is your tape running?

Yes.

VS: I just want to say, for this book, that I loved my father very much. That he was a good man, and I miss him terribly. And whatever he did with that woman, he did it because he wanted to look after us. He just got muddled up. That was typical of Dad. Couldn't bear the fact that he couldn't do enough. Thought we didn't care about him any more. So he went to see that crazy woman.

Do you not feel angry with him?

VS: We did. We were angry with him for getting himself killed. For leaving us. But we're not angry any more. Not with him, anyway.

The passage of time helps.

GS: It's nothing to do with the passage of time!

VS: Guy, hold on a minute. Just let me finish what I'm saying. That Dad loved us and would never have done anything to harm us. And that, whatever he did, we forgive him.

Guy, is this how you feel? You seem very angry.

GS: *I'm fucking angry. Angry enough to come here and visit a parasite like you.*

VS: *It's not his fault, what happened, Guy. He's just trying to find out the truth.*

GS: *He's not interested in the truth. He's a fucking writer!*

Why don't you try me?

VS: *Look, why don't you just say what you want to put on the record for the book? Then we'll give him what you want to give him.*

GS: *What **we** want to give him.*

VS: *Then we can go.*

[There is a long pause.]

GS: *I can't say it.*

VS: *Please, Guy. Please. For the book. For Dad.*

GS: *OK.*

[Guy begins to sob uncontrollably. Victoria puts her arm round him to console him. Eventually, he speaks.]

I love you, Dad.

[They hold each other for perhaps twenty seconds. Then they separate, and make as if to leave my office.]

Is that all you have to say?

GS: *Mum's doubtless said everything else.*

You sound as if it's her you're angry with.

GS: *I wonder why that could be?*

[He spits out these words with almost unutterable bitterness. Then he takes a 10x8 Jiffy envelope out of his shoulder-bag, and puts it on my desk.]

We got this in the post a few days after my dad died.

What are you –

GS: *We couldn't tell anyone about it. We thought Mum might be be arrested.*

VS: *That's enough. Come on, Guy. He can draw his own conclusions. We need to leave. Thank you for talking to us.*

But what's on it?

GS: *You'll like it. You'll **love** it.*

But . . . but you've had this tape for a year and a half! Why now? Why?

[Guy Seymour gives me a hard, resentful stare.]

GS: *Because she's pregnant. By* **him**. *And this time she's not going to get away with it.*

[Then they leave, Guy sobbing again.

I open the packet, already sure of what I will find.

A videotape.]

Unmarked Tape, Monday, 28 May, Time Code 16.30

The tape is from Adams Street. It begins with a shot from the external camera, which shows Samantha Seymour approaching the front door and pushing the bell. At first it is ignored, but eventually Sherry Thomas answers. She does not unlock the front security grille.

– *Are you Sherry Thomas?*

– *You know who I am.*

– *I'm Mrs –*

– *I know who you are. The innocent victim of a terrible transgression.*

– *I don't know what that means. But I'll tell you what I'm not. I'm not a fool. I know what's been going on.*

– *How did you get this address?*

– *It doesn't matter. You already know more about my business than you have any right to.*

– *Look, I think you might have got things every which way here. Nothing has happened between me and your husband.*

– *I know that. He wouldn't sleep with someone who looked like you. You're not his type.*

– *Aren't I?*

– *You're too ugly.*

– *Have you come here for a cat fight?*

– *Not really.*

– *What, then?*

– *Are you going to let me in? Since you've been inside my home, and met my family – at least at a distance – you could do me the service of showing me your . . . private domain.*

There is the sound of a door unlocking. The internal cameras show Sherry Thomas entering her flat with Samantha Seymour behind her.

– *Would you care for a cup of tea?*

– I don't want a Tupperware party. I just want to say a few things to you straight. Before all this ends.

– It's going to end?

– Alex has had enough. He thinks you're crazy. He's never going to see you again.

– Is that so? Shall we sit down at least?

– I prefer to stand. Interesting place you've got here. Homely, in a very bleak, minimalist kind of way. It's like a monument.

– To what?

– Aloneness. Have you ever tried buying a copy of The Rules *rather than going through all this?*

Sherry Thomas sits down. She seems relaxed and unflustered. She takes out a cigarette – not the Marlboros she had when Dr Seymour was with her but a Virginia Slim – and lights it.

– I presume you've talked to Alex about your shocking discovery.

– Not only do I have a husband, I share everything with him.

– Yeah. That's right.

– If you could hear yourself! You don't know anything about either of us.

– Actually, Samantha, it's you who doesn't know anything about your husband. The thing is, I can see what's there. I knew him immediately. You just have him in two dimensions. You simply have an idea of him that you use to keep your world nice and cosy. But he's much more than you think. Much braver, much stronger than you think he is. He's just got some issues he needs to –

– I'm not interested in your American psychobabble.

– If you're not interested in what I have to say, what is it **you** want to say, Samantha?

– Don't call me Samantha. You don't know me.

– I know a little about you, I would say.

– This is all going to stop. Then you can go and commit suicide or whatever people like you do when they get abandoned. That's what you do, isn't it? Get abandoned.

– Is that what Alex is going to do? That's a pity. He's nice to have around. A good guy. He cares about you very much, Samantha.

– I don't need you to tell me how much he cares about us. Just because you've watched a few videotapes doesn't mean you know anything about me.

– Is that right? But Alex has talked to me quite extensively. Confided in me a great deal.

– Not any more.

– Tell me again, because I'm really not clear on this. Why is it going to stop?

– Because I'm going to break up his stupid cameras and throw them in the bin.

– I don't think you'll do that.

– What makes you think that you have any say in the matter?

– Because if you try to stop me seeing him again, I'll tell him about you and Mark Pengelly.

– What are you talking about?

– Your affair with him.

– That's absurd.

– Is it? You're telling me that there was never anything between you and Mark Pengelly?

– Absolutely. Anyway, I don't have to justify myself to you.

– No, but I know what I know. I'm an expert. Worse for you, I'm a woman.

– That's hardly conclusive proof of an affair.

– Does it matter? I can easily point Alex in the right direction. And I know I'm right. I know the body language. I know the mating ritual. People like me – lonely, abandoned people – study this kind of thing at night school. I can tell him all about you, even if you do try to rain on our parade. And if he's thinking of stopping seeing me, I advise you to talk him out of it. I'm sure you're capable of it. You're good at psychology, Alex says.

– I am not having an affair with Mark Pengelly.

Now Sherry Thomas goes to a chest of drawers in the corner of the room, takes several 10x8 photographs out of it, and throws them on to the table in front of Samantha. She picks them up, inspects them and puts them down again. She seems unfazed. Sherry Thomas inspects the photographs where they lie.

– *That Pengelly looks like he works out.*

– *He does. He's got an amazing body. They're good photographs. Quite artistic.*

– *Sometimes digital technology just can't beat the traditional methods.*

– *Could you let me have the negatives, do you think? They really are nicely shot.*

– *Why on earth should I do that?*

– *Because you're a killer.*

For the first time, Sherry Thomas looks taken aback. She lights another cigarette and says nothing.

– *My husband told me everything, you see.*

– *What the fuck are you here for?*

– *To meet the enemy. To even things up a little. Before the endless pattern of your life asserts itself once more.*

Here there is a long silence as Sherry Thomas and Samantha regard each other like fighters before the first bell. Finally, it is Sherry Thomas who speaks.

– *You're a piece of work, Samantha. I'll give you that. The video camera doesn't do you justice.*

– *I think I should go now. I've said my piece. Give me the prints and the negatives.*

Sherry Thomas, apparently defeated, returns to the chest of drawers and fetches a roll of negatives, which she places on the table in front of Samantha.

– *You should brighten this place up a bit. Just because you're on your own doesn't mean you have to make the whole room a tribute to the fact.*

– *Anything else? I have a terrible headache.*

– *Could you show me round the flat, please?*

– *What?*

– *You've had a good look at where I live. I want to see the sorry state you live in.*

– *I don't think I can do that.*

– *Yes, you can. You'll do anything I want you to do. Unless you want a very unwelcome phone call from the authorities back home in . . . wherever the hell it is you come from. Anyway, what have you got to hide?*

– *It's not* –

– *Any of my business? That's funny. Just show me round the flat.*

Reluctantly, Sherry Thomas complies, leading her into kitchen and bathroom. They emerge some minutes later. Sherry Thomas is massaging her temples.

– *Satisfied now?*

– *Are you joking? You think I'm going to miss out on the high point?*

– *There's nothing of interest in my bedroom.*

– *Is that so? There should be no problem, then.*

Again, they disappear briefly. When they return, Sherry Thomas is wringing her hands and her head is bowed.

– *That's quite a video collection.*

– *I suppose.*

– *I came across 'enthusiasts' like you when I was studying at college. We'd see them when we had field trips to institutions.*

– *Can you go now? My head is really . . . Please . . .*

– *In a moment. First, give me the tape.*

– *What are you talking about? What tape?*

– *You've taped this. All of it. I know what you're doing. I know what you're like. I want the tape of this . . . meeting before I go. Internal and external.*

– *If I have to do what you say, why do you need the tapes?*

– *One can't have too much of the truth, don't you think?*

Sherry Thomas gives a resentful nod.

– *And bring me a couple of tapes from your bedroom collection. Just a dozen or so. For entertainment purposes. No, hold on. I'll choose them myself.*

Sherry Thomas visibly turns white with rage. But nevertheless she sits still while Samantha goes next door and reappears with an armful of videotapes.

– *It's going to be a lot of fun getting to know you better. Now, give me the tape of us. And when you get the phone call from my husband telling you he never wants to see you again, don't breathe a word to him about this meeting. Or someone else will be getting a phone call, someone whose idea of treating your headaches might be a little different from*

Alex's. *I believe it involves some form of injection. One hundred per cent effective.*

Obediently, Sherry Thomas rises from the sofa and disappears from view – presumably to wherever the receiver for the cameras is set up so that she can retrieve the tape. Seconds later, the recording ends.

Author's Note: That this tape, apparently taken by Samantha Seymour at the time of recording, was posted to Victoria and Guy Seymour is puzzling but explicable. I would have to assume that Sherry Thomas backed up her tapes simultaneously to their recording on a computer hard disk. Examination by an expert confirms that it was dubbed on to magnetic tape from computer digital impulses.

I can also conclude that the person to whom Sherry Thomas was saying her ironic goodbye in the last seconds of her life was Samantha Seymour, knowing that she would eventually view the tape. And that Sherry Thomas sent the tape to Guy and Victoria, understanding that by attacking her children – mainly through the allegation about Mark Pengelly – she would hurt Samantha Seymour most.

That this strategy was effective is confirmed not only by my meeting with Guy and Victoria, but also the discovery that they had been living for some time with their uncle, Toby Seymour, and have refused consistently to meet or talk to their mother since shortly after their father's death. Not only did it reveal her affair with Mark Pengelly, it suggested that, by goading Sherry Thomas, she might have been partly responsible for Dr Seymour's death.

Immediately after I had viewed the tape I approached Samantha Seymour.

She reluctantly agreed to meet me one last time.

Interview with Samantha Seymour

Hello, Samantha. Nice of you to come.

I'd like you to return the tape.

Why on earth should I?

Because it's my property. Because you don't need it any more. Because Victoria and Guy are minors and have no legal rights in this respect.

Of course I need it. Do you think I can keep this out of the book?

Haven't you any feeling for people at all? For Guy? For Victoria? For me, even? How can you be so ruthless?

That's a little ironic, I think, coming from you.

What do you mean? Are you going to give me the tape or not?

Apart from anything else, it's not only the public who might be interested. The police would find it fascinating.

[At this point Samantha Seymour looks genuinely shocked.]

Why? I've committed no crime.

How about blackmail? Or even accessory to murder?

[Samantha Seymour does not reply. Then she leans over and is sick into the wastebasket.]

Jesus, Samantha.

[I hand her some tissues and she wipes her face.]

How could you possibly think that I – that I would –

You got the life insurance. You got Pengelly. You got to sell your story. You had the motivation and the perfect opportunity.

How on earth could I have had the opportunity? How could I have known what she was going to do? And I didn't 'get' Mark.

Let me be completely upfront, Samantha. You've lied to me all the way through our interviews. At best you deceived your husband. At worse, you've been complicit in a murder. Now you have to tell me the truth. Right down to the last detail. Or I'm going straight to the police with this.

You really are full of surprises, aren't you? And I chose you because –

Because you thought I'd be soft. An 'author' rather than a reporter.

I suppose so.

I am soft. But that's not quite the same as stupid. Listen to me. When we first met, you told me you had a Ph.D. in psychology. What did you specialize in?

Why is that relevant?

There's no point in lying any more. It's too late for that. I know the answer anyway. It's a matter of record.

Criminal psychopathology. That doesn't prove anything. I'm not a genius. I don't have a crystal ball.

You didn't try very hard to stop what you must have known *might* have been unfolding. You knew she'd committed one murder. So presumably you could work out how crazy she was. Especially after you'd seen the room full of videotapes and even taken a selection home to watch, which, apart from anything you knew, would make her seem just that little bit *more* crazy. It wouldn't take a genius to work out that the woman was seriously disturbed. Incidentally, how *did* you find out you were being taped? And when was it exactly?

[Samantha Seymour sighs, and sits up straight in her chair.]

Alex. So organized, but hopeless at hiding anything. Because he thought that people would always play by his rules.

Was it just luck?

A bit of luck. A bit of suspicion. It was that day when Alex confronted Guy over the mobile phone.

May the tenth.

I can't recall the exact date. That day, anyway. When Guy broke down and . . . It was so extraordinary. And that strength – it was so untypical of Alex. So out of character. I was immediately suspicious. He seemed so sure of himself. Of course, I didn't think anything about cameras. But I did remember that the loft room stretched over the ceiling of Guy and Vicky's room. And I wondered if he'd done something sneaky like finding a little spyhole so he could see what they were up to.

So you went up to have a look.

Yes.

I thought Alex's room was out of bounds.

I'm his wife. No secrets.

'No secrets'. That might be a good title for the book.

It wasn't until the following week I went up to have a look. Just on impulse. He'd left the door ajar, and I fancied a bit of a snoop. Simple as that. It was a few days before he went off to that Sunday medical conference.

And?

There was no spyhole. But I did notice the video-cam up there and wondered what it was doing in his room. I'd been looking for it a few days previously and was surprised to find it there. Alex had never shown the remotest interest in either making or watching videotapes of the family. So I was curious. And I had a look. The diary tape was in there. Very soppy. The sort of thing I would do, not Alex.

So you saw his video diary.

Which made it plain that there were more tapes. I found them quickly. Alex hadn't hidden them very well. They were nicely filed, but badly hidden. He was obviously confident that his domain was secure. I sat down there and then and I watched them.

How did that make you feel?

I was incredibly shocked.

Was it then that you realized what Sherry Thomas was capable of? Perhaps that was the moment it all fell into place for you. You suddenly had your chance and you ran with it.

No. I didn't know what to do. It was shattering. I thought of that woman having power over me. I thought of her watching footage of our kids. I found it unbearable. I know I should have confronted Alex straight away, phoned him, screamed at him. Divorced him.

But you didn't.

No.

Why on earth not?

Because I realized I didn't love him any more.

At that moment?

*I think so. Not stopped loving him, you understand. Just **realized** that I'd stopped loving him. And any last vestiges of loyalty I might have had disappeared as I watched the tapes. Because I wanted to stay with Mark Pengelly but not smash up our home – and if I'm honest, not lose the financial security that came with it. And if it was going to break up, I wanted Alex to be responsible.*

Why?

Because the kids were going to blame someone. And I wanted it to be him rather than me. Also, if I did call a halt to it there and then – well, I'd still have a suspicious husband on my hands, given what he'd seen on the videotapes up to that point. And I really didn't want that.

So you decided to stage a performance for him.

I was just fighting fire with fire. I had nothing to lose by letting it all continue between Alex and Sherry Thomas and everything to gain. It could continue indefinitely, as far as I was concerned. Apart from anything else, it was making Alex a better father, ironically enough. He was happy, the kids were happy, and I was happy. I thought I could control the situation. All Mark and I had to do was keep out of the front room.

Samantha Seymour sighs deeply and lights a Silk Cut Ultra.

Look. I'm no angel, I admit. I've made mistakes. Mistakes I bitterly regret. All right, I was bored with him. All right, our marriage wasn't what it used to be. And obviously I put on that little act with Mark, which was pretty cheap of me.

– And the act you put on when he told you about the cameras? The surprise, the outrage, when in fact you'd known about them for weeks? That punch in the face was convincing.

It was convincing because I was genuinely incensed. He'd ruined every-thing – decent, moral, can't-even-cheat-on-his-wife-properly Alex. Just had to confess. Bloody Catholics. Anyone else would have just kept on and everything would have been fine. I'd still have Mark and Alex would still be alive. And don't forget I had a long-standing grudge against him, boiling away inside me. Even before any of this happened, he'd betrayed me. You must understand that I had been angry for some time.

About what?

About that thing he did with Pamela Geale, of course.

235

I thought you said you'd overreacted.

*No, I didn't overreact. It was disgusting. I still **am** disgusted. What was the use of Alex if he wasn't solid and reliable and faithful? He was boring, washed-up. He was impotent, he didn't earn enough money. But at least I could always rely on him. That's important in a family. God, I would never have had a fling with Mark if –*

You didn't get involved with Mark Pengelly until after the kiss between Alex and Pamela Geale?

*Certainly not. Mark had been trying it on for ages, but I had rebuffed him time and again. I was tempted, but I didn't want to sell out Alex. But then the thing with . . . Geale. I lost all respect for Alex. Something went out of me. Some key element of my willpower. A few days later I gave in to Mark. And I was overwhelmed – **overwhelmed**. I don't think I've ever been in love before, actually. Not really. But with Mark – it was like everything I'd read about in those silly romantic novels was possible. The lights, the fireworks. Incredible. After that I was lost. We were all lost. So, yes, I had an affair with Mark Pengelly.*

Had?

It's over now. It had to end. The guilt after Alex's death destroyed everything. So my heart was broken twice. But I had no choice. The children would never have stood for it. And I didn't want it any more. The price had proved too high.

Right.

I swear to you on the life of my children. Follow me, track me, do what you like. It's finished. He's left London. I don't even miss him now.

That's strange, because Guy says you're pregnant with his baby.

*He says **what**? Poor Guy. He's just not dealing with the whole thing very well at all. Retreating into a kind of paranoid fantasy life.*

You're not pregnant, then?

He just hates me because, for the first time ever last week, I wouldn't send him the money he wanted. The money he demanded. For some stupid gaming console. They won't talk to me, but they're always hassling me for cash.

Victoria says the same. About you being pregnant.

She'll go along with whatever Guy wants. She's idolized him since

Alex died. Funny, isn't it? Her younger brother a father figure. Well, I suppose he does look like Alex.

You're not pregnant, then?

Of course I'm not. Do I look pregnant?

I can't tell.

What kind of woman do you think I am? I admit that I did fake the scene with Mark to keep the affair safe. I admit I went to see Sherry Thomas out of curiosity and a desire to equalize the power balance between us before Alex ended it all – as he announced he was going to do in his video diary. I admit I let the thing go on far longer than it should have. I admit that I didn't understand Sherry Thomas as well as I thought I did. But my copybook is no more blotted than Alex's is. And, at the risk of being infantile, he started it.

Why *did* you decide to go and see Sherry Thomas? After all, the whole thing was coming to an end anyway. Why not let it run its course? You could have kept Alex in the dark about you and Pengelly easily enough. And you'd have had the moral high ground to boot.

An impulse thing. A woman thing. I'd had enough. I'd wanted to go and slap that woman's face since it had all started. But I couldn't, without giving the game away. Once Alex said she'd got away with murder, though, I had a weapon.

When did this 'impulse' come over you?

It was after Alex came home that Saturday, having seen Sherry Thomas, and decided he was going to put an end to it. He said as much in his video diary the next afternoon – and I watched it later that evening. Then I decided I wanted to see her the first chance I got. I couldn't bear the thought of her thinking that she had got away with all this. It was a compulsion, if you like. To shame her. To punish her. And I wanted to find out what she knew about Mark and me. It was possible that she had spotted some detail Alex had missed, and would be able to expose us if she chose to. Although she never got round to doing that.

I wonder why not.

Maybe she really did love Alex. Though bludgeoning him to death was a funny way of showing it. Anyway, I sometimes think the murder, the tape sent to Guy and Victoria, wasn't about Alex but about me. It was me she hated. Because I had what she didn't.

How did you find out who and where she was?

It was easy. There was a business card in Alex's miscellany file. I put two and two together. Sherry Thomas, managing director, Cyclops Surveillance Systems. And an address. Then I checked the telephone directory. Sherry is an unusual name. She was listed living a mile away from the shop. I was pretty sure I'd find her there.

What was your plan?

I didn't have one. Other than revenge.

You say you didn't love Alex any more. You'd allowed the whole thing to continue when you could have stopped it. It seems a bit unfair to take revenge when you were complicit in the whole thing.

Fairness has nothing to do with it. Property is property. Alex was mine, not hers. The kids were mine, the house was mine. And she was watching it all. As I've said before, she was a rapist.

What did you feel when you saw her?

The first thing I thought was, She's not Alex's type. One of those hard-bitten Americans. 'How to Get A Husband in Thirty Days', that sort of thing. I couldn't imagine him going for her, I must say. Anyway, I wanted her to know who was boss. To give her a piece of my mind.

What made you so sure she wouldn't tell Alex?

I wasn't absolutely sure. But she was a murderer. If she did anything I didn't want her to do, I'd go to the police.

You manipulated her and put her under such pressure you knew she'd turn violent.

No.

You pulled the strings. She just wielded the weapon. You knew that Alex was about to call her. You stood next to him while he did it. You guessed she would threaten suicide. You knew Alex would want to go round there. You had a pretty good idea what might happen. And you let it, so you could have Pengelly, the pension, the kids, the serial rights to the story, whatever you wanted.

How can you think that? I would never have done anything to harm Alex. I might have stopped loving him, but he was the father of my chil-

238

dren. *We were married for twenty-odd years. I just didn't understand the rules of the game she was playing.*

Who won, by the way?

I suppose Sherry would say that she did. Except that she's dead, of course, which must sour the victory a little.

Did you honestly think you could control someone you must have known was a psychopath? A killer? An unstable woman with a history of damage and disaster behind her?

Yes. Because of the murder. Because she'd confessed to it. She knew that I could get her into deep trouble.

Surely that should have put you on your guard. Surely then you must have realized that Alex was in danger.

I swear I never thought she was going to hurt him!

[Samantha breaks down, crying, and collapses on to the floor. I can do little other than put my arm round her shoulders and, in a pathetic gesture, she reaches out and takes my hand.]

Haven't I suffered enough for my stupidity? I've lost Alex. Mark's gone. My family is in ruins. Guy and Victoria don't ever want to talk to me again. Polly hardly sees her brother and sister. Only the four of us know about the tape. Won't you return it to me? Please.

I don't know. I think you still need to convince me.

In what way?

In a legal, contractual and financial way.

[There is a long pause.]

I see what you mean.

I hope so.

I really did get you wrong, didn't I?

Perhaps you're only good at criminals.

Or perhaps I started believing your PR.

Always a big mistake. Writers are no more noble than anyone else. Less so.

All right. All bets are off. OK. I'll tell you what I'll do. Those confessions you made, that I insisted on, you can edit them out.

I don't care about them.

So, if you're not after that . . . then – oh. I see.

239

Do you?

*I don't need a psychology degree to read **your** mind. OK. OK, then.*

OK then what?

On behalf of the Seymour Institute, I will agree to forfeit the world-wide rights to the book. All profits from the book will go to you.

I see. So you'll manage to get by on Alex's life-insurance policies. And your modest salary.

You'll get a fax from my lawyer this afternoon.

[There is a long pause.]

I'll look forward to it.

Right.

Once the paperwork is done, you can come back here and pick up the tape. I'll put in with it a sworn affidavit that no copies have been taken. And one last thing, Samantha.

What's that?

I'd like the bank details of the Institute.

Why?

I'd like to make a donation.

A donation?

Because it's a cause I wholeheartedly support.

[She gives a forced smile and a resigned nod.]

I'll send you a form. Are you really going to leave all your confessions in the book, by the way?

No.

So much for your commitment to truth.

I *am* committed to the truth. To my truth, anyway.

Is that so?

Absolutely.

Then why?

I'm taking out the confessions because they're not true.

Sorry?

I made them all up. My uncle, my brother, the beating. All just stories. Stories, Samantha. My stock-in-trade. My living. My vocation, if you want to be solemn about it.

I don't believe you. Those stories were true. You were weeping. You

240

were hurting.

It doesn't matter whether you believe me or not. It's my book now. So I decide what the truth is. To put them in would be dishonest. And I'm not prepared to compromise my integrity, I'm afraid. As I told you right at the beginning. Goodbye, now. And thanks for your co-operation. It's been invaluable.

[Samantha Seymour walks slowly to the door, turns, makes a brief, obscene gesture, then goes out, slamming the door behind her.]

The End

I see you.

I do not judge; I do not pass comment.

I do not think; I do not reflect.

I watch you from the moment of your birth to your last breath.

I am in the hospital as I am in the graveyard.

I watch you on the streets, on a twenty-four-hour loop. I watch you in the shops, in the car parks, in the cinema lobbies.

I watch you in your car, using the bus lane. Exceeding by three miles the permitted speed limit. I watch you in the airport. I watch you as you fly through the air five miles above Earth.

I capture you on the miniature camera on your videophone. I track you in the corridors of your schools. I see into every corner of your workplace.

Nowadays, I have no limits.

I watched when the author rang the publisher.

This was time code ten days, three hours, ten minutes and twenty-three seconds ago. He said that he would come to her office. He had uncovered some important new material.

Two days, six hours and seventeen minutes after he made the call, I watched a woman leave the author's office.

She had straight, brown, highlighted, shoulder-length hair and wore casual, well-cut high-street clothes in dark blue and white. There was a small food stain on her lapel. She was smoking a Silk Cut Ultra cigarette.

In her bag was a videotape. I watched her put it there.

Just as I watched when she cried in front of the author.

After that, she walked down the steps and into the street. She stopped. She wiped her eyes and smiled. She walked again. Her pace was faster. She looked behind her. She walked round a corner.

I do not reflect on this, I do not judge it. I only observe it.

I followed her round the corner. A man was waiting for her. He had carefully messy mid-length black hair and was clean-shaven. His skin was olive and he had a bold, almost Roman nose, and full, Cupid's-bow lips.

They embraced. Then she stood back.

He smiled and cupped her stomach in his hands.

I followed them as they walked down the street towards a coffee shop. They come here often. It's on tape. I am there to stop the *baristas* pocketing change.

I have been responsible for three dismissals and a caution.

She ordered a cappuccino. He ordered a *latte*. With Nutra-sweet™. He is on a diet. She likes slender men. She can't stand it when they get overweight. Overweight and old.

They order what they always do. It's on tape.

They laughed and joked. There was high background noise. My microphones could not pick up their conversation so I cannot know what they are saying.

But I will find out.

Sooner or later, everything will be revealed to me.

She laughed and threw her head back. She kissed the man.

I do not know what this means. I only watch.

Unblinking.

I watched the author again. Time code four days, one hour and seven minutes later.

He was wearing a blue suit that he bought the previous day at time code 15.03 at Wodehouse in Kensington High Street for £275. I was there.

It was a lousy suit. Or so the sales assistant said after the author had gone.

He left his office. I followed him for most of the three miles he covered on foot to his publishers.

He arrived time code thirty-five minutes and seventeen seconds later. His publisher greeted him. She wanted to hear about the progress of the book. She had had positive reactions from other executives at the publishing house. She was excited about the new revelations he had promised her.

He told her that the new revelation was that the children had agreed to an interview.

She asked what they said.

He replied that they said they loved their father.

She asked, What else?

Nothing much, he said.

Is that it? she said.

Yes, he said.

Then he blew his nose.

She seemed disappointed.

He placed a new manuscript on her desk.

He told his publisher that the personal confessions the woman had forced out of him in the course of the interviewing had now been cut out.

He told her that he had negotiated a new contract beneficial for himself and the publishers, and that his agent would be in touch regarding the terms.

I do not know what the publisher thought. I cannot read minds. I can only watch.

She argued with him. She said she thought he was committed to the truth. She wanted to know what the children really told him.

She said she did not believe that the 'new developments' had turned out to be so slight. She said that he was not telling the truth.

He argued with her. He said that he would take the book to a different publisher if she failed to agree. He said there was no such thing as the truth anyway.

The publisher agreed to the cuts. I did not know about her motivation. I only watched and listened. They shook hands. He left. Did he looked uneasy? I cannot tell.

★

I watched a boy on his way to school. He was a tall, lanky boy, with high cheekbones, and floppy brown hair similar to that of his father. He displayed an almost perpetual expression of surliness and disappointment. He was with his friends, who were laughing and joking.

But his face was serious.

He made an excuse and broke away from the others.

He disappeared down an alley, almost, but not quite, out of my range. For although I could not see him, I could hear him.

If he was sobbing at a normal level, my microphones would not have been able to pick it up. But it was not a normal level: he was crying loudly. The remaining boys heard him and looked uncomfortable. They moved away.

It was a private moment.

Those are my special interest.

The other boys moved swiftly on in the direction of the school, where they could no longer hear the noise.

But I could.

It continued for time code three minutes and seven seconds.

I saw a girl stare at her mobile phone when it rang. She was not a pretty girl. She had a phoenix tattooed on the upper part of her right arm. I have seen her pause like this eleven times before. My lens is sometimes close enough to see the name display.

Many times, recently, it has rung with the name display showing one word.

'Mum'.

She never answers. I watched her, as, once again, she switched off the phone.

I was there when they gave that woman an autopsy. She blew her own head off with a gun.

That was interesting.

She didn't look too good.

But better than that man who got hit with a hammer.

They were dead.
This means nothing to me.

I see you.
Reading a book.
Finishing the book.
Closing the book.
Thinking yourself
Of course
Unwatched.